Christine Rimmer came to writing [...] long way arou[nd...] to teaching t[o...] found work th[at...] never had a p[...] gaining "life experience" for her future as a novelist. Christine lives with her family in Oregon. Visit her at christinerimmer.com.

Books by Christine Rimmer

Harlequin Special Edition

Bravo Family Ties

Hometown Reunion
Her Best Friend's Wedding
Taking the Long Way Home
When Christmas Comes
His Best Friend's Girl
The Marriage Plan

Montana Mavericks: Behind Closed Doors

The Maverick's Dating Arrangement

Montana Mavericks: The Trail to Tenacity

Redeeming the Maverick

Wild Rose Sisters

The Father of Her Sons
First Comes Baby...
The Christmas Cottage

Montana Mavericks: Brothers & Broncos

Summer Nights with the Maverick

Montana Mavericks: The Real Cowboys of Bronco Heights

The Rancher's Summer Secret

Visit the Author Profile page at Harlequin.com for more titles.

The Marriage Plan is dedicated to Sharon Hoch and her lively, affectionate Bengal cat, Voodoo, who is the inspiration for the Bengal cat in this story. Sharon informs me that Voodoo is a big boy who loves to climb, takes commands (when he wants to) and never gives up trying to convince the family dog to play with him. Voodoo's a busy guy who will rarely sit still to be photographed. Full of mischief, Voodoo is leash trained and loves to go for walks.

Thank you, Sharon, for sharing Voodoo with me. He's the perfect companion for my heroine's six-year-old daughter, Ana, and I had such fun writing about him.

THE MARRIAGE PLAN

CHRISTINE RIMMER

Harlequin

SPECIAL EDITION

If you purchased this book without a cover you should be aware that this book is stolen property. It was reported as "unsold and destroyed" to the publisher, and neither the author nor the publisher has received any payment for this "stripped book."

Harlequin® SPECIAL EDITION™

Recycling programs for this product may not exist in your area.

ISBN-13: 978-1-335-18016-2

The Marriage Plan

Copyright © 2025 by Christine Rimmer

All rights reserved. No part of this book may be used or reproduced in any manner whatsoever without written permission.

Without limiting the author's and publisher's exclusive rights, any unauthorized use of this publication to train generative artificial intelligence (AI) technologies is expressly prohibited.

This is a work of fiction. Names, characters, places and incidents are either the product of the author's imagination or are used fictitiously. Any resemblance to actual persons, living or dead, businesses, companies, events or locales is entirely coincidental.

For questions and comments about the quality of this book, please contact us at CustomerService@Harlequin.com.

TM and ® are trademarks of Harlequin Enterprises ULC.

Harlequin Enterprises ULC
22 Adelaide St. West, 41st Floor
Toronto, Ontario M5H 4E3, Canada
www.Harlequin.com

HarperCollins Publishers
Macken House, 39/40 Mayor Street Upper,
Dublin 1, D01 C9W8, Ireland
www.HarperCollins.com

Printed in Lithuania

"I am considering getting married again."

Macy sipped her drink and set it back down. "Wow. Okay. But not dating?"

"That's right."

"So you're thinking a mail-order bride, maybe?"

"Didn't I just say that I'm not getting anything going with some stranger?" Joe asked.

"Gotcha. So what exactly *are* you planning?"

"It's simple. Falling in love is dangerous. I need to choose a woman I can trust. Love is not the point."

"Yes, it is. Love *is* the point."

Joe corrected her. "Macy Lynn, it's the devotion. The mutual trust. The dedication. The ride or die. I want that, not the romantic love crap. Falling in love just messes you over. I don't want that. I need to know that all the promises that are made will be kept."

Macy drew a careful breath and let it out nice and slow. "Be realistic. No one can guarantee a life of unbroken promises. Things happen. People change. It's just the way it is, Joe. You won't get any guarantees. Life doesn't work that way."

"But it *could* work that way, with someone you trust...

"Someone like you, Macy..."

Dear Reader,

Best friends to lovers? It's one of my favorite themes. In this Christmas love story, it's actually best friends... to husband and wife.

Joe Bravo has been in love twice. Both times, the one he loved shattered his heart. He's never falling in love again. But Joe does very much want a family. And who better to make a family with than his best friend, Macy Storm?

Divorced and raising her bright, quirky six-year-old daughter on her own, Macy's not interested in getting married again. Maybe someday, but not now. The hurt from her ex-husband's betrayal is still far too fresh.

But her dear friend Joe can be very convincing. Joe is quick to remind her of the strong bond between them. They're in business together; they count on each other. Their mutual trust is unbreakable. Though they are not in love, they do love each other very much.

Joe promises that they can create a beautiful life together raising Ana, building their business and having more kids. They will share all the good things that marriage has to offer—without the heartbreak Joe has suffered in the past because he was foolish enough to fall in love. It's the perfect plan, one built on trust, respect and love. Really, what could possibly go wrong?

I'm wishing you and yours a merry Christmas and the brightest of New Years—and I hope Joe and Macy's story gives you all the holiday feels.

Happy reading, everyone,

Christine

Prologue

Fourteen years ago...

Dear Macy,
Okay, I'm doing it. I'm writing you a letter. One letter on actual paper with an actual pen. And I know your game. You think if I write one, I'll just go ahead and write more. Wrong.
Because, come on. Really? Why write a letter when we're in the same class and I could just talk to you in person? Think about it. This is a pointless assignment and sometimes you have to just say no. And that's why I think we should just say no and not do it. Mrs. Kubblemeyer can find some other way to torture us.
Yours truly,
Joe Bravo

Dear Joe,
See? You did it. You even spelled all the words right. That wasn't so hard, was it?
Please write me another one because I want an A in freshman English and for that to happen, we need to write at least six or seven letters each. Joe, it's just not okay for you to mess this up for me—or for you,

either. I mean it. We got assigned to do this together and if you don't get with the program, you're bringing your grade down and mine, too.

I promise you it won't be that hard. Because think about it. You're already doing it. You just wrote me a letter and it did not kill you. You might even surprise yourself and find out you're good at this.
Sincerely,
Macy Lynn Oberholzer

Dear Macy,
I'm onto your plan. You got me to agree to write one letter, now you're pushing me for more. And don't act like it's a big deal that I know how to spell. That's flat-out insulting.

I just don't get it. How does you and me writing letters to each other help us in any way whatsoever in real life? It doesn't.
Joe

Dear Joe,
Oh, come on, you know why we're doing this. The Guernsey Literary and Potato Peel Pie Society *is an epistolary novel, a story told in letters. Writing letters of our own helps us to appreciate the book more.*
Macy

Dear Macy,
Well, I am feeling zero, zip, nada appreciation-wise from writing these letters. I read the book. We spent a whole lot of time talking about it in class. And I even wrote a book report. It's enough.
Joe

Dear Joe,
Just write me another letter, please, one that's at least a page long. Write me a letter and I'll write back and we'll keep doing that until we have enough to finish this assignment.
Macy

Dear Macy,
I give up. You'll be sorry, but here goes...

Eight years ago...

Macy,
All these years since those first letters you made me write to get yourself that A. And here I am, still writing letters to you. Never knew that would happen. Sometimes I think I should quit but I just can't stop myself.

Because I'll get to thinking of what you wrote me last time or what's going on in my life right now and before you know it, I grab the nearest Uni-Ball and a fresh sheet of paper, and the words just come rolling on out. Wouldn't Mrs. Kubblemeyer be proud?

And damn. Here I am in Mainhattan, Frankfurt, Germany, actually picking up more than a few words in the language, fifteen months into my two years of active duty, getting through it, you know? And then...

Macy, I don't even know how to tell you this. It's all gone to hell for me. It's Lindsay. I don't know if you heard yet, but she dumped me. She's been seeing some guy from Cheyenne and he's asked her to marry him. He's moving back home and she's going with him.

I guess I should have known this would happen. I mean, it's happened before with her. You know that her childhood was crap and she's got a boatload of issues. But, Macy, she swore to me never again. And I believed her when she promised she would wait for me.

But over the past six months, the care packages and letters slowed to a trickle and then she stopped answering my DMs...

I should have known. But I didn't know and now I'm feeling really down. I'm just a chump and I hate it. I swear to you, Macy, never again. I'm going to be single the rest of my life. Because love? It's not worth it. Not to me, anyway.

Write something funny to me. Cheer me up a little, will you please?
Joe

Joe,
I am so sorry. I mean, really sorry. Sorry enough that I can't think of one funny thing to say.

And of course you feel down. How could she do this to you? I always liked her and now I just...

All right. I'm not going to hate on her—not in this letter, anyway. But you know what? Call me when you can, okay? We'll talk. I would like to hear your voice. And to tell you out loud that whatever you're feeling right now is exactly what you should be feeling and whatever's going on in your head, let it happen. It's okay. It's part of the process of dealing with a messed up situation.

And all right, I did consult wikiHow just now so I

wouldn't say anything that could scar you for life at a bad time like this. Don't laugh.

Or wait. Do laugh. It's good for you, especially now when I'm guessing you're feeling like you'll never laugh again.

Just, you know, feel what you feel and be okay with it. I'm still here and I got you, ride or die and all that. Watch for my care package coming your way soon. In it you will find all the random crap you never knew you needed.
And call me when you can.
Macy

Six years ago...

Joe!
Thank you! For being my best friend and my man of honor. Having both you and Riley stand up with me on my wedding day, well, it was perfect. I was already the happiest woman alive to be marrying Caleb and looking forward to the baby coming (in less than a month now, can you believe it?). Having you there for our wedding has made me even happier...

Macy,
You have to know that I would never let you get married without me there to make sure it all went according to plan. And it did. Caleb Storm is a lucky, lucky man.

I really did hope you might move home eventually—after college and then again after last year when you decided to get out and see the world. Now that I've seen the world a little myself, I know for sure

I wouldn't ever live anywhere else but right here in Medicine Creek.

I get it, though. Caleb has to be where the snowboarding is and you love Caleb and want to stay by his side. I was rooting for Jackson Hole because at least it's in-state. But Seattle makes sense. It's got so much going on and there's great snowboarding in all directions.

Just be happy, all right? And keep writing me letters. And above all, reach out when Ana comes. Send me word the day she's born and I'll be on my way to Washington State because I can't wait to meet my goddaughter up close and in person...

Four years ago...

Macy,
How's my goddaughter? Send more pics immediately. I miss her and I need to get out there to Seattle again soon. Because I know she's growing fast and I missed some stuff with her—first step, first word. That's just wrong. Please give her a big hug and a kiss for me and tell her I will see her soon.

And Macy Lynn, I have news. Big news. I've met someone. Her name is Becca Wright. She moved to town two months ago and works up in Sheridan as an insurance agent at Bighorn Life and Casualty. I met her at Arlington's Steakhouse. She was sitting at the bar and I asked if the seat next to her was taken—and I know, I know. Not my best pickup line.

But guess what, Macy? It worked out fine. Becca patted that seat and gave me a smile that made me forget how to talk for a minute there. That girl. She does love to party. We did too many shots and we laughed and laughed. Since that night, I can't stay away.

I know you are grinning because you love being right. Yes, after Lindsay, I said never again. And you said to be patient, to sit with my feelings, to give it time. I said to hell with that. I was done with love.

But, Macy, I was wrong. Becca Wright is the woman for me...

Three years ago...

Dear Joe,
This is one of those letters, the kind it hurts a lot to write.

Caleb's found someone else. Her name is Jaquel— that's right. Jaquel. Like Jaqueline but minus the last three letters. He and Jaquel have been together for months, or so he tells me. And buckle up, because you will not believe this...

Jaquel is having Caleb's baby. Déjà vu all over again? You'd better believe it.

He wants a divorce. Which is fine. I wouldn't stay with him now if he begged me on hands and knees.

And you know how you've said that you wished I'd move home? Well, surprise! Caleb's agreed to give me full physical custody of Ana. So my little girl and I are coming home.

The other good news in this mess is that I'm in excellent shape financially. I got the house which I've now decided to sell. And Caleb may be a cheater, but he didn't put up much of a fight when it came to the divorce settlement. At first, I thought I would stay here in Washington State. But no. I want to go home. And when I get home, I'm putting my business degree to use helping Mom out with the flower shop. I have big plans for Betty's Blooms, believe me. I'll be dragging the shop into the twenty-first-century retail world. For starters, I'll be taking over the store's nonexistent online presence and developing a plan to bring in more customers, a plan that will start with a redesign of the store itself. Mom says she's on board with whatever I want to do—and I have to tell you, I actually believe her. She's excited to get more free time and to have her granddaughter and me back home to stay.

And that's not all. Joe, if you meant what you said about wishing I were there to help you out at the hardware store, I'm in. No pressure, I promise you. Just let me know either way.

And give Becca a hug for me, please. I am looking forward to getting to know her better.
Yours always,
Macy

Dear Macy,
I don't know where to start. What I would love to do most right now is to track down Caleb and beat the ever-loving...

Okay. Never mind. Violence is not the answer—or so I've been told.

Do you need my shoulder to cry on? I'm here for you anytime. But somehow I get the feeling you've zipped right past the crying stage and moved on to the action phase. Did you call Riley? I hope you did.

Sometimes a woman just needs another woman to talk to.

But I'm here for whatever you need. You only have to let me know.

And I hate that Caleb has turned out to be such a complete and total waste of space as a man and a human being. Not to mention a fool to give a woman like you no choice but to walk away.

Was that too harsh?

Sorry, not sorry...

On a happier note, I am so damn glad you and Ana are coming home to stay. And it's great that you'll be working with your mom at the flower shop.

As for the hardware store, yes! You're hired—which you will already know when you get this letter. Because I'm going to text you right now to set up a time to talk it over in detail.
Joe

Two years ago...

Hey Joe,
Even though I live right here in town now, even though we work together and I see you just about every day, sometimes I miss your letters and I miss sitting down and writing to you. Sometimes, like now, I just want to put what I'm thinking on paper. I want to slap a stamp on it and send it off to you through the US mail like people used to do way back in the day. Sometimes, I just need to write down on paper what I feel in my heart.

What I feel is pain, Joe. And I know the pain I feel

can't come close to the hurt you're going through right now.

I also know you're not going to want to hear this right now. So you don't have to hear it. You don't have to read it. You can tear it up, throw it in the trash, set it on fire.

But I hope you won't. I hope you'll save it for some day in the future, someday long after you've lived through the awfulness you're feeling now.

Because you will live through it. And you will be all right. Eventually.

Joe, Becca did love you. So much. I know it hurts to remember that she promised you to give up the drinking—and then didn't. I get how you feel. You said it out loud to me. You said, "She blew off her promise. She drove drunk and now she's gone." You said, "She's dead. She's dead and I can't forgive her." You said, "I thought she was the one for me. I thought we would get married, have kids, be happy together. But all that is never going to happen now. She broke me, Macy. She broke me so bad."

You also said that you were never falling in love with anyone ever again, and that you meant it this time. That getting over Lindsay was nothing compared to this.

I heard you, Joe. I heard every word. Each one is burned into my brain.

I know that you're hurting and I know that it's bad. I know you mean what you say when you say, "Never again." But Joe, hearts heal. Just wait and see.

You will find the woman for you, the one to spend your life with. I know you will, Joe. And I will always be there for you, I promise you, just like you've always been there for me—and for Ana, too.

Will you be angry with me when you read this? Will you feel that I don't understand?

Probably. Because I am kind of stepping over the line, promising you that eventually it will be all right. Telling you what you're going to feel sometime in the future.

But I just...

I love you lots, Joe. And I want to make it better even though I know I can't.

Just know that I'm here, okay? Just know that when you need someone to listen, you can always count on me.
Your Friend Forever,
Macy

Chapter One

Two years later, present day

The doorbell rang just as Macy stuck her head into the large upstairs bathroom to encourage her six-year-old daughter to get a move on.

Ana, floating on her back in the tub with her eyes closed and her long black hair drifting out around her, sat up with a splash. "Doorbell, Mom," she said with a look of great patience as bathwater ran down her face and glued her hair to her narrow shoulders. "Better go see who it is." Grabbing a red plastic cup as it bobbed by, she scooped up tub water and poured it over the top of her head.

On the bathroom counter next to the sink, Voodoo, Ana's Bengal cat, sat calmly licking his left front paw. Voodoo was seventeen inches tall, weighed twenty-two pounds and had been known to open doors and turn on faucets with those big paws of his. Last year, Ana had taught him to walk on a leash. The two of them were a pair, Ana and Voodoo. If Ana had her way, she would take that cat everywhere. Voodoo felt the same. Wherever Ana went, he wanted to be.

The doorbell rang again.

"Better see who it is," Ana lisped. She'd lost her two

front baby teeth recently and all her *s*'s came out a bit mangled.

Macy checked to see that the bath towel was in reach and Ana had brought her pj's into the bathroom with her. Yes, on both counts. "Need help?"

"'Course not."

Macy stifled a grin. Her six-year-old daughter was amazingly self-reliant. "Get out before you turn into a prune. You need to get ready for bed."

Another chime of the doorbell. "Out," Macy said. "Now."

"I *am*," Ana replied with an eye roll.

Downstairs, Macy opened the front door to find Joe Bravo standing on the welcome mat in the chilly October darkness. She wasn't the least surprised to see him. He dropped by unannounced all the time—to discuss work or just to hang out. Sometimes he came by to see Ana.

Bracing one hand against the doorframe, he swept off his hat with the other. "You're home. Good. I saw the lights on, but after ringing the bell three times, I was starting to wonder."

"Just trying to coax Ana out of the tub." Macy stepped back. He came in and she shut the door. "If I let her, she'll fool around in there for hours." She watched as he hung his buckskin jacket on a peg, then hooked his hat on the next peg over. "What's up?" she asked.

"Just want to talk."

"About…?"

He cast a glance toward the stairs. "Once Ana's in bed."

"Is it about the store?"

"Nope."

"Well, then, what?"

"What'd I just say?"

"Alrighty, then. I guess I'll have to wait till Ana's in

bed." She looked at him sideways. "But really, this is sounding very mysterious—maybe just a hint?"

He chuckled. "No way."

"Fine. Coffee? A drink?"

"I'd take a whiskey if you have it."

"Come on, then." She led him across the great room to the kitchen beyond it. "Sit."

He pulled out a chair at the table as she took a bottle of Jim Beam from a high cupboard. Grabbing a glass, she set it and the bottle in front of him. "You're not drinking?" he asked.

"You need me to have a drink so you can say whatever it is you plan to say to me?"

"That's right, I do."

Macy had a thousand questions. "Joe, I..." The look on his face said, *Just pour yourself a damn drink.* A jolt of alarm went through her. "Joe, really. Is everything okay?"

He looked at her steadily now. "Everything is fine. I promise. I want to talk, that's all. But after Ana's in bed."

"Okay then." She grabbed another glass and set it down next to his.

He poured for both of them and then raised his glass. She tapped her drink to his.

"Joe!" Ana, dressed in her Green Lantern pajamas, her damp hair loose on her shoulders, stood in the arch to the living room. "You came to see me!"

"Oh, yes I did!" He held out his arms.

With Voodoo at her heels, she went to him. He scooped her up and set her on his lap as Voodoo detoured to his water bowl. "How's my girl?"

"Good." She sent Macy a sly look. "I want Joe to tuck me in."

Macy shrugged. "Ask him nicely." Ana did as instructed

and Joe, of course, said yes. As if he'd ever say no to her. Macy nodded. "Okay, then. But first let's go back upstairs and dry your hair..."

Macy followed them up to blow-dry Ana's hair, then left them alone. A half hour of tucking-in later, Joe came downstairs where Macy waited by the fire in the great room.

"I topped off your drink just in case." She nodded at the glass on the coffee table.

"Thanks." He sat on the sofa beside her, picked up the glass and sipped. "Ana and I read a few chapters of *Revenge of the Dragon Lady*—and by that I mean, she read them to me."

"She loves those books." *Dragon Slayers' Academy* was currently Ana's favorite series. "She reads at a fourth-grade level now."

"Wicked smart."

"Some days I have trouble keeping up with her." Macy sat back against the armrest and studied her friend's handsome face. Joe Bravo had broad shoulders, blue eyes and a devilish smile. "Okay. I've got a sip or two of whiskey left and I'm listening, Joe. What's going on?"

Several way-too-quiet seconds elapsed. Then, finally, he said, "You know, thanks to you, Bravo Hardware and Building Supply is now a real moneymaker."

She scoffed. "So you *are* here to talk about the store."

"No, I'm not. But I do want to say that you are amazing."

"Why, thank you!" She pressed her hand to her heart. "I've done my best."

"Smartest thing this cowboy ever did, partnering up with you."

Four years ago, the local hardware store had gone belly-up due to bad management. The store, along with all the equipment, stock on hand and a fifteen-year lease remaining on the building, were offered for sale at forty-thousand dollars.

A few months before that, Joe had received an inheritance of eighty thousand after the death of a distant Bravo relative. He'd put half that money into buying the store and the other half into building his house on his family's ranch, the Double-K. Then, for the next year, he'd struggled to keep the store going. During that time, he'd written Macy long letters full of frustration and growing panic as he tried to run the store, make progress on his new house and also hold up his end on the ranch.

But then Macy had moved home and started working for him. She was proud of how, together, they'd managed to turn things around.

"We've done well," she said.

"You bet we have. And we both know that you're the reason the store is a success."

She gave him an encouraging smile. "Thank you again—and get to the point, please."

He knocked back another gulp of whiskey. "You know how much I want a family."

"I do, yes." However, since Becca's death, he remained absolutely certain that he did not want a wife. In the past eighteen months, he'd registered with more than one adoption agency.

"Joe. Just tell me what's happened."

He gave her a shrug. "Nothing. That's the problem. The adoption thing is going nowhere."

Mildly, she reminded him, "You do know that it usually takes longer than you've been at it, even for married couples."

"Yeah, well, I keep thinking there has to be a better way to do this."

"What about fostering to adopt? You could try that again."

He'd fostered an eight-year-old boy, Aiden, for five months the year before. But then Aiden's mother had worked out her problems well enough to get her son back. And then she'd promptly packed up her life and her son and moved to Wisconsin to be near her family.

"I don't think so," Joe said, his elbows braced on his spread knees and his eyes on the floor between his boots. "It hurts too much to get my hopes up." He lifted his head. "I can't take the uncertainty at this point. I still miss Aiden, I really do, and I don't think I'll ever see him again."

What could she say? "I know it's hard…"

"Yeah, well…" He looked straight into her eyes. "I've been thinking."

She was thinking, too—thinking of the letter she'd written him right after Becca died. He'd never once mentioned that letter. And neither had she.

Had enough time passed to broach the painful subject at last?

He was watching her so steadily. "What?"

She blinked. "It's just… Well, have you considered dating again? If you found a nice woman, you could—"

"Macy."

All he'd said was her name and yet she felt marginally offended. "What?"

"How many times have we talked about this?"

"I know, but—"

"No buts. Please. I'm not looking for a stranger to make a life with."

"But, Joe, everybody's a stranger at first. Let me just state the painfully obvious and say that you would get to know her. In time, she wouldn't *be* a stranger."

"No kidding."

"Don't give me sarcasm, Joe. Please."

"Oh, come on. I tried it the usual way, with Lindsay and then with Becca. It didn't work out either time. What happened with Lindsay was bad. But Becca..." He looked away. "Please don't push me on this."

"But if you—"

"I mean it. Stop finding new ways to tell me that I need to try again. *You* need to believe me when I say that trying again with some stranger, learning to trust and believe in her and then having it all go wrong? That is the last thing I'm ever going to do."

"But if you did try and it worked out, you and that nice woman you eventually fell in love with could just let nature take its course. You could create a family together—and if somehow, making babies didn't happen, well, adopting a child would be at least a little bit easier than trying to do it all on your own. Plus, you would have each other and that would count for a lot."

"Do you know that you sound exactly like my mother right now?"

She groaned. "No..."

"Pretty much—and I meant what I said. I don't want to go the trad way. Not again. Think about it. They call it *falling in love* for a reason. And the reason is that you fall. And if the *nice* woman you think I need to *find* turns out to be someone who can't be trusted to catch me, I'm screwed. Uh-uh. This time I'm taking a whole different approach."

She sat up straighter. "This time? So then, you are considering dating again?"

"No. I'm considering getting married."

She sipped her drink and set it back down. "Wow. Okay. But not dating?"

"That's right."

"So you're thinking a mail-order bride, maybe?"

"Didn't I just say that I'm not getting anything going with some stranger?"

"Gotcha. So...what exactly *are* you planning?"

"It's simple. Falling in love is dangerous. I need to choose a woman I can trust, not some stranger I met online. Not some woman a friend set me up with. And definitely no one I met during happy hour. What I want is what my folks have—devotion and commitment."

She couldn't stop herself from reminding him, "Your parents are in love, Joe."

"Yeah, but that's not the point."

"Yes it is. Love *is* the point."

"Macy Lynn, it's the devotion that matters. The mutual trust. The dedication. It's the ride or die. I want that, not the romantic love crap. Falling in love just messes you over. I don't want to fall. When you fall, it's too easy to break something. I am not getting broken again."

She drew a careful breath and let it out nice and slow. "Be realistic. No one can guarantee a life of unbroken promises. Things happen. People change." She thought of Caleb and wished she hadn't. She'd believed him when he promised her forever. And she'd been so wrong. She was doing fine now. But Caleb's betrayal had cut her to the core. "It's just the way it is, Joe. You won't get any guarantees. Neither life nor love work that way."

"But it *could* work that way, with someone you trust. Someone like you, Macy..."

Macy shut her eyes. Should she have known from the first where he was going with this? Probably.

Straightening her shoulders, she faced him. "Look, Joe..."

"Come on. Just think about it."

"Uh-uh." She was already on her feet and backing away from him with both hands up. "You can't be serious."

"Oh, but I am." He smiled then, slowly.

"Joe. No. The two of us are not getting married."

For the longest time, he said nothing. They stared at each other. It was excruciating.

Finally, he said, "All I'm asking is that you think about it."

"No, I—"

"Consider it realistically. We could have it all. Best friends are the best bet for marriage. We know everything about each other. We trust each other with no conditions. We work together. And Ana really is like a daughter to—"

"Stop." She said it flatly. "I mean it, Joe."

He went quiet, just sitting there, staring up at her through pleading eyes.

She struggled to find the words that would get through to him, words to make him see his plan couldn't work. "Joe. We're just not like that with each other. We're…buddies, you know?"

"Yeah." His eyes were somber now. "We're buddies and I want you to marry me. I want you to let us be a real family—you, me and Ana."

She folded her arms across her chest and scoffed. "Oh, right. Piece of cake. Is that all?"

"No. It's not all. I want us to try for more kids, too. The natural way, for sure. Maybe by adopting, but I don't know about that. I'm sick of all the red tape, the waiting and wondering. But maybe we could talk about the adoption thing later, see how we feel after we've been married for a while."

"But, Joe, we're not getting—"

"Hold on. I'm not finished."

She sighed, but she gave in. "Fine. Finish."

"The way I see it, if you and Ana are with me, if the three of us are a team, I can wait as long as it takes for more kids. If more kids didn't happen, I would be okay with that. Because family is what matters and that's what we'd be."

She backed away until her calves hit the easy chair across the coffee table from him. "Joe. No." With a hard sigh, she collapsed into the chair. "Absolutely not."

He sat forward, braced his elbows on his spread knees and pinned her with a look of sheer determination. "Just think about it. Please. Don't make a decision right now."

"But there is no decision to make. Joe, I'm almost as disillusioned as you are when it comes to true love. But that doesn't mean getting married without it is a good idea."

He stood. "I'm going to go."

"What?"

"Please just think it over."

"No, wait. Hold on. Joe, you can't do this—just come over here and lay this on me and then get up and go…"

He came around the coffee table to stand in front of her. "There's nothing more to say right now. Think about it. Take your time."

"But I don't need time." She stared up at him, willing him to accept her answer as final. "It's not going to happen."

He bent close. "Macy…"

"I mean it, Joe. No."

And then he cradled her face between his two rough warm hands and brushed a soft barely-there kiss across her upturned mouth. When he pulled away, her lips tingled where his had touched them. "'Night, Macy Lynn."

She sat there staring blindly into the middle distance as

she heard his boots retreating across the great room floor. The front door opened and then clicked shut.

With a groan of pure exasperation, she slumped back in the easy chair. Where in the world had he come up with a wild idea like this one?

She didn't really want to know.

Eventually, it would pass, she told herself. He would give it more thought and realize that this disappointment at losing Aiden and the challenges of the adoption process in general had him grasping at straws. In the end, he would come to accept she was right. He would end up wondering what he could possibly have been thinking to have suggested that the two of them should get married.

Too bad she had no idea how long it would take him to change his mind and let it go.

Rising with a sigh, she picked up their glasses and carried them to the kitchen.

Joe woke before dawn the next day with a big smile on his face. Because he had a goal and the goal was to get Macy to marry him.

So what if she'd said no last night? He would keep trying, keep showing her all the ways it was going to be great for them to make a family together.

Eventually, she would get on board with his plan.

He threw on his work clothes, filled a steel thermos with coffee and headed out to handle morning chores with his sweet-natured Goldador, Rosie, at his heels.

His dad caught up with him at the chicken pen. "Breakfast at the main house," Nate Bravo said as he bent to give Rosie a quick scratch behind the ears. "Your mom's making pancakes."

"I'll be there," Joe replied.

"Good." His dad headed off toward the barn and sheds.

As Joe gathered eggs and then helped his brother, Jason, with the horses, he considered how best to finally convince Macy that marrying him was a brilliant idea.

The main thing was to get her to see how good they could be together—maybe write her a letter that wowed her with all the reasons they would make a great team.

Because, as he'd correctly pointed out to her the night before, they were already a team. Getting married would only make them more so...

Damn. He should have asked her to marry him weeks ago. Months ago, even. If he'd only seen the light sooner, they could be married now. He, Macy and Ana would be a family already.

Now that he knew what he wanted, it seemed as though he'd always known it deep down. He'd only been waiting for the idea to rise to the surface.

Because the two of them, him and Macy, they could have all the good things together—companionship, understanding. Someone to count on no matter what. Fun, too. She made him laugh. She also made him think.

Macy made everything better, she really did. And then there was Ana. In so many ways, Ana was like his own kid already. Caleb Storm might be a world-famous snowboarder with money running out his ears. But when it came to what mattered in life, that fool didn't have a clue.

Macy was the real deal. A woman a man could count on—and smart and pretty, too. Caleb hadn't appreciated what he had with Macy—or with his own little girl. The man paid child support, period. Yeah, it was a serious chunk of change that he handed over every month. But it wasn't anywhere near enough. A child needed so much more than money from her dad.

Joe could do better for Ana—he already was doing better for her. Who'd gone to her Bring Your Dad to School Day last year? Who brought her out here to the Double-K every chance he got? Who'd put her on a horse for the first time that summer? Who stepped right up whenever Macy had too much going on and needed someone to drive Ana to the dentist up in Sheridan or the pediatrician in Buffalo?

Joe did, that's who.

And it wasn't only about Ana. Joe knew he could be a good husband to Macy. He could be the man she deserved. And he would be.

Yeah. The more he thought about him and Macy together for life, the more he knew it was a great idea. He had his own house now with plenty of room right here on the family ranch. Macy could rent or sell her place in town. Or if she really wanted to live in town, he would move in with her and Ana. It wasn't that far from town to the Double-K.

It was going to work out; he could feel it. He would be patient. In time, she would see the light.

"Joseph Nathan, what's going on with you?" his mom asked at breakfast. "You're a thousand miles away."

Joe blinked and looked around the table. His brother, Jason, and Jason's wife, Piper, had brought their two kids over to share the pancake feast this morning. Four-year-old Emmy was busy licking syrup off her fork. Miles James, who'd had his first birthday three months ago, sat in his high chair shoving precut bites of pancake and bacon into his mouth with sticky little fingers.

Not far from the table, Rosie was sprawled on the floor next to Jason's dog, Kenzo. Both dogs appeared to be sleeping. But Joe knew they were ready to spring into action the moment somebody dropped a hunk of pancake or a bit of bacon.

He thought of Macy again. He definitely should have married her a year ago. If he'd had enough sense to get going on his plan earlier, she and Ana would be sitting right here at this table now.

His mom shared a look with his dad and his dad said, "Your mom asked you a question."

Joe couldn't decide what to say. No way was he going to be discussing his marriage plans with the family at this point. He would do this the right way—by getting Macy firmly on board first.

Everyone at the table was watching him now, even the kids.

He shrugged. "Just thinking that it's time to change the oil in the Chevy C/K." It was only halfway a lie. The ancient ranch truck did need an oil change.

"Truck maintenance makes you smile?" His mom scoffed. "Nobody's buying that story."

Joe gave her a smirk. "Hey, Ma. I'm a happy guy."

And he was. He was a man with a plan. Now he only needed to convince his future wife of what a fine plan it was.

All that morning, Macy felt on edge.

She knew Joe like she knew the face she saw every time she looked in a mirror. And she had a very strong feeling she'd been lying to herself last night. Just because he'd gotten some wild, impossible idea in his head, didn't mean he'd wake up the next morning and realize he was wrong.

Uh-uh. When Joe had walked out on her the night before he'd had that look he got sometimes—a stubborn look. Thinking about that look made her realize he would not give up. He would keep after her, checking in constantly to ask if she'd changed her mind yet, coming up with new reasons they just *had* to tie the knot. Because when Joe got that stubborn look, he never backed down.

For instance, when he bought the hardware store, everyone had warned him he was taking on too much. Macy reminded him that he had no experience in retail, that he really ought to invest that forty-thousand dollars in something else. That he'd be much better off just putting it in savings.

He'd bought the store, anyway. He'd insisted that, one way or another, it would all work out.

And it had. Eventually. Partly because Macy had come home and gone to work for him. But also because he didn't give up when things got dicey. Joe worked hard. True, he made mistakes, but he also learned from them.

He was such a good man. And she loved him, she did. He mattered to her. A lot. And he mattered to Ana, too. No way they could afford to screw up the good thing they had together by suddenly deciding to take a walk down the aisle. Somehow, she had to make him see that if she gave in and agreed to his plan, they *would* screw it up.

There were just too many ways it could all go wrong. And if that happened, if their marriage didn't work out, they could lose their friendship. She could end up with a second ex-husband in place of her best friend Joe.

No. Just...no way. It could never work.

After dropping Ana off at Medicine Creek Elementary, Macy went to Betty's Blooms. She spent the early morning rearranging a few of the displays. When her mom came in at ten, Macy headed to the small office in the back of the shop to update the website and get caught up with the payables.

At eleven o'clock, she and her mom shared an early takeout lunch from the Stagecoach Grill. They were sitting in the back room, eating and chatting, taking turns getting up to deal with customers whenever the bell over the door to the street rang.

It wasn't that busy. The conversation had lulled and they'd been sitting in silence enjoying grilled chicken sandwiches when Betty looked up and asked, "You okay, honey?"

Macy put on a smile. "Of course. Just, you know, lots to do as always." *Including heading over to Bravo Hardware where I truly hope my best friend, the boss, won't be lying in wait with more reasons why I should marry him.*

"You look a little stressed." Betty sipped from her can of Polar Seltzer.

"No more than usual," she said.

"If there's anything I can do to help, you let me know."

"I will, Mom. Thanks."

Right then, the bell rang out in the shop. Her mom patted her knee. "Finish your sandwich. I'll get it."

At noon, Macy walked into Bravo Hardware and Building Supply.

A year before, Joe had given her 10 percent of the store as payment for the way she'd turned the business around. That extra 10 percent was in addition to the generous salary they'd agreed on when she first came home from Seattle.

Nowadays, Macy managed the books, including payroll and inventory. She made decisions on seasonal sales promotions. She created and arranged the displays. She also clerked whenever necessary.

They had two other employees to stock shelves, wait on customers and man the register, so her schedule was flexible. It was working out great. She had time to keep on top of her responsibilities at both shops.

When she walked in, Myron Finkel stood at the register ringing up a sale. Myron always wore overalls and had been working at the store for more than two decades.

"Afternoon, Myron," she said.

"Macy." Myron gave her a nod as she went through the arch to the small office in back where she hung her jacket by the door and stashed her purse in the bottom drawer of her desk before booting up her laptop. She was just letting herself feel relieved that Joe didn't seem to be around so she wouldn't have to deal with him when he spoke from the open doorway behind her.

"Hey."

She turned and forced a careful smile. "Joe."

There was a weird moment. They just looked at each other. She waited grimly for him to start in about the marriage thing again.

But he surprised her. "Riley called from the Statesman." Riley Thompson was not only Macy's other best friend, but she also co-owned the Statesman Hotel with her mother-in-law, Annette. Joe went on, "She ordered some cabinet hardware a couple weeks ago. It finally came in. I thought I would run it over there for her."

"You want me to do it?"

He put up both hands. "No way. You've got that laptop open. That means bookkeeping and spreadsheets. You're the expert at that stuff. Plus, I've got a couple of other errands to run."

"Okay, then," she said briskly, breathing easier now she knew he wouldn't be sticking around—and that they could talk about business as usual without him bringing up that *other* topic.

He sent a wave back over his shoulder as he left.

For an hour or so, she paid invoices. At 2:30 p.m., she

took a break to pick up Ana at school and drop her off for a playdate.

When she got back to the store, Joe stood behind the register. Her heart sped up at the sight of him—which was absurd. Especially considering that all he did was give her a quick wave as she ducked through the door to the office.

As she worked at her laptop, she kept expecting to hear the sound of footsteps behind her, kept imagining his warm deep voice telling her she worked too hard. And then, when she replied that she liked working, he would teasingly order her to relax for a minute.

And then he would start in again about how they should get married....

But that never happened. Joe avoided her office. When she left to get Ana at five o'clock, he was back in the Electrical aisle with his second cousin, Josh, who owned Bravo Construction there in town.

Macy could hear them back there, talking and laughing. They seemed to be having way too much fun for a couple of guys discussing light fixtures or breaker boxes or whatever.

Then again, Joe and Josh were good friends. In fact, they'd all been in the same class in school—Macy, Joe, Josh and Riley, too. Over the years, from kindergarten through high school, the four of them had become something of a crew. They remained so to this day.

And Joe and his cousin almost always kidded around when Josh came into the store to buy materials. The sound of their laughter had never bothered her before. Today, though, it annoyed her no end that they were having such a fine old time when all she could think of was Joe and his ridiculous marriage proposal.

At home, she cooked dinner for her and Ana. It was like any other night. She helped Ana with a class assignment.

They watched two episodes of *The Thundermans* together with Voodoo sprawled on the sofa between them.

At eight thirty, she kissed Ana good-night and then went back downstairs thinking she would...

What?

She didn't want to watch another show. She wanted...

Really, she had no idea what she wanted.

Upstairs in her bathroom, she washed her face and brushed her teeth. She got in bed and considered reading for a while. The thick juicy novel of a glamorous actress in the 1950s and her many loves and losses should have had her glued to the pages.

But she just wasn't feeling it. Not tonight.

All day, she'd dreaded the moment when Joe cornered her and started in again about his outrageous marriage plan. She'd been a bundle of nerves just waiting for him to bring it up.

Instead, he'd said hi and headed off to the Statesman to take Riley some drawer pulls. And then later, he'd yukked it up in Electrical with Josh.

On the nightstand, her phone buzzed with a text from Joe.

Just checking in. You okay?

She reminded herself to hold firm, say no, as she hit the phone icon.

He picked up on the first ring. "Hey."

"Hey."

"You all right?" he asked.

"I am just fine." And she was. Definitely.

"Have you been thinking it over?"

"I have no idea what you're talking about."

"Liar," he said teasingly.

And she couldn't help it. She smiled. "Stop. We're not doing that."

"Doing what?"

"You know what. It's not a good idea, Joe."

"No...?" He drew the word out, teasing her with it.

"No."

"I disagree." His voice was oddly pensive now. "In fact, I've been thinking about it all day."

A mocking laugh escaped her. "Even while you were back there in Electrical having a fine old time with Josh?"

"Yup. Even then. I've been thinking and the more I think, the more certain I am that marrying you will be the best decision I ever make."

She felt a flare of heat. It swept up her neck and warmed her cheeks. "Will be? You say it like it's already a done deal."

"You're thinking I'm overconfident, aren't you?" he asked—and then he answered for her. "I'm not. I know it won't happen if you don't want it, too. But I like to keep a positive attitude, especially about something as important as marrying my best friend."

She opened her mouth to say slowly and clearly that she was not going to marry him and he'd better stop assuming she would. But her throat felt tight and for a second or two, she was scared she would cry. But why? She had absolutely no reason to cry.

Before she could pull herself together, he asked again, "You sure you're okay?"

"Of course."

"All right, tough girl. Just checking."

She cradled the phone close. "Thanks for checking in."

"No problem."

"'Night, Joe."
"'Night, Mace."
And then he was gone.
She sat there for several minutes with the phone in her hand wondering what had just happened, sniffling a little but never quite letting a single tear fall.

Chapter Two

Five minutes after she hung up with Joe, Macy called Riley.

Her other best friend answered with, "It's been days. How are you?"

"I'm good. You?"

Riley blew out a hard breath. "I've been better. Dillon has a cold." Her little boy was three. "Also, yesterday at the hotel two of our housekeepers walked out."

"Why?"

"Apparently, they hate each other. Too bad they failed to report the issue to their supervisor until they were walking out the door. But the good news is that Annette came over this evening. She spent some time with Dillon, dosing him with PediaCare and reading him his favorite stories. When he finally went to sleep, I opened a nice bottle of red and Annette and I griped about the living hell of running a hotel." Riley and her mother-in-law were close. Not only were they business partners, but they were also both widowed. Annette's husband, Trevor, had died years ago. Her only son and Riley's husband, TJ, had been thrown from his ATV during a weekend camping trip in the Bighorn Mountains two years ago now.

Macy commiserated with her friend. "Poor Dillon has

a cold *and* you lost half your housekeeping staff? That's awful."

"Yes, it is. Cleaning rooms is not my favorite activity. But we hired a couple of temps. Fingers crossed that at least one of them might actually work out long term."

"You do sound frazzled."

"Hey. It's not easy being a hardworking single mom."

"Amen to that. And Dillon…?"

"He's a little better today. I'm crossing my fingers he'll be back at day care on Monday."

"Give him a hug for me."

"Absolutely."

"Riley, we need to sneak away and get lunch next week—or at least coffee. No excuses."

"You're right. Tuesday. Lunch at Frackelton's." The deli-style restaurant on Main Street had great salads and sandwiches and wonderful coffee—wine and beer, too.

"It's a date," Macy said.

They talked for another half hour, catching up on the details of each other's lives—well, except for the part about Joe proposing marriage. Macy didn't know how to even start with that so she put it off. Tuesday at lunch, she would be telling all.

The next morning, Macy woke with cramps. When she checked, she found that yes, indeed, her period had arrived. She showered and took some ibuprofen. By the time Ana knocked on her bedroom door, she was feeling almost human.

"Scrambled eggs, please," said her daughter as they went downstairs together with Voodoo in the lead, wagging his long tail as he went. "And cocoa and cinnamon toast…"

"Fruit, too," Macy reminded her.

Ana fed Voodoo, set the table and sat down to peel herself an orange while Macy got the coffee going and scrambled them some eggs.

As they ate, they discussed how their Saturday would play out. Macy had the day off from both the hardware store and her mom's shop. But a day off for a working mom really meant doing all the things she rarely had time for during the week.

That morning, she and Ana ran errands and stocked up the fridge. In the afternoon, Ana hosted a two-hour playdate with three of her "very best friends." Macy did laundry and made sure no one was injured or crying as Ana and her besties built a blanket fort in the living room, snacked on Fruit Roll-Ups, pizza pinwheels and granola bites, and played dress-up with their dolls.

All three of Ana's best friends left smiling and with the same number of fingers and toes they'd started with, so Macy considered the playdate a success. She swallowed more ibuprofen and was sticking a chicken in the oven to roast when her phone beeped with a text. It was Joe.

Can U talk?

She called him and put it on speaker to keep her hands free for cooking. "What's up?" she asked cautiously.

"Miss me?" he asked when she answered the phone.

"Desperately," she replied, heavy on the sarcasm.

"Are you at home?"

"Why?" she tried to sound suspicious, but the truth was she was grinning. She loved hanging out with him, even now when the odds were pretty high the conversation would eventually work its way around to the subject of marriage.

"Myron's closing the store for me, so as of right now, I'm available."

"No kidding?"

"Nope. I just want to know what's for dinner?"

She gave it up. "Roast chicken."

"One of my favorites."

"Joe. They're *all* your favorites."

He was quiet.

She knew he was waiting for her to tell him to come over and she managed to hesitate for all of three seconds. "You coming now?"

He chuckled, the sound low and rich and full of good humor. "I'll pick up a nice bottle of white and see you in twenty minutes."

Joe arrived right on time. He poured the wine and then played Go Fish with Ana, then helped her set the table. After dinner, Macy got out her laptop and the three of them played Minecraft. It was fun and the evening went by fast. Too soon, Ana was dressed in her Beetlejuice pajamas and demanding that Joe tuck her in.

"'Night, Mom." She gave Macy an obligatory kiss on the cheek, grabbed Joe's hand and pulled him up the stairs.

Macy hadn't felt edgy or nervous all evening. But somehow, the minute Joe, Ana and the cat disappeared upstairs, she was suddenly a bundle of nerves. She knew he would start in about the marriage thing sooner or later, and she just wasn't up for it.

Joe stayed till after midnight. They talked about what he would get Ana for Christmas, about Bravo Hardware, which had enjoyed a very profitable year, one that was likely to be even more so because of the busy holiday season that was still to come.

They talked about Caleb—in hushed voices in case Ana came downstairs unexpectedly.

"I feel bad," Macy confessed. "It's like he never existed

for Ana. She doesn't talk about him—not even a mention now and then. He sends the money like clockwork. At this rate, she'll be able to buy a house when she turns eighteen—and not only that, but she'll be also able to afford any college that grants her admission."

Joe turned toward her and rested his elbow on the back of the sofa. "Look at it this way. She's a happy kid. Macy, I honestly don't think she misses him."

"Not that we can see on the outside, anyway."

"She never mentions him to me, either. Was he ever around? Seems to me he was always busy with his career."

"You're right. Caleb was constantly heading off somewhere, chasing powder or working on sponsorship deals and endorsements."

"My point, exactly."

She wanted to argue that Caleb wasn't that bad as a husband and father. But really, he was. Caleb wasn't mean. He wasn't abusive. He was merely...absent. His personal goals and priorities always came first and his ambition to be the best in his sport and to monetize his fame meant he didn't have much time for anything else—*except maybe cheating on his wife*, Macy thought with a touch of lingering bitterness.

And they needed to change the subject. "It's good she has you and her grandpa."

Macy's dad was a burly man with a ready laugh. Curtis Oberholzer ran the produce department at Big Country Grocery there in town and helped out at the flower shop, too. He adored his wife, his daughter and his granddaughter—and he was right there for all three of them anytime they needed him.

As for Caleb's parents, they were like their son—rarely around. They'd divorced when Caleb was ten and each had remarried more than once. Caleb had several half-siblings he barely knew. Neither his siblings nor his parents showed any interest in being involved in Ana's life.

"It *is* pretty sad that Ana might never really know her own dad," Macy admitted softly.

Joe caught her hand. "Hey."

She blinked at him, suddenly on guard. Was this it, then? Was he going to bring up getting married now?

But then he said, "I get pissed at the guy whenever I think about how he had it all and just threw it away."

"Okay, now," she said sternly. "Enough about Caleb."

He rubbed his thumb across the back of her hand. It felt good, his touch—reassuring, calming. And also, for the first time that she could remember, more than just friendly…

Or maybe that was only her imagination.

But no. It did somehow feel different this time.

And the truth was, she didn't hate that it felt different. Far from it. She liked it.

It was so strange. All these years they'd been friends. She had touched him often—hugged him, taken his hand, felt his fingers brush her shoulders as he helped her into her coat.

Never once in all those years had she felt anything resembling the special kind of awareness a woman experiences when there's more than friendship going on with a certain man.

Never once…

Until now—and last night, too. Last night, when he called her and asked her if she was okay. Last night, when his voice was tender and teasing and gentle. And kind—the way it had always been.

Everything was the same. And yet it was completely different somehow.

"You've got that look," he said.

"Which look is that?"

"Edgy. Like you wouldn't mind if I hung around a while, but you really think that I should go."

She had to hand it to him. "Yikes. Nailed it."

"Okay, then." He got up. "Thanks for dinner."

"Anytime." Her throat felt tight with the need to urge him to stay. But she kept her mouth shut. Instead, she followed him to the door and waited as he pulled on his jacket and plunked his hat on his head.

"'Night, Mace."

"'Night, Joe." She trailed along behind him out onto the porch and then just stood there until he got in his truck and drove away.

Back in the house, she wandered from the great room to the kitchen and back to the great room again. Was it odd that he hadn't even mentioned the marriage thing tonight?

Yeah, she decided. It was odd—not that she'd wanted to talk about it.

She hadn't.

But that he'd failed to bring it up made her wonder. Had he given up, then?

If he had, she should be glad.

But she wasn't. Right now, she didn't know what she felt.

Sunday, she and Ana stuck close to home. It was nice, just the two of them for most of the day. They walked around the block to Grandma's house for dinner. After the meal, they played a rousing game of Sorry, which Grandpa won.

It was chilly out and already dark when they walked

back home together. Voodoo greeted them at the door, purring loudly, making those chirping sounds common to Bengal cats, as though he was filling them in on how his day had gone. He followed Ana up the stars, chirping and chittering all the way.

Once Ana was in bed, Macy spent a couple of hours dealing with minor bookkeeping issues for both Betty's Blooms and the hardware store. As she worked, she realized she was waiting for her phone to buzz with a text from Joe.

That didn't happen.

She considered reaching out. But she held back.

It seemed more and more likely that he really had given up on the marriage thing. She should definitely be relieved about that.

But she went to bed feeling crampy and generally out of sorts. By morning, the cramps were fading, but the feeling of being uncomfortable in her own skin?

It was still there.

She dropped Ana off at school and headed for the flower shop, where the workday dragged. Mondays tended to be a little slower at both stores.

At eleven o'clock, when she arrived at Bravo Hardware, Myron was back in Power Tools. Macy could hear him delivering a treatise on cordless drills to a customer. She manned the register until Myron and the customer came up front together. Then she headed for her office and got to work at her desk.

"Hey," Joe said from behind her at a little after one o'clock.

She turned to find him standing in the doorway to the storeroom. "Hi."

"How was your Sunday?"

"Great!" she replied with far too much enthusiasm. "We went to dinner at my folks' house. Played Sorry."

"Sounds fun."

"It was!" she replied with the same weird excess of fervor. *Chill*, she silently reminded herself and then managed to ask more calmly, "And your Sunday?"

"Good." Was he looking at her funny?

She almost asked him what the matter was, but then he tapped his knuckles on the doorframe and said, "I've got some deliveries. And then I need to head back to the ranch later, help my dad out with a few things."

"Okay..."

"Have a good day."

"I will, Joe. You, too."

And that was it. He was gone and she suddenly felt a little sick to her stomach. He'd seemed so...careful. Like he had no idea what to say to her.

It had to be the marriage thing that was bothering him, right? He'd definitely changed his mind about it, decided that it was a bad idea and he never should have suggested it.

With a long sigh, she pressed her hands to her suddenly hot cheeks. Now she was miserable. Because things were weird between her and Joe—and looking back over all the years she'd known him, she couldn't remember a single time when she'd felt uncomfortable around him.

Not until now.

Not until his impossible, out-there marriage proposal that now he seemed eager to forget.

She gave a little cough to clear her suddenly tight throat, squared her shoulders and focused on the spreadsheet in front of her. Everything would be all right, she promised herself.

Because they would talk about it sometime soon and

clear up any weird feelings. For right now, she would concentrate on work and get through the damn day.

When she left the store to pick up Ana at school, she told Myron she would see him tomorrow. Lucky Tremayne, the other clerk, was back in the storeroom pulling stock for a delivery. Between them, Lucky and Myron could handle things just fine for the rest of the day.

As for Macy, she picked up her daughter and went home. When she pulled into the driveway, the USPS mail truck was out in front.

"I'll get the mail, Mom!"

"Okay." Macy stopped to let Ana out before putting the Subaru into the detached garage.

Ana was waiting on the front porch with both small hands full of junk mail when Macy walked up the front steps. "Nothing good," Ana announced—and then deftly pulled a #10 envelope from the pile. Smiling hugely, displaying the wide gap between her front teeth, she announced, "'Cept you did get a letter from Joe."

All the rest of the afternoon and into the evening, Joe's letter lurked in the back of Macy's mind. She'd decided to put off reading it until Ana was in bed.

That way, if there was bad news in it, she wouldn't have to hide her feelings from her daughter. She'd have until tomorrow morning to deal with whatever he'd written. She could maybe call him, talk to him about it, whatever *it* was...

Or maybe not.

All that endless afternoon and evening, she tried not to imagine what Joe's letter might contain. At least Ana never once asked about it.

At bedtime, as Voodoo made biscuits on Ana's green and purple *Wicked* bedspread, Ana asked, "Mom, are you sad?"

"What? No, sweetheart." It was true. She wasn't sad. But she was preoccupied. And worried about what she would find when she opened Joe's letter. "I just have a lot on my mind, that's all."

"Like what?"

"Grown-up stuff."

"Like what?"

Macy decided that two could play that game. "Grown-up stuff."

Ana wrinkled her nose. And then she sighed. "Just give me a hug."

"I would love to." Macy held out her arms.

Ana sat up and snuggled close.

A few minutes later, Macy turned off the light and went downstairs. She sat on the sofa in the great room and stared at the unlit logs in her fireplace until curiosity won out.

Rising, she turned off the lights on the main floor, climbed the stairs again and entered the small front bedroom she used as a home office. After silently shutting the door to the hallway, she sat at the desk by the window, took Joe's letter from the pencil drawer where she'd stuck it earlier and sliced the envelope open.

Dear Macy,
It's Friday night—the night after I asked you to marry me and twenty minutes since I hung up the phone with you tonight.

Gotta say, this whole waiting for you to decide whether or not to say yes to me? It's no fun at all.

I'm trying really hard not to put pressure on you—not to demand an answer now. Not to follow you around asking, "Have you decided yet?" over and over and over again, hoping each time that you'll give me that big beautiful smile of yours and say, "Yes, Joe! Let's get married!"

So far, I've managed to keep a lid on my enthusiasm for this brilliant idea of mine. But I need to make sure I've put it all on the table, all the excellent reasons we should make a family together.

So I'm writing you a letter. Because letters are what we do, you and me. I'm going to lay out my case for marriage right here on paper and then I'm going to back the hell off—or try to, anyway.

First off, let me just say that whether you decide to marry me or not, we already are a great team and I don't want that to change. I hope you see it that way, too.

Also on the subject of us as a team, I honestly believe that getting married will only make us stronger together than we already are.

That said, I've got bullet points.
- *You've mentioned once or twice that you would love to live at the ranch.*
- *Ana has said she would love to live on the Double-K, too.*
- *If you came to live at the ranch, you could do whatever you want with the ranch house, fix it up just the way you like it.*
- *But if what you really want is to stay in town, we could make that work and I would move in with you.*
- *Ana loves me so much and I love her right back!*
- *I can cook, and I will.*
- *I pick up after myself.*
- *I'm a hard worker.*

> - *A hard worker who has enough sense to accept his teammate's guidance when it comes to things I'm not very good at—like marketing, store design and keeping the books.*
> - *We could be happy together. I know this because we already are.*
>
>   *And for now, I'll leave it at that. And I'll leave you alone on the subject of marriage until you decide how you want it to be.*
> *Yours always,*
> *Joe.*

Macy set down the letter, picked up her phone, pulled up Joe's number and almost hit the call icon.

But then, at the last possible second, she stopped herself.

Because she was tempted—so tempted to say yes. All of Joe's arguments rang true. She really could see it, the two of them as a team in every way.

But she needed a sounding board first. She needed to talk about this with Riley, to see how her other bestie reacted to the idea of her and Joe saying *I do* to each other.

Tuesday, she was on the schedule for the morning hours at Bravo Hardware. Lucky opened up that day. She told him she had work to do in back and to give her a holler if he got jammed.

Riley called at nine thirty. "Things are hectic here at the hotel," she said. "I need a raincheck on lunch."

Macy tried to tamp down her disappointment. She really needed Riley's take on the situation with Joe. "Bad, huh?"

"I can't even. Today, I'm cleaning rooms on top of my usual duties..."

"Well, that's not fun."

"Tell me about it."

"How 'bout dinner? My house. Six o'clock. You, me, Dillon and Ana."

"Wow. That would be great. I can do that—you sure?"

"Oh, yeah. We are on."

"What can I bring?"

"Nothing—except Dillon. Ana can look after him—you know how much she loves to boss him around."

"Hey. He loves it, too. Go figure."

"All right, then. The kids can hang out together. And you can give me some advice."

"Advice on…?"

"I'll tell you everything at six."

"You got it. See you then."

They said goodbye and Macy went to work. It was a pretty busy Tuesday, so she spent a lot of the morning out on the floor either manning the register or helping customers decide which tool they needed or which brand of toilet seat to buy.

Joe showed up at noon. When he walked in the door, Macy was ringing up a sale. She glanced over and their eyes met.

He had a look—both hopeful and a little bit hurt.

She wanted to leave her current customer standing there waiting for his receipt and run to Joe, to tell him it was okay. She understood. She'd gotten his beautiful letter and yes, she would marry him and they could build a happy life together…

Somehow, she restrained herself. She would talk to Riley first. There was no need to rush this. Talking it over with someone she trusted would be a good thing. The *right* thing.

"Thank you," she said and gave the customer his receipt.

When she looked for Joe again, he was nowhere in sight.

She rang up two more purchases and helped Mr. Callahan, who lived down the street from her, choose a socket set.

And then it was time to go. She was due at Betty's Blooms for an hour or so to give her mom a lunch break before she went to pick up Ana.

But she felt bad about leaving before she'd at least touched base with Joe. She tracked him down at the store's loading dock out back. He was driving the forklift, loading lumber on a flatbed truck.

He didn't notice her and she decided not to interrupt him. He would know from the schedule that she was done for today and she would see him tomorrow. They could talk then.

Detouring to her office to grab her purse and coat, she headed for her mom's shop.

The rest of the day went by fast. She left the flower shop at 2:20 p.m. and picked up Ana at school. They stopped at Big Country Grocery where she said hi to her dad and bought what she would need to cook dinner that evening.

At home, Ana asked to have a friend over for a couple of hours. The two girls played happily upstairs for a while and when they came down, Macy fed them a snack.

When Ana's friend left, Ana set the table for four.

Riley and Dillon arrived right on time. Dillon was sweet and talkative as always. Riley looked exhausted. They sat down to Macy's famous retro tuna noodle casserole—retro because her grandmother used to make it when Macy's mom was little. The kids loved it and adults never seemed to have much trouble scarfing it down, either.

There was ice cream for dessert. After that, Ana led Dillon upstairs where she would no doubt boss him around mercilessly and probably dress him up as a Stormtrooper or possibly Dracula. Dillon never objected to anything Ana wanted to do. Both Dillon and Josh Bravo's three-year-old son, Shane, idolized Ana. To them, she was magic and could do no wrong.

In the kitchen, Macy refilled Riley's mug with more decaf and took the chair across from her.

"You look beat," Macy said.

"Yeah, well…" Riley guided a curly swatch of red hair back behind her ear. "Today was a nightmare. If I ever have to make one more hotel room bed, I think I'll run out the lobby doors screaming—but there's good news. We hired two new housekeepers today. Annette and our head of housekeeping both seem confident the newbies will work out."

"I'll bet that's a relief."

"You have no idea—and enough about making beds." Riley leaned closer across the kitchen table and lowered her voice. "What's going on with you?"

Macy shook her head. "Where to even start…"

"Just go for it. Lay it on me."

"You asked for it—Joe wants to marry me."

Riley's blue eyes got wide as bread plates. "No…"

"Yeah. It's not romantic—he's not in love with me and he doesn't expect me to fall in love with him—but he thinks we could have a marriage that's more of a partnership. He thinks we'd make a good team—I mean, he says we're already a team and he just wants to take it one giant step further. He's frustrated because he's gotten nowhere so far with the adoption thing. The way Joe sees it, we can make our own family, him and me and Ana…"

"So okay," said Riley when Macy finally finished.

Macy scowled at her friend. "*Okay?* That's all you've got for me?"

"Well, give me a minute to take it all in—I mean, wow. Just wow... You need advice?"

"Oh, you bet I do."

Riley hitched up one shoulder in a half shrug. "I think it's a good idea."

Macy almost spewed coffee but managed to swallow it instead. "You *what*?" Yes, she'd been starting to think the same thing, especially after getting his letter, but she'd never expected Riley to agree with her.

"Oh, come on." Riley waved a hand. "My reaction shouldn't surprise you. Think about it. You two are together constantly. You run the hardware store as a team. You and Ana spend a lot of your spare time with him—here, or out at the Double-K. I mean, please. We both know that you're halfway in love with the guy and have been forever."

Macy groaned. "Wrong."

Riley cast a glance toward the ceiling like she was hoping for help from above. "Hey, I'm not going to argue with you. You asked for my opinion and I gave it to you. If you don't like my advice, don't take it."

"Halfway in *love* with him? Riley, that's just wrong. I mean, yes, I love Joe—just like I love you. But I'm not *in* love with either of you."

Riley rubbed the bridge of her nose, as though she might be getting a headache. "Okay. Whatever you say. You are *not* in love with Joe."

About then, Macy started feeling a little foolish. "Sorry—and you're right. I shouldn't have asked if I didn't want to hear what you had to say."

"Exactly."

"But you still think I should go for it, that I should say yes?"

"Not if you're going to jump down my throat about it, I don't."

"Point taken," Macy replied, sheepish now. "I really am sorry..."

Riley pushed her mug to the side, rested her forearms on the table and laced her fingers together. "Okay, then. I think you would be happy as a couple. You and Joe are besties same as you and me. You get along. You always have your heads together, making plans for the weekend—or for Bravo Hardware. He loves Ana and would do anything for her."

"But...we're really not in love, Joe and me. Shouldn't two people who get married be in love?"

"Oh, you mean like truly, madly and deeply...?"

"Well, yeah."

Riley sighed. "I'm going to say this and you better not jump all over me when I do..."

"I won't. I swear to you."

"Okay, then. Truly, madly and deeply in love like you and Caleb were? Because look how great that turned out..."

"Ouch," Macy said mildly. She was determined not to jump down Riley's throat, but she couldn't deny that the words hurt.

"It's the truth and you know it."

"Okay, okay. I hear you, I do. I really did love Caleb."

"And that jerk was too busy and self-important to be there for you or your little girl—not to mention, he cheated. Joe would never do that to you—or to any woman."

Macy closed her eyes and nodded. "You're right again. I've known Joe forever. I know him to the core. He's honest and straightforward. And when he commits, he's all in and he stays the course. Joe Bravo is a man a woman can trust."

"Yes, he is." Riley asked cautiously, "So then, what are you going to do?"

Now Macy was smiling. "Don't you think I should talk to Joe about this first?"

"Hmm. I really want all the deets and I want them now. But yeah, you should be talking to Joe about this—and soon, too. Because whatever you decide, it's wrong to keep a good man hanging."

Chapter Three

Joe sat at his kitchen table and considered having a third drink. He'd had one at Arlington's Steakhouse, where he'd gone for a quick meal at the bar before driving home. Once he got home, he'd poured himself a second one and nursed it for over an hour.

That second drink was supposed to be it. Ever since Becca died, he drew the line at two drinks a night. More drinks, as he knew from having been in love with Becca, only made a problem worse.

But on a night like tonight, getting stupid drunk sounded pretty damn attractive. All he could think about was Macy and he needed something to ease his growing disappointment.

It wasn't going to happen, he was pretty sure of that by now. She must have gotten his letter. It should have been delivered yesterday. He'd had high hopes that the letter would finally convince her—that she'd come in the next day and give him the answer he wanted.

Instead, she hadn't even let on that she'd received it. Probably because she didn't know what to say to him, how to let him down without making things worse.

His guess? She wished that the whole problem would simply go away. That was embarrassing to say the least.

In fact, he had a growing fear that proposing to her had messed things up between them permanently.

He stared down into his empty glass...

No. Another drink wouldn't fix his damn problem. He needed to talk to Macy, to tell her he understood. He needed to remind her of what he'd written in that letter—that if his big idea didn't work for her, so be it.

He just wanted things to be the way they had been. He just wanted his best friend back.

On the floor near his feet, Rosie stretched and yawned. He reached down and gave her a scratch around her collar. Her tail thumped the floor.

He clicked his tongue at her. "C'mere..."

Rosie got up and plunked her head in his lap with a big doggy sigh. He told her she was beautiful and scratched her ruff some more.

By then he was feeling marginally better. After all, life goes on. One way or another, he and Macy would work it out.

His phone buzzed with a text. From Macy.

Can we talk?

He hit the call icon and tried to make his voice light and unbothered. "Talk about what?"

"I, uh, got your letter yesterday. It's a beautiful letter, Joe."

Okay, the phone wasn't cutting it. What in the hell was she trying to tell him? He needed to see her face. "I'm coming to your house."

"Uh, now?"

"Yeah. Now. Say that's okay."

She laughed and the sound of that laugh—the easiness

of it—reassured him. Would a woman about to turn a man down laugh like that?

Dear God in heaven, he hoped not.

"It's okay," she said. "Come on over."

Twenty minutes later, he was walking up her front steps. She pulled open the door before he reached the welcome mat.

"Hey," she said.

"Hey."

They grinned at each other.

Oh, yeah. Things were definitely looking up. Even if she turned him down, that smile told him they would still be Macy and Joe, best friends and business partners—and there for each other no matter what.

He asked, "Is Ana already in bed?"

"Are you kidding? She would never forgive me if I let her go up to bed without telling her you were coming over."

As if on cue, Ana appeared in the arch to the great room. "There you are, Joe," she said sternly. "I'm all ready for bed. Come up and tuck me in."

He followed her up the stairs, where she insisted on reading him two full chapters of *Revenge of the Dragon Lady*.

When she finally set the book aside, she threw her little arms around his neck and whispered, "I'm glad you came to see me."

"Me, too." He tucked the covers in around her. "Thanks for reading to me."

"You're welcome." Those big dark eyes stared up at him solemnly. "I like it when you come over."

Joe couldn't help thinking about Caleb Storm right then. The man was a damn fool for letting Macy get away. But his neglect of his daughter was unforgivable. Ana deserved a real dad, one who would always be there for her.

Joe turned off the lamp by the bed. "'Night, Ana."

"'Night..."

Downstairs, Macy was waiting for him on the sofa. "Coffee?" she asked. "Or a drink?"

"Nah. I'm good." He edged around the sofa table, sat beside her—and instantly felt awkward, completely out of his depth. "So..." The word trailed off. He couldn't think of what to say next.

She stared at him, those brown eyes enormous. "About your letter..."

"Yeah?" He gulped. Hard. All his self-confidence had gone MIA. He felt like he was fourteen again, fourteen and working up the nerve to ask Belinda Littlefeather to be his date for the homecoming dance.

Macy said, "I... Well, I read that letter and I read it again. And I thought about the things you said. And then tonight I talked to Riley about it."

Was that good news—or bad? "What did Riley say?"

"A lot. But the downstroke is, Riley thinks that you and me together is a good idea."

"She does?" Riley's approval counted for a whole lot with Macy.

"Yeah, Joe. She does."

So was this going to be a yes? His pulse pounded in his ears. She needed to cut to the chase before he had a heart attack right then and there. "But the big question is what do *you* think, Mace?"

She looked down at her hands, which were folded tightly in her lap. "Well, I think it's a good idea, too."

He blinked. For a moment, he forgot how to breathe. But then the tightness in his chest eased. He realized he was smiling. "Macy Lynn. Was that a yes?"

She straightened her shoulders. "I do have...questions."

Questions he could deal with. "Good. I mean, we need to talk about it, right? We need to make sure we're in agreement about what we're getting into."

She nodded. "Yes, we do."

"So go for it. Lay those questions on me."

"Well, in your letter, you mentioned Ana and me living at the ranch with you."

"Yeah. But I thought I was clear that I would be willing to move into town. I can work it out so that I put in my time on the Double-K and also live here with you."

She gave him the sweetest smile. "I'm just clarifying, Joe. As far I'm concerned, yeah. I would be willing to move to the ranch and I'm almost positive that Ana would, too."

Was this really happening? He could hardly believe it.

And what were they talking about? Right. "I was thinking you could rent this house," he suggested. "Or sell it."

"Probably one or the other. I would need time to think about that, though."

"Sure. I, uh..." Why where they talking about her house? Damn. He was so excited his brain had gone offline. "Never mind about the house," he said. "You'll decide what you want to do with it and when you want to do it. And as for, uh, growing our family, I'm hoping you would be open to that?"

"Yes, Joe. I would."

"Really?"

"Yes," she replied with zero hesitation.

"Wow." He plunked both hands on his head, fingers laced together.

She laughed. "Truthfully, Joe, I haven't thought much about more kids since it all went wrong with Caleb. But if you and I are together, well, that changes everything."

He couldn't get over it. She'd said yes—to his proposal

and to trying for more kids. They stared at each other. He realized it was his turn to speak. "I'm just glad, Macy. So damn glad."

"I'm glad, too." Her brown eyes were misty. Joe realized he hadn't felt this happy in a long damn time. "So then," Macy said, "just hypothetically, how long would we be dating—I mean, if we actually did get married, when do you see the marriage happening?"

"I'm thinking Friday, a week from tomorrow, at the courthouse up in Sheridan."

"*What?*" she yelped. "Didn't we just agree to take our time?"

He wanted to grab her and hold her and promise it was all going to work out just fine. But she was looking stressed. Grabbing her might freak her out even more.

So he kept his hands to himself and said in as even a tone as he could muster, "What I meant was that we would take our time *after* the wedding."

"But what about dating? Shouldn't we date at least for a while first?"

"You really want that, a dating period?"

"Well, it just seems logical, don't you think?"

"Macy. If you need us to date, we'll date."

She was studying his face. "But you don't think it's necessary?"

"No, I don't. It's not like we need to know more about each other. Think about it. We know it all when it comes to each other—the good, the bad, the deeply embarrassing. We know all the secrets nobody else knows. Like I said, if you want to date, we'll date. But I'm ready to jump right in, tie the knot, and then get busy finding out what it's like to be married to each other."

"Wow. Just like that."

"You said it. Just like that."

"But, Joe…"

"What? Tell me."

"Well, we've never had sex together. What if we're not… compatible that way?"

"I don't think it'll be a problem—not for me, anyway." He went ahead and laid the truth right on out there. "I've always found you to be sexy as hell."

She let a squeak of surprise. "Come on, seriously? Since when?"

"Seventh grade—maybe end of sixth. Not that I ever would have said that out loud to you at the time."

"Whoa. Joseph Nathan, I had no idea."

"Yeah, well. It's true. And I need you to be honest with me. Have you ever in your whole life had a single sexual feeling about me?"

"Joe!" With a goofy little laugh, she whacked him lightly on the knee with the back of her hand.

He decided to take her laughter and that slap on the knee as a good sign. "You're blushing again."

"Well, I mean, sex isn't what we're about, you and me."

He leaned a little closer to her, close enough that he could see the ring of amber around the iris in those deep brown eyes of hers. "Answer my question."

"Fine," she said. "Yeah, I have been…attracted to you."

"When?"

"Eighth grade."

"Ha!"

She wrinkled her nose at him. "I might even have had a crush on you—not that I ever would've told you. You were so annoying in eighth grade, so loud and full of opinions that you couldn't wait to share whether a girl wanted to hear them or not. And then you had that farting contest with Josh in third period social studies. That was when I decided I had no idea why I still thought you were cute."

"But you did still think I was cute?"

"Yeah. But I got over it."

"When?"

"It was that same year—when you started holding hands in the hallways with Marilee Cooper. That did it. I hardly spoke to you until freshman year when I had no choice."

"Right..." He caught both her hands and leaned in until their foreheads were touching. "Freshman year when Mrs. Kubblemeyer paired us up to write letters to each other."

"Exactly—and this little detour down memory lane aside, that we have both found each other attractive at some point in our lives doesn't mean that we're sexually compatible."

He honestly didn't see the problem. He'd always found her desirable. He truly believed that they would be good in bed together.

But they'd friend-zoned each other early on. And Macy was a great friend. The best. Until lately, he'd seen no reason to mess with a relationship that he didn't ever want to lose.

Now, though...

Well, he just wanted *more* with her and he was willing to take a chance and change things up between them. He just hoped she might be willing, too.

"How about this?" he said. "If you want to date for a while and get to know each other sexually, we'll do that first."

She made a thoughtful sound. "I just think we need time before jumping into marriage."

He put his arm around her—and she let him. They sat

back against the cushion and he asked, "Did you miss the part where I said we could do it your way?"

"No. I heard you."

"Then what?"

"I just... Well, now that I've convinced you to do it my way, I'm suddenly seeing the plus side of handling it your way."

"This is getting confusing." Not that he really minded. She was working through it and that was what mattered.

She met his eyes directly. "We do know each other. And we each know...what we like."

"In bed, you mean?"

"Yeah. In bed. So when the time comes, if we're both honest about what each of us wants from the other, I think it will be all right. I mean, a lot of people choose to wait for marriage to have sex...not that we'd be waiting all that long if we end up getting married next week."

"Macy."

"What?"

"We'll do it however you want to do it."

She drew a deep breath and said, "Okay, then. The more I think it over, the more I like your idea. We wait for our wedding night. And we get married soon."

"Done."

"Joe, you're so easy."

"I aim to please—especially when you've talked your way around to seeing things the same way I do."

She slanted him a sly look. "Yeah. I can't believe I did that."

"I *love* the way you did that." He took her hand.

She threaded her fingers with his and it felt good. Right. "So we need to decide when to talk to Ana," she said briskly. "If the wedding's next week, we should talk to her soon."

"How about tomorrow night for that?"

"Okay, tomorrow night. If she's on board with it and she's good with us getting married right away, we can get a license. And then I'll do my best to be ready in a week."

He seemed puzzled. "Are you saying you're not sure?"

"No. What I'm thinking is that it will be a civil ceremony and take about ten minutes, but I still have to buy a dress and deal with a thousand other things."

"What things?"

"The things I haven't even thought of yet."

Should he have figured that out for himself? Probably. "Right! *Those* things."

"So we're agreed. Given that Ana is on board and ready to go, we'll get the license right away and the wedding will be at least a week after that—longer if I need more time to pull it all together."

"Of course," he said. "I'm good with that."

"Great." Now she seemed worried.

He leaned in extra close again. "Why do you still look unsure?"

"Well, Joe. I'm just nervous. I mean, what if it's bad?"

"What if *what's* bad?"

"Well, the sex, you know?"

"Tell you what. If it's bad, we do it some more. It's bound to get better."

"Be serious." She scowled at him.

"But I am serious."

Now she gave him one of those looks—like she couldn't believe how another human being could be so dense. "Think about it. What if it doesn't get better? Then we're married and we're having bad sex for the rest of our lives?

Or we get divorced? Or we…cheat? None of those options are the least bit attractive to me, Joe."

"Whoa," he said as soon as she paused for a breath. "Slow down. Macy, it's all right to have doubts."

She shook her head. "Joe, I haven't had sex with another person since things blew up with Caleb. But still, I was really hoping that maybe someday that would change, you know?"

"I get it, I do. And Mace, if I've rushed you and you just need more time to—"

"No. I don't need more time. I really don't. I want to marry you. It's just…" Macy pressed her hands to her cheeks. "This is a lot, that's all."

He took her by the shoulders and pulled her close. "I promise you, it's going to be fine."

"Easy for you to say…" She groaned as she sagged against him. He breathed in her sweet clean scent and smiled as he realized he could pick her out blindfolded in a crowded room without her uttering a single word. All he needed to do to recognize Macy Lynn was to get close enough to breathe her in.

"If you need more time, you'll get it," he promised as he rubbed her back. "If you change your mind, that's okay. However it works out, we'll still be the best of friends and business partners. It really is going to be fine."

Macy believed him. He was her best friend. They had a lot of love between them, for each other and for Ana.

And what about shared history? She had that with Joe, too. And they had trust that got stronger year in and year out.

Even if he didn't end up rocking her world between the sheets, his big arms felt just right around her.

And, well, great sex wasn't everything. Sometimes mind-blowing physical attraction only led a girl down a disappointing path. Take Caleb. In their first couple of years together, the sex had been fantastic. And he'd burned their marriage to the ground, anyway.

Which reminded her of something else she and Joe needed to get crystal clear about...

She pulled back. "Look at me Joe."

He blinked down at her, worried now. "What'd I do?"

She put her hand against his cheek. It was warm—and rough with beard scruff. Fondness filled her. He was such a good friend. He was also a fine man in his own occasionally oblivious way. "So far, you've done only good things and I trust you in every way. But I need to make this crystal clear..."

Now he met her eyes steadily. "I'm listening."

"You absolutely cannot cheat on me. Ever. If it's not working for you and you want out, you have to say so. We'll deal with it honestly. Don't go falling into some other woman's bed like it's some kind of accident. I hate when men do that."

"I get it." His gaze was steady, unwavering. "I know exactly what you mean."

She remembered then. "Right. Lindsay..."

"Macy, I would never pull that crap on you. And I know you would never do that to me."

"Good. Just so we're on the same page."

"We are." And then he grinned. "So, what else is holding you back?"

She was thinking that she really did like it when he held her in his arms. "Nothing. I'm in."

"We're doing this?" he asked.

"Oh, yes we are."

***

The next day, Macy drove Ana straight home from school and lured her into the kitchen with a snack of cheese, crackers and apple slices.

Her daughter washed her hands, climbed onto her chair and dug in. "Thanks, Mom."

"You are so welcome." After pouring herself a glass of sparkling water, Macy sat down, too. "And I have something I really want to talk to you about…"

Ana crunched on a cracker. "Okay. What?"

"Well, Joe and I have been talking…"

"'Kay."

Macy's throat was tight. She'd spent over an hour today reading up on how to tell your child that you were getting remarried. She'd thought she was ready.

But now that the moment had come, her mind had gone blank. Even as she guzzled more sparkling water, her mouth felt so dry.

"Mom."

"Hmm?"

"What's the matter?"

"Nothing, honey. Nothing at all…"

"You look really nervous." Ana popped a cheddar cube into her mouth.

Honesty. That was always a good start. "Yep. I *am* nervous."

"How come?"

"Because Joe and I… Well, Ana, Joe and I have been thinking about getting married…together." When Ana wrinkled her nose in obvious confusion, Macy rephrased that last part. "What I meant was, Joe and I are thinking about getting married to each other."

Ana set down her half-eaten cracker. "Married?" she

whispered, as though she didn't dare say that word too loud. Her dark eyes were enormous. "You and Joe might get *married*?"

Macy gulped and bobbed her head in a nod. She hadn't been especially nervous about this conversation—at least, not until now, when it was actually happening and her daughter was staring up at her with wide unbelieving eyes. It was important that Ana be on board with this. If she had objections, they would have to be dealt with to everyone's satisfaction before any wedding could happen. How that would go, she wasn't sure.

Right now, she wasn't sure about a single thing.

On the floor at Ana's feet, Voodoo started chirping.

Ana leaned sideways in her chair and instructed in a soft tone, "Shh, now. Mom and me are having a little talk." Voodoo chittered again. Then he darted out from under the table and zipped off to the great room. Ana ate a bite of apple. "Mom?"

"Hmm?"

"Where is Joe?"

Macy felt oddly disoriented—and younger than her own child. "Well, we agreed that I would talk to you alone first." Every article she'd read about discussing remarriage with one's children had mentioned that the parent should talk to the child alone first. "You know, so this can be just between you and me and you can feel completely comfortable talking about whatever you need to talk about."

"Okay. But where is Joe?" Ana asked again.

Now Macy felt foolish—because Joe was right outside waiting for her to say what she needed to say before he joined the conversation.

"Mom?" Ana prompted with growing impatience.

Macy gave up. "He's out front waiting in his truck. He

wanted to be right here in case you had any questions for him or...anything."

"But he isn't right here. He's out sitting in his truck." Ana set her half-eaten apple slice back on her plate, picked up her paper napkin and rubbed it across her lips. "So can we just go get him and bring him inside now?"

Macy wasn't sure what she'd expected from this potentially difficult conversation, but she was starting to think she'd been a whole lot more concerned than she needed to be. "Uh, sure."

Ana dropped her napkin beside her plate and climbed down off her chair. She held out her hand. Macy took it.

Joe was parked in the driveway. He rolled down his window when Ana and Macy came out the front door.

"Joe!" Ana called and waved him forward. "Come inside!"

His gaze shifted to Macy. . "Now?" He mouthed the word at her.

"Yeah!" Ana answered for her. "We need to talk."

Joe's mouth twitched with the grin he was trying to hide—and okay, maybe it was kind of funny. Macy had wanted to protect her daughter, to give Ana space to say what she really felt. But Ana had never needed a buffer from Joe. She told him what she wanted and he tried to make sure she got it.

"Come inside now!" Ana insisted.

Joe's grin spread wide. "You bet!" He pushed open the door and swung his boots to the ground.

Chapter Four

Inside, big decisions were agreed on and finalized at the speed of light. Ana had no problem at all with her mom and Joe getting married. She announced her approval and then asked, "Can we move to the ranch?"

When Macy answered yes, Ana hugged her. Macy explained that the wedding would be soon—and no, not at the little brick church a few blocks from the house but at the county courthouse, just the three of them and two witnesses, probably Riley and Josh.

"And maybe we'll have a small reception afterward," Macy added. "With just close family and friends…"

Ana wasn't all that interested in the details of the wedding day. What she really wanted was to live at the ranch—and adopt a puppy. She turned those big brown eyes on Joe. "Joe, now that you're getting married, can I get a puppy, please?"

"A puppy?" Joe had that look, the one that made Macy nervous. He just couldn't wait to give Ana whatever she asked for. "Well, I think we can probably—"

Macy cut him off with a firm hand on his arm. To her daughter, she said, "You have Voodoo and now you'll have Rosie, too. It's enough."

Ana stuck out her lower lip and pleaded, "But, Mom. I want a puppy. I *really* do."

Now Joe was looking hopefully at Macy, too. The guy was putty in Ana's small hands. He opened his mouth to speak.

Macy grabbed his arm again before he got a word out. She said to Ana, "Honey, right now we need to get settled in at the ranch as a family. We're not adding a puppy to all that. We're just not." Should she have simply said no? Probably. But her daughter's pleading looks worked on Macy almost as well as they worked on Joe.

Ana put on her saddest face—for about two seconds. And then she gave a tiny sigh and asked hopefully, "Not now, but maybe later…?"

"We'll see," replied Macy, all too aware that the puppy question was in no way put to rest.

"Man, I have to say it." Josh Bravo, Joe's cousin, raised his mug of Bomber Mountain Amber Ale. "You look stoked!"

Joe tapped his mug to Josh's. "I am." They both drank.

It was a little past six o'clock on Thursday evening, the day after Ana had given her eager approval to Joe and Macy's upcoming marriage. Joe had called his cousin before he left the store and asked him to meet him in the bar at Arlington's Steakhouse for a beer.

When Josh set his mug down, he asked, "So when's the big day?"

"We're shooting for a week from today, at the county courthouse up in Sheridan."

"That's quick."

"Hey. Macy and me, we don't fool around. And it will

just be us—Macy, Ana and me at the courthouse—and you and Riley for witnesses. That is, if you're willing…?"

"You bet I am. What time?"

"Two in the afternoon?"

"I'm in."

"Thanks, man."

"Hey. I wouldn't miss it. No way…" Josh's voice trailed off. Suddenly, the sounds of the busy restaurant seemed louder—laughter, the constant chatter of the customers, the clatter of flatware against plates.

Joe leaned in and spoke for his cousin's ears alone. "I want a family, Josh."

"I know you do." His cousin understood. They'd known each other all their lives.

"I was beginning to think there was no way I could make that happen." Not without falling in love again—or lying and telling some nice woman that he felt something he didn't. Neither of those options would have worked for him.

Josh's gaze didn't waver. Like Macy, Josh knew it all—about Lindsay and about Becca, too. "I hear you."

Joe lowered his voice another notch. "Damn. Sometimes I wondered, you know—if I'd ever be happy again. And now, here I am marrying my best friend. Smartest move I've ever made. Trust is everything. And I trust Macy."

"Congratulations."

"Thanks. I'm happy now, Joshy."

"I know you are," Josh said with feeling. "And I'm glad." Then he narrowed his eyes and spoke in a gravelly whisper. "But call me Joshy one more time and I'll wipe the floor with your face—Joey."

Joe laughed and so did Josh. They'd grown up with those nicknames and hated them. Nowadays, nobody ever used them—except for Joe and Josh whenever one of them felt like yanking the other's chain.

The next day at noon, Joe and Macy drove up to Sheridan together to get their marriage license. Wyoming required no waiting period, so when they left the county courthouse, Macy had the license in her hand. They returned to the hardware store and got on with their day.

That evening, he went to Macy's for dinner. He had a great time just hanging out with his soon-to-be family. He and Ana played a board game called Taco vs. Burrito. She beat him easily. Throughout the game, that big cat of hers was sprawled on the sofa beside her purring like a motorboat. Ana said she couldn't wait to move to the ranch—and she *really* hoped to get that puppy soon.

Once Ana was in bed, he and Macy discussed the weekend ahead. Tomorrow, after dropping Ana off at Riley's, Joe and Macy were driving out to the Double-K to break the news of their marriage to his parents and his brother's family. Riley had volunteered to keep Ana overnight, so that evening Macy and Joe would talk to Macy's folks.

"I asked Riley to be a witness for us," Macy said. They were sitting on the sofa in the great room by then. He'd built a fire. It was nice, just the two of them working out the logistics of telling their families, getting everything in order so they could get married in a week.

"And?" he asked.

"Riley's in."

"Excellent. Josh said yes, too."

"Perfect. And I'm going to need Monday off from the store. I'll be shopping for a dress—and I have an appointment with Dr. Hayes on Monday, too."

Joe knew what that meant. Birth control. "You think you'll need Tuesday off?"

"Depends on how well the shopping goes. Ana already has the dress she wants to wear, so that's handled. But there's always something, so I'll keep you posted." She slanted him a teasing look. "Would you say I'm taking advantage of my relationship with the boss?"

"Absolutely. Never stop." He wanted to kiss her and he almost did. But then he thought it over for a little too long and the moment got away from him.

She was studying his face. "What?"

"I wanted to kiss you," he replied with zero hesitation. Because with Macy, he could say anything and she would just roll with it.

She tipped her head to the side, studying him. "*Wanted?* Past tense? You changed your mind?"

He answered honestly. "No. I chickened out."

"Don't be afraid, Joe," she teased with a sly grin. "I won't bite."

"You sure?"

"Try me."

He went for it. Pressing his mouth to those soft cool lips of hers, he breathed in the fresh scent of her perfume.

She pulled back first. "Was that weird?"

He thought, *I'm marrying this woman.* And he was glad.

"Are you with me, Joe?" she whispered, a hint of nervousness creeping in.

"Yes, I am," he said. "And no. Not weird. Not weird in the least."

For Macy, the weekend that followed flew by.

Saturday, as planned, they dropped Ana off at Riley's

and then headed for the Double-K Ranch where Joe's mom served a hot lunch and Joe and Macy broke the big news.

Nate, Joe's dad, seemed really happy for them. His mom was more reserved. Meggie Bravo had a lot of questions—mostly about why they'd suddenly decided to get married after all these years as friends.

Joe spoke right up. "Mom, I think every man should marry his best friend." He took Macy's hand and brought it to his lips. His warm breath touched her skin and his eyes held hers—just for an instant, long enough to let her know he was on her side today, tomorrow. And always. Then he pinned his mom with a meaningful look. "There's love and there's trust between good friends," he explained. "Macy will never let me down and I'm going to make damn sure I'm right there whenever she needs me."

Meggie Bravo sat back in her chair. She glanced at her husband and Nate gave her a slow knowing smile. When Meggie smiled back, Macy breathed a sigh of relief.

And then Joe's mom said, "When's the wedding?"

"Friday," Joe replied. "At the courthouse."

"That's quick—and the courthouse? They hold *trials* there."

"Mom," Joe said patiently. "It's *our* wedding and we want to do it our own way."

Meggie slid another glance at Nate before replying, "Of course you do and so you should."

Macy said, "We were thinking we would keep it simple. Just the three of us—Joe, Ana and me—with Josh and Riley as our witnesses."

Meggie asked, "But don't they frown on bringing children to the courthouse?"

"It's not like Ana's going to be in court," Joe said. "We'll probably just stand before the county clerk."

"So you'll be married in an office." Meggie clearly did not approve.

"Mom. Macy and I are fine with the courthouse. We really are."

"And I'm not objecting to the courthouse. I just want to be there. I really do, and I know that you can only bring so many guests to a courthouse wedding."

Joe had no comeback for that. Macy felt slightly embarrassed and more than a little thoughtless. Of course his folks would want to be there. She and Joe should have considered that. But they'd put their focus on getting the wedding out of the way so that they could start their life together.

His mom went on, "The way I see it, there are any number of good reasons to get married in a courthouse." She sent her husband a fond look—one with a lifetime of memories in it. "As a matter of fact, Nate and I got married down in Buffalo at the Johnson County Courthouse. Looking back, I kind of wish we'd chosen another setting." She glanced at Macy then. "And you know, Macy. I'll bet your mother and dad would love to be there, too…?" Meggie pressed both hands to her chest. "Honestly, I get it. I do. You want to get married and you don't want to wait for months or make a big production out of it."

Macy realized she was nodding as Joe said, "Then you do understand."

"Yes, I do," said Meggie. "And so I was thinking, why not have the wedding next Saturday afternoon, here at the house? I would take care of everything, and we'd make it really simple, just the families and any close friends you want to invite. It will be a casual reception after a simple ceremony."

Macy hardly knew what to say. "That's… Well, that's

just so kind of you to offer, Meggie. But really, it's a lot, to put something like that together in less than a week."

"It's honestly not that much," said Meggie. "And I would love to do it. I mean that sincerely."

Macy believed her—but it really was a lot to ask in such a short time frame. "Someone has to officiate—doesn't it have to be a minister or a judge?"

"That's right." Meggie didn't miss a beat. "And I know two ordained ministers and also Judge Crawford up in Sheridan. I'll bet one of them will be available next Saturday."

Joe was frowning. "But what if none of them can do it?"

"Oh, Joe. Just give me until Monday to find out. If I can't make it happen, you can always go back to the original plan, have that civil ceremony on Friday and then come here for a little celebration on Saturday."

By then, Macy had a serious case of the warm fuzzies. She couldn't help loving that her future mother-in-law really wanted them to have a family wedding on the Bravo ranch.

She'd had a big, fancy wedding when she married Caleb—and the marriage, in the end, had crashed and burned. She didn't want another fancy wedding. This time she was marrying her best friend. This time, they would make it work. And the family should be there—she wanted them there. She honestly did.

She turned to Joe. "I would love to be married here on the ranch."

To her left, Nate Bravo chuckled. "Looks like the women are ganging up you, son."

"You're sure about this?" Joe asked, his eyes locked with hers. "You want to marry me next Saturday right here on the Double-K?"

"I do, Joe. I really do."

"Okay, then." He turned to his mom. "Let us know by Monday whether or not you can find the minister."

Meggie let out a gleeful, "Yes!" and clapped her hands. "I'm so glad. It's going to be simple and easy without any fuss, wait and see." She beamed at Macy. "Give me your phone number and a list of who's coming?"

"I will. And thank you, Meggie."

Joe's mom pushed back her chair and held out her arms.

They stopped by Joe's brother's house before they drove back to town. Both Jason Bravo and his wife, Piper, were home. So was their toddler, Miles, and their four-year-old, Emmy. The little girl had a friend over. The two girls appeared wearing paper crowns and ballerina outfits with Jason's dog, Kenzo, herding them from behind. They greeted Joe and Macy with big smiles and then headed right back to Emmy's room.

Piper offered coffee and the four adults sat around the table.

Joe got straight to the point. "It's official. Macy said yes—to me, of all people."

Piper gasped. "You two are getting married?"

"You bet we are. It was going to be a courthouse wedding. But we talked to mom before we came to see you."

Jason laughed. "Let me guess. You're getting married here at the ranch."

"Bingo, big brother—that is, if Mom can find a minister. If not, she'll still be hosting a party for us next Saturday so save the date."

There were hugs and congratulations. Piper said she'd talk to Meggie and help out wherever needed. "And I know a minister down in Buffalo at Summit Fellowship just in case Meggie's options don't pan out—and come to think of it, I know a pastor in Casper, too. So I'm pretty sure you two will be getting married Saturday at the main house."

By the time she and Joe climbed back into his crew cab for the drive home, Macy was feeling really good. Joe's family had been right there, ready to do what they could to make the wedding a day to remember.

It was going to be lovely and she couldn't wait.

Halfway to town, she remembered Joe's sister, Sarah, a nurse who lived in New York City with her wealthy husband and stepkids. "I suppose we really should fly to New York to share our big news with Sarah," she teased.

Joe laughed. "I can't believe I almost left my baby sister out of the loop."

"For shame," she scolded.

"Don't worry. I'll reach out to her in the morning and let her know that my single days are numbered—and that I couldn't be happier about it."

Their eyes met. She thought what a good-looking guy he was, with his thick brown hair, broad shoulders and fine blue eyes. A sweet shiver ran through her and she realized all over again that this was really happening. In seven short days, she would marry her best friend.

That night, Macy's parents came to her house for dinner. As soon as they sat down to eat, Macy shared the news that Joe had asked her to marry him and she'd said yes.

"Omygoodness!" Betty Oberholzer jumped up, pulled Macy from her chair and wrapped her in a hug. "I'm so happy for you, honey!" And then she turned to Joe. "Come on. Get up here."

There was more hugging. Her dad joined in, too. When they all took their seats at the table again, Macy and Joe told her folks about Meggie's offer.

Her mom beamed. "A wedding at the Double-K. What

a terrific idea. I'll call Meggie, let her know I'm on board and that I'll help with whatever needs doing."

Macy warned, "Don't get too carried away, okay? It's just supposed to be simple, you know?"

Her mother sighed. "I'll try, honey." And then she snickered. "But weddings are so much fun. And there will have to be flowers. I'm doing at least a few arrangements. You know you can't stop me."

Macy reached across the table and squeezed her mom's hand. "Love you, Mom. So much."

"It's October. I'm thinking burgundy and burnt orange, bronze calla lilies, cymbidium orchids and eucalyptus leaves..."

Her dad leaned toward Joe. "She'll settle down, don't worry," Curtis muttered.

"Not worried in the least," Joe replied.

Betty said, "It's so lovely that the two of you have finally realized how much you mean to each other."

For a moment, Macy felt a little bit guilty that she and Joe didn't love each other quite the way her mom seemed to assume. But then again, they did mean the world to each other. So maybe her mom had it right, after all.

When it was time to go, Macy's mom caught her hand and gave it a squeeze. "So, then. We need to get a running start to be ready by Saturday. I'll get in touch with Meggie right away."

"That's wonderful, Mom. But don't take on too much. It's a really short time frame and we're keeping it simple."

"Simple. Right. I'll try my very best..."

Joe pulled her in for a side hug. "You *are* the best, Betty."

"Thanks, Mom," said Macy. "For everything."

"You are so welcome, always. Just be happy, honey."

"You bet I will." As Macy said the words, she realized

she believed them. She and Joe might not be *in* love. But they had love—and a whole lot of it, too. And she was sure they'd be happy together.

As Joe pulled to a stop in Macy's driveway, her phone chimed.

She checked the display. "It's your mom..."

Of course it is, he thought. "Once she makes up her mind to do something, watch out."

Macy put the call on speaker so that he could hear, too. "Hi, Meggie."

"I've found our minister!" his mom practically shouted. "Sandy Crowe, the pastor of Grace Community Church right here in Medicine Creek has said she would be happy to officiate."

"Terrific," said Macy.

"So..." Meggie sounded very proud of herself. "Are we on for Saturday here at the ranch?"

"Yes. Absolutely," Macy agreed. "And I have to say, that was fast."

"Hey. I don't fool around." Joe's mom went on to report that she'd already heard from Piper and Betty, too. "They're working with me now, making it even easier than I expected."

"That's great," said Macy. "Meggie, I can't thank you enough."

"You are so welcome. I'm excited to be able to do this, I really am. You two are perfect for each other. I've always thought so and wondered why you never..." Her voice trailed away and a soft laugh escaped her. "Sorry. I'm pretty sure you don't really need to know what I've always thought. What matters is, you two are getting married and Nate and I are so happy about that."

Macy was looking at Joe. He made a face that telegraphed, *Hey, she's my mom. You know how moms are...*

Meggie said, "And yes, I am rambling. I'm guessing my son is there waiting for me to shut up and get off the phone."

Macy laughed. "No worries. He can wait a little longer."

"Okay, I have to ask. Am I on speaker?"

"Yep," Joe said. "I'm right here, Mom."

"I thought so," Meggie said dryly—and then shared more of her plans.

As she talked, Joe and Macy interjected brief responses, all of them in agreement with Meggie's recommendations.

Finally, to move things along, Joe said, "Thanks, Mom..."

"I'm just so excited!" Meggie cried. And then, finally, she let them go.

"Sorry 'bout that," Joe said when Macy tucked her phone away.

"Sorry? Your mom's the best. I love all her plans."

"That's good, because she has definitely taken charge."

Sunday, Macy picked up Ana from Riley's at 8:00 a.m. At home, Ana showered attention on Voodoo and gave Macy a detailed rundown of all that had happened during her sleepover at Dillon's house.

Meggie called more than once that day and Macy said yes to everything Joe's mom suggested. Meggie had great ideas and really she was so sweet to be making the wedding an extra-special event.

Monday, before shopping for her wedding dress, Macy tried texting Caleb to share the news that she was getting married that Saturday—and also to remind him once again that he hadn't seen his daughter in a very long time.

But after typing and discarding three different messages, she decided that a text wouldn't cut it. She called instead.

As usual, it went straight to voicemail.

When the beep sounded, she said, "Hi, Caleb. A couple of things. I'm marrying Joe Bravo on Saturday, just, uh, so you know. Ana and I will be moving out to Joe's ranch to live. I'll text you the address there. And I... Well, Caleb. Time's going by and your daughter misses you..."

Did Ana miss him, really? Hard to say. Ana rarely mentioned the father she hadn't seen since she and Macy moved back home. Truthfully, he hadn't been around much before the divorce. But maybe he was different now and behaved like a real dad to his two-year-old son. For that little boy's sake, Macy hoped so.

And what else had she wanted to tell him? "Ana's at school today. But if you'll call back this evening, you can catch up with her, find out how she's doing and what's going on in her life now..." Macy almost groaned when she said that. Caleb and Ana were hardly great pals who'd recently lost touch.

But honestly, how was she supposed to handle this crap?

At first, she'd pushed Caleb gently to keep in contact with his daughter. And then she'd gotten tougher, insisting that he make some time for Ana. More than once in the past three years, when she heard that voicemail beep, she'd shouted her message at him, demanding he take some damn responsibility for his child beyond the big bucks he threw around.

Nothing worked. Caleb sent money and that was all Caleb did for his daughter.

"Caleb," she said into her phone, desperation creeping in. "Please..." Great. Now she was begging. Why plead with the guy? It never did a bit of good. "Call your daughter. Goodbye."

She hung up, wishing she hadn't bothered to reach out

at all—and then texted him the address at the Double-K, as promised.

There, she thought. Caleb was dealt with. The parenting ball was firmly in his court. Time to go buy herself a pretty wedding dress.

At a little boutique up in Sheridan, Macy found the perfect dress. It was floor-length. A simple crepe sheath in lustrous ivory, it had a boat neck and long sleeves. The fit was perfect, sparing her the trouble of trying to get alterations in such a short time frame. At a shop down the street, she found a gorgeous pair of lace-up ivory wedding boots.

Then, back in Medicine Creek, she kept her appointment with Dr. Hayes. From there, she went to State Street Drugs to pick up her birth control prescription.

Tuesday morning, she took the first pill. When she opened the medicine cabinet to get the blister pack, the condoms she'd bought were right there on the shelf next to the pills.

It was now four days till the wedding. She wouldn't be fully protected for seven so she'd bought the condoms just to be on the safe side, though Joe no doubt already had them. It never hurt to be ready for anything.

Joe...

She washed that first pill down with water, took the condoms from the cabinet and wandered into her bedroom. With a sigh, she sank to the edge of her bed.

Yesterday, she'd been a busy little bee, buzzing around, finding just the right dress and the perfect shoes, visiting her doctor and the pharmacy.

This morning, though, doubts nagged at her. Had they made the right choice? Because, really, two lifelong buddies suddenly deciding to become husband and wife...

Was this a bad idea?

Closing her eyes, she breathed in and out through her nose until the panic eased. She was in this now and she would give it her all. But still, staring down at the strip of condoms in her hand, she wondered if Joe was having second thoughts, too.

Saturday, he'd seemed so sure about this—and she'd felt sure, too. Right now, though, she hoped that she wasn't just enabling him, helping him to avoid learning to love again.

For a year after Becca's death, Joe hardly went anywhere socially. He'd come out of his shell a little when he started fostering Aiden. But then Aiden went back to his mother and Joe retreated into loneliness once more. Macy had worried about him a lot during that time. She and Josh used to take turns coaxing him out for a beer.

But in recent months, Joe had seemed to emerge from his shell a little...

She looked down at the strip of condoms again and recalled how she used to nag him to get out and meet someone.

He'd shut her up by informing her, "I *have* met someone, and more than once. When that happens, the woman and I have a nice night together after coming to a clear understanding that it is just that, one night. And Macy Lynn, I have to ask. When do *you* plan to get out there and meet someone special?"

She'd gotten his message loud and clear—finally. "I stand admonished," she'd softly replied. "Because you're right. I have no more intention than you do of falling in love again."

Macy trusted Joe with her life and the life of her child. And she found him attractive, too. Very much so.

But she couldn't quite picture herself getting naked with him. It made her blush just to think of it—and mostly in an uncomfortable way. Because he was Joe, her bestie forever, and she didn't have sexy thoughts about Joe...

However, she *would* be getting naked with him—and very likely on Saturday night. Even though they'd agreed to wait a while before trying for a baby, she'd gotten the impression that he'd imagined them getting intimate right from the start, so she needed to be fully protected from pregnancy right now. To make sure of that, she tucked the strip of condoms into her weekender bag.

Chapter Five

On Saturday morning, Macy woke from a dream she couldn't quite remember.

But then it came to her. She'd been flying, hadn't she? Soaring like an eagle high in the sky. In the dream, it was springtime. She sailed, weightless, on thermal winds, the world a rolling expanse of green below her.

Macy smiled. She hadn't dreamed of flying in years.

Tossing back the covers, she went to the window that faced her front yard. Parting the curtains, she looked out at her front walk and the tidy redbrick house across the street. The morning sky was overcast. It was the last Saturday in October and snow was predicted, though probably not enough to stick.

I'm marrying Joe today...

The thought made her smile. Last night she'd been mired in doubt, but now her misgivings had somehow evaporated, chased away by the morning light. It was happening and she realized she was ready.

"Mom, you awake yet?" Ana tapped on the bedroom door.

Still smiling, Macy turned toward the sound. "Come in!"

The door swung inward. Anna stood on the threshold in her green Elphaba pajamas carrying her giant chirping cat.

"Okay, okay," she said to the cat. Chittering impatiently, Voodoo wriggled free of Ana's grip, landed soundlessly on the rug and bolted back out the bedroom door. Ana asked, "When are we going to the ranch?"

"In a few hours." The ceremony was scheduled to occur at two in the afternoon—outside, weather permitting.

"You look happy, Mom," her daughter said.

Macy laughed. "Hey. Today, I'm a bride. Aren't all brides happy?"

"Not the Corpse Bride."

"Right. I forgot about her."

Ana padded across the rug to join her at the window. "It's going to snow. I hope we get snowed in at the ranch."

"Sweetheart, there isn't going to be *that* much snow."

"You never know about snow, Mom. If we're snowed in, we can drink cocoa, make popcorn and watch videos. And I'll bring Zombie Kittens." Ana loved the card game in which kittens exploded but could come back to life—as zombies. Wearing her most hopeful and angelic expression, she asked, "Can I please bring Voodoo?"

Macy wished she could say yes. "Sorry, sweetheart, but nope, not today."

"But if we get snowed in—"

"Not going to happen." Not according to the weather report, anyway. "But we'll leave him extra food and water and a super-clean litter box, just in case. And when you get back to town this evening, Grandma and Grandpa will bring you here first so you can take Voodoo to their house for your sleepover."

Ana pooched out her lower lip. "Voodoo will be sad not to watch you and Joe getting married."

"Voodoo will be fine, all cozy and safe right here at home—now come on, let's fix ourselves some breakfast."

"I want French toast."

"Great. Me, too—let's get cooking, okay?"

When Macy pulled her Subaru to a stop in front of the main ranch house at the Double-K, the front door swung open. Betty, Meggie, Piper and Riley came out onto the porch. Two dogs, Joe's golden Labrador, Rosie, and Jason Bravo's big black Sheprador, Kenzo, bumped out behind the women.

Ana was out of her booster seat and running to the base of the steps before Macy could tell her to slow down. Spreading her arms wide, Ana cried, "We're here! And I'm wearing my special magic peacock dress." With that, she opened her puffer coat to reveal one of her favorite outfits—a sparkly peacock-blue ballerina skirt, a long-sleeved leotard top, black tights and black knee-high riding boots. For this special day, Macy had fashioned Ana's hair into a corona of braids accented with a peacock-feather rhinestone comb.

"You look gorgeous!" Grandma Betty scooped her up in a hug and carried her inside as the other women came down the steps to greet Macy and help her carry in her things.

They all trooped back up onto the porch, where Meggie held open the door. "Rosie, Kenzo, come." The dogs went inside. Meggie ushered the rest of them in after that. The house smelled delicious. Whatever they were having later, Macy couldn't wait.

"This way." Riley, looking gorgeous in a moss-green velvet dress, grabbed Macy's hand and led her upstairs to the bedroom that would serve as her dressing room.

The other women wandered in and out as Macy got ready. It was fun, catching up with Piper, who ran the library in town. And Macy got lots of fond wishes and advice from her mom and Meggie. Riley stuck by her side. Those two hours before the ceremony flew by in an instant.

Happily, the weather had held.

At two o'clock, Macy walked down the porch steps on her dad's arm. Joe was waiting for her in the yard in a black jacket, black hat, a crisp white shirt and jeans along with a black tie, black boots and a white rose boutonniere. He was smiling so wide. When she reached him, Riley held out her hand and Macy passed her the enormous bouquet of fall-colored flowers.

"Mom…" Ana whisper-shouted from her spot on Riley's other side.

"C'mere," Macy whispered back.

There were chuckles from the others watching from up on the porch as Ana slipped around Riley to get to Macy, who bent to kiss her little girl's velvety cheek.

"Mom, you've got diamonds in your hair…"

"You like them?" Riley had swept her shoulder-length waves to one side and pinned them there with a big rhinestone clip.

"You look so pretty, Mom."

Macy bent to press a kiss to her little girl's soft cheek. "Thank you, sweetie…"

"Psst," signaled Riley. "Ana…"

Ana darted back into place on Riley's other side.

Joe took Macy's hand. His was big and work-roughened. Warm, too—even on such a chilly almost-winter afternoon.

Together, they faced the tall slim brunette with the open Bible. She introduced herself as Pastor Sandy and instructed them to face each other, which they did.

The vows were short. They promised forever, no matter what, in sickness and in health. And when Joe pulled two rings from his pocket, Macy stifled a gasp of surprise.

The rings! It had all happened so fast she'd forgotten they needed to choose their rings.

But Joe had remembered. He took her right hand, turned it over and set the larger ring in her palm. It was a band of gold, thick, smooth and lustrous, the kind of ring a working man could safely wear out fixing fence or moving cattle.

A moment later, he guided the smaller ring onto her finger. It fit just right, a perfect circle of gold. She loved it so much she had to blink away happy tears as she took Joe's hand again and slipped his ring into place.

Pastor Sandy said, "You may kiss your bride."

As Joe pulled her close, Macy was happy, truly happy—to be right here, right now, with this man. To face the future at his side.

His big strong arms surrounded her and his warm lips met hers. He smelled of leather, soap and clean skin. Macy felt safe. Loved. And completely understood.

Back there on the porch, their family and their friends were smiling.

Pastor Sandy said, "Ladies and gentlemen, Mr. and Mrs. Bravo!"

Everybody started clapping. In unison, Riley's son, Dillon, and Josh's little boy, Shane, shouted "Hooray!"

Laughing with happiness, Macy tipped her head up to the gray sky. It was starting to snow.

On the porch, her dad waved his camera. It was his pride and joy, a Canon EOS, and he seized any chance he got to use it. "Okay, everybody! Let's get some pictures before the weather gets too bad…"

The wind kicked up, but Macy's dad ignored it. He kept them all out there for another half hour. Macy's mom urged him more than once to hurry it up, but he just waved a hand and kept on taking pictures.

Macy loved her dad's dedication to the job of wedding photographer. She and Joe might not be passionately in love, but still, it was a big day and her dad made sure she would have lots of photos to remember it by. The snow was a little soggy, though, and she worried a bit about ruining her dress.

However, when they finally trooped inside and she ducked into the downstairs bathroom, her dress looked fine—a little damp at the hem, maybe. But it would dry quickly enough. She fiddled with her hair and beamed at herself in the mirror.

And right then, her phone buzzed. She should have just ignored it. But no. She pulled it from the clever hidden pocket of her wedding dress and checked the display.

A text from Caleb.

Because the guy couldn't get back to her last Monday when she called him. Oh, no. He had to interrupt her wedding day.

Was she bitter?

Possibly. Just a little.

She read the message. It didn't take long.

Congratulations, Macy. Will call when I have the time.

Shaking her head, she stuck the phone back in her pocket, freshened her lip gloss, needlessly smoothed the skirt of her dress and fiddled with the rhinestone comb in her hair.

As she primped, she reminded herself that her daughter was happy, a quirky little wonder, a whiz at school and beloved by her family. Ana had lots of friends who invited her to playdates and loved to come to her house, too. The absence of her father from her life wasn't affecting her one damn bit.

By the time Macy went back out to join the party, she was smiling again. Because Caleb was Caleb and what could she do about his behavior, anyway? Nothing. She doubted the guy would ever change.

The afternoon and evening went by too fast. There was food and wine and lots of laughter. Her dad took more pictures.

Near the end of the party, she held out her hand. "The camera, please."

Her dad gave it up. Macy set it carefully on a built-in bookshelf in Meggie's living room and then grabbed him in a hug.

"Thanks, Dad," she whispered, "I love you."

"Love you, too, Sugar Pie." And he snatched up his camera again and took yet another series of shots of her laughing and waving her hand at him, ordering him to quit messing around.

At a little after nine o'clock, she threw her bouquet at Riley, who caught it with a laugh, though she always swore she was never getting married again. She'd loved TJ with her whole heart, she often said, and she would never find another man like him.

As for Macy's dad, he didn't quit. He kept taking pictures till the very end, when Joe swept her up in his arms and carried her out the door to his waiting crew cab as everyone, dogs included, filed out to the porch behind them.

Macy laughed and waved. "Thank you! I love you all so much!"

They shouted back, "Love you, too!" and "Don't stay up too late!"

Ana yelled, "See you guys tomorrow!"

When Joe set her down to open the passenger door, she remembered her weekender. "Yikes! Joe, I left my suitcase in the house—"

"It's in the back seat," he said as he pulled open the door for her. "While you were upstairs getting ready, my mom shoved it at me and said *put this in your truck*."

"Thank goodness for Meggie. She thinks of everything... Joe!" Macy let out a shriek of surprise as he swept her off her feet again and deposited her on the seat.

"Buckle up," he advised, already shutting the door and heading for his side of the truck. A minute later, he opened the back door on his side and Rosie hopped in. Then Joe got up behind the wheel and started the engine.

"What's that godawful clattering?" she asked as he turned onto the circular two-track that would take them to his house.

"Cans," he replied. "Your dad and my dad snuck out a couple of hours ago and tied cans to the trailer hitch."

"Some men never grow up," Macy said fondly, picturing the two older men tiptoeing around, trying not to let the cans rattle as they tied them on the back.

It was a short drive to the two-story house with redwood siding and a pair of dormer windows on the upper floor. The clattering cans fell silent as Joe pulled to a stop in front of the porch that ran the width of the house.

"Stay there," he commanded when she reached for the door handle.

This was getting silly. "Enough with the carrying me."

"I mean it." He was faking a scowl. "Don't move."

So she sat there as he let Rosie out and then came around to scoop her from her seat and carry her up the steps to the front door.

She was laughing by then. "I can't wait to see how you get the door open with me taking up both your hands."

"No sweat," he replied as he bent at the knees, got hold of the door handle and gave it a push.

The door opened onto the living room, with its slanted cathedral ceiling, a stone fireplace on the right and stairs to the second floor on the left.

"We're here," she said dryly. "You can put me down now."

"Your wish is my command."

"Yeah, right."

He set her on her feet. "I'll get your things."

She stood by the door, staring at nothing in particular, suddenly a bit overwhelmed at the idea that she would live here now. Joe's house would be her house—and Ana's, too...

He was back in no time. He paused to hang his hat on a peg, kick off his boots and put his jacket away in the entry-area closet.

She gazed ruefully down at her lace-up white boots.

"Let me help." He knelt right there and she gathered her skirt, pulling it high enough so he could undo the laces and slip off both boots.

"Thank you," she said.

"Anytime." Rising, he picked up her bag again.

Still feeling oddly disoriented, she followed him across the big living room, through the wide arch that framed the kitchen and into the short hallway on the left that led to the downstairs bedroom. He went in and switched on one of the table lamps by the beautiful Amish-style bed that he and his brother had made from reclaimed barnwood. Just looking at that bed had Macy going suddenly breathless.

Tonight she would sleep there—with Joe.

Hesitating just outside the door, she watched him set her weekender by a chair.

He came to her then and took her hand. "Come on. Let's get something to drink." She let him lead her back to the kitchen. "Have a seat," he said when they reached the central island. He even pulled out a stool for her.

She perched on the stool and then didn't really know what to do with herself. The familiar room seemed suddenly alien. She stared at the big table in the dining area to her right. Joe and Jason had made it, too, in the same simple, perfect style as the bed in the other room. On the far side of the island from where she sat, the L-shaped butcher-block counters surrounded a farm sink with a now dark window above it.

"I've got soda, plain water, coffee, tea—or something stronger," he offered as he took off his tie, draped it over one of the chairs at the table and then undid the top buttons of his white dress shirt.

Conflicting urges assailed her. She wanted to laugh at the sheer strangeness of this moment at the same time as she longed to leap up, gather her heavy skirts in both hands, spin on her heel and sprint out the front door. She'd been here in this house with this man a hundred times, at least. And yet right now, it all felt bizarre, completely unreal.

"Should we have done this?" she heard herself whisper.

"Aw, Mace…" He took the stool beside her and touched her shoulder. "You going to be okay?"

She forced herself to meet his eyes. "I'm not sure," she whispered.

He didn't look away. "To answer your question, yes, we should have done this. And I'm glad we did."

She tried to smile. Too bad it ended up feeling like more of a grimace. "You sound so certain."

"Because I am. We're going to be great together, just wait and see—I mean, come on. We already are."

"Well..." Her throat felt tight with a thousand different emotions. She gave a little cough to loosen it up. "We *are* a good team. You're right about that."

He smiled at her. Slowly. "Whiskey? Wine? Beer?"

"This calls for the big guns."

"Uh-oh," he said, but she could see the smile in his eyes.

She commanded, "Break out the Jim Beam."

"Done." He got the whiskey and two glasses and poured them each a stiff one.

"Here you go."

She took the drink. "To...us," she offered lamely.

"To us." He reclaimed his stool.

They were both silent as they drank. She was careful to sip slowly and it eased her mind to note that he was, too. The last thing they needed was to get wasted tonight. That would be too pitiful—best friends getting married and so scared to sleep together they had to get drunk to even attempt such a thing.

No. They were not getting drunk. She wanted to remember tonight, remember their first time together—or not, if they didn't quite pull it off.

The thought of that, of being too on edge to have sex with her new husband, probably should have made her feel awful.

But as she looked in his eyes now, it didn't. Because he was Joe and she could tell him anything.

So she did. She told him the truth. "I'm freaking out," she said. "Just a little."

He set his drink down and leaned closer until their foreheads touched. "No kidding."

"Hey," she grumbled. "The least you could do is act

surprised. How about saying that I seem so cool and collected—and beautiful? Don't forget that. Times like this, a woman needs to know she's hot."

With a slow gentle finger, he guided a loose wave of hair behind her ear. A warm shiver went through her at his light playful touch. "Damn. You *are* beautiful, all sweet and perfect."

"Perfect, huh?"

"You bet." He let his finger stray over her cheekbone and down to her lips, which he touched lightly with two fingertips. "Perfect. And so hot."

"Now you're talking…"

"I do my best." He leaned closer again.

When his lips touched hers, she smiled against them, suddenly happy. Warm all over. "Joe…"

"Macy Lynn." His mouth strayed from hers. He kissed one cheek, then the other, his lips featherlight against her skin.

With a gentle finger, he guided her chin up—and kissed her again, softly. And so carefully at first.

But then he caught her lower lip between his teeth in a quick light bite.

She whispered, "Joe…" and opened for him as heat flared through her, followed immediately by sweet relief as a sudden, intense yearning sparked to life within her. *It will be all right*, she thought. *It will be just fine…*

He tasted of whiskey and safety and heat. She could sit here forever with him—with her good friend, Joe—just kissing and kissing.

And kissing some more.

But then he took her hand. Rising as he kissed her, he pulled her along.

Suddenly she was in his arms and he was still kissing

her, holding her close. She slid her hands up and wrapped her arms around his neck, pressing herself even closer. She was breathless now, and she smiled against his parted lips as he kept on kissing her.

It felt so delicious, so right. All her doubts and fears just melted away. It had been so long for her—a lifetime, it seemed, since she'd kissed a man deeply. She never wanted to stop. She could do this forever, just stand here, kissing Joe on their wedding night.

But then he started moving. Walking backward, he pulled her along with him toward the bedroom, kissing her endlessly as he drew her on.

She closed her eyes and let it happen, because it felt good. It felt wonderful. It had been so long for her—years— since she'd felt a man's deep hungry kiss. She'd told herself she was fine with that. She didn't need a man. She could take care of herself, even in bed.

And she had. She owned more than one sex toy and she knew how to use them. She could bring herself pleasure, including multiple orgasms...

But this, tonight, with Joe of all people...

They'd done no more than kiss and flirt. Yet somehow, already, it was good. Real. And deeply exciting.

To be held in his strong arms, to feel his lean body pressed close to hers. There really was no substitute for this—for intimacy. For a man she could trust who wouldn't ever let her down.

Joe stopped walking. She looked up at him. He was watching her, his eyes twin blue oceans, his mouth turning up at the corners in a slow knowing smile. "Hey, there."

"Joe..." They were in the bedroom now. Rosie had gotten there before them. From her bed in the corner, she lifted her head and yawned.

"You doing okay?" Joe asked. His hands rested on her shoulders, steady and reassuring.

She studied his face—so familiar. So dear. "You're a good kisser."

He chuckled. "Thank you."

"Just thought you should know…"

He leaned closer, nipped at her earlobe and whispered, "You, too." He was watching her so closely.

Was she blushing all of a sudden? "Is my face red?"

"Nah."

"You're lying."

They both laughed then. "Maybe," he confessed. "A little."

She straightened her shoulders and turned around. "Unzip me?"

For a moment, he was absolutely still behind her. She held her breath and knew that he was holding his, too.

She glanced over her shoulder and into his eyes. "Is everything okay?"

"Okay doesn't even begin to cover it…" He ran the back of a finger along the nape of her neck, sending shivers racing up and down her spine. And then, at last, he pulled her zipper down. It was a long one, descending to well below the small of her back. He was careful and it didn't snag.

She peeled the snug sleeves off her arms and stepped out of it. Carrying it to the leather chair in the corner, she carefully laid it out. From there, she went to the ancient pine dresser a few feet away. She took off her diamond earrings and the rhinestone comb in her hair and set them both on the dresser top.

Finally, feeling awkward again, she turned to face him wearing her white lace stockings, lace panties and bra.

Joe came to her. He cradled her face between his palms and kissed her again.

Then he caught her hand and led her back to the bed. She stepped in close and got busy helping him off with his shirt. When she carried the shirt and tie to the other chair, he took over, pulling off his socks, rising to unbuckle his belt and drop his jeans.

When she faced him again, he tossed the jeans toward the chair. Now they were both left in nothing but their underwear. He came around the bed to her. They stood facing each other.

And then, in an instant, he whipped off his boxer briefs and tossed them over his shoulder.

She laughed as the faint lines around his eyes deepened with his shameless grin. When he reached for her, she reached back.

He kissed her slow and deep, his arms going around her. She felt his deft fingers unhooking her bra. When he lifted his mouth from hers, he tossed the bra away.

Kneeling before her, he took down her white lace stockings. He stared up at her as he did that, heat in his eyes. "I like all this white lace," he said in a rough whisper. "I want to rip it off you with my teeth—but it's too pretty to ruin."

She felt weak in the knees when he said that. Weak and excited and so ready for him—for Joe.

Joe who, as of tonight, was her husband.

It all felt unreal, scary, to be here like this with him. But scary-good, like a wild ride on a fast horse beneath a sky thick with stars.

He took one foot and then the other and peeled the stockings all the way off. Her panties came last. He slid them down slowly, his head tipped up, his eyes still locked with hers.

She gasped when he moved in and started kissing her,

nipping at her lower belly as she stood above him there at the side of the bed. He kissed the faint stretch marks, silvery-white below her navel and then tender grooves under her hip bones, on one side and then the other, biting a little, scraping his teeth lightly over her skin.

She might have whispered his name at that point—and then moaned it, too.

He looked up. "Say my name again."

And she did—"Joe..."—again. And again. He went on kissing her, sliding his fingers into her, stroking her, then kissing her there, wrapping his hands around her hips, grasping one cheek in either hand, pulling her in close, his tongue doing things...

Wonderful things...

She shoved eager fingers into his thick hair, yanked him even closer and held on for dear life. For a wild, scary moment, she feared she might have smothered him.

But no. He was still kissing her, still doing things with that tongue of his that she hadn't believed ever actually happened in real life.

She said his name again, because she couldn't stop. She said it over and over. Because this couldn't really be happening, could it?

When she came, she unraveled. There was no other word for it. Her climax radiated through her from the flat of his tongue and the insistent stroking of those highly skilled fingers of his.

She begged him. She cried, "Yes!" And, "That!" And, "Oh, Joe, please Joe, please..."

And he did exactly what she pleaded for. Impossibly, he took her higher, made every perfect sensation sweeter, hotter, more overwhelming.

When she hit the peak, her knees got wobbly. He caught

her before she crumpled to the floor—caught her and helped her down to the rug slow and easy and then stretched out beside her.

It took her a moment to catch her breath. "I think I died and went to heaven," she whispered.

"Nah." He braced up on an elbow and rested his free hand on her bare belly. "You're still breathing." His hand strayed upward to cup her breast.

"Heaven," she whispered. "No doubt about it." She let out a ragged little sigh.

"Come on." He nuzzled her cheek. "Let's get in bed."

"Great idea."

He helped her up and then said, "Give me a sec." She didn't argue, just stood there on the rug, her arms wrapped around her naked middle, watching him as he pulled the covers back, thinking how handsome he was, so broad and strong, with the powerful legs of a horseman, the lean chest and arms of a guy who worked hard for his living. "Okay," he said. "Slide on in."

She climbed onto the bed and scooted to the far side. He got right in with her and settled the covers over them. His hairy leg brushed her smooth one.

She shivered in delicious expectation of yet more pleasure on this, their wedding night. By then, her orgasm-addled brain had started to function again. She remembered that she wasn't yet fully protected from pregnancy.

And she realized that she didn't even want to be.

"Don't bite that pretty lip," he said tenderly, bending close to give her a sweet, swift breath of a kiss. "What's wrong?"

She looked up at him, thinking how good this was, being here like this with him. She wondered why they hadn't thought to get married earlier—but then, no. Neither of them had been ready for this giant step. Not until now.

And she'd been silent too long. He let out a groan. "Sheesh, Mace. What's wrong? Just say it. Put me out of my misery, won't you?"

"I don't know where to start."

Carefully, as though he feared she might shrink away, he guided a few errant strands of hair back off her forehead. "Just jump right in. Whatever it is, we'll work it out like we always do."

"Oh, Joe…" She reached up, wrapped her fingers around the nape of his neck and tugged him down for a slow sweet kiss. "I want to suggest something."

He pulled back a little, his eyes alert now, watchful. "Uh, sure."

"If you're not ready for it, that's fine. We'll stick with the plan."

He scanned her face, so clearly looking for clues as to what might be going through her mind right now. "What plan?"

"The one where we wait a year to start trying to get pregnant."

His brows drew together in a frown. "You don't want to have more kids?"

"Joe!" She caught his face between her hands and lifted up enough to press a hard quick kiss on those fine lips of his. "Give me a minute. Just let me say what I need to say."

He was still frowning. But then he said, "Okay. I'm listening."

"It's like this." She kept her eyes steady on his. "From Tuesday when I started taking the pill, it takes seven doses to be fully protected."

"Okay, so…"

"So as of tonight, I'm not fully protected."

"I have condoms," he said, fast and with feeling, his eyes narrowing a little, as though he feared she might be backing out.

Fat chance. She almost smiled. "I have condoms, too."

"All right, Mace. Then what is the problem?"

"We said we'd wait a year to try for a baby."

"Right..."

"Well, I'm wondering what we're waiting for, that's all."

That stunned him. His mouth dropped open. "What are you telling me?" His voice was so quiet, so carefully controlled.

"I'm saying, we're married. We both want more kids. If you're up for it, I'll just stop taking the pill and we'll start trying now, tonight, on our wedding night."

"Whoa." He fell back to his pillow and stared at the ceiling as though something really alarming was happening up there.

"Joe? You okay? Because honestly. If you don't want to change the plan, that's fine. We'll wait. I understand, I really do. It's probably not fair of me to spring this on you tonight. I just thought we—"

"Macy." He cut her off in a strange flat voice.

"Um. Yeah?"

Finally, he turned his head and looked at her. His eyes burned into hers. "You mean that? You're sure?"

"Yes. I wouldn't have said anything if I wasn't."

"Macy..." He seemed at a loss.

For once, she couldn't read him. And really, she should have just left things alone. But no. She had to open her big mouth and mess with the plan. "Joe, listen. Never mind, okay? We'll just stick with the—"

"Yes."

She hadn't realized she was holding her breath until she let it out in a rush. Scooting closer, she rolled to her stomach and braced up on her elbows so she could look him squarely in the eyes. "Yes?"

"Yes!"

"You sure? Because I—"

"Macy." He wrapped his big hand around the back of her neck and slid his warm fingers up into her hair. His eyes burned into hers. "Take yes for an answer."

Now she was halfway on top of him, his bare body so warm beneath hers, his erection pressing, firm and insistent against her upper thigh. It felt so good, just to be here with him, to be suddenly more than the best friends they'd been for so long. It felt right—to be his and to know that he was hers. To feel certain that she could trust him in all the ways that mattered most.

To know beyond any doubt that her daughter could count on him to do what fathers do—back her up no matter what, paint her bedroom *Wicked* green, protect her from scary things like spiders, nightmares, monsters of every kind. For Ana, Joe would do all the things he was already doing.

But now he would do them as part of their family.

No, they weren't *in* love. But they *had* love, together, Macy and Joe. The best kind of love. One based on trust, respect and shared history, on the absolute certainty that neither would let the other down.

"Okay, then," she said, breathless now. "How about we get to work on our new plan?"

He laughed, the sound low and rich and full of sexy promises. "Done." And then he kissed her, a long kiss, which felt like a vow, a promise as binding as the words they'd repeated when they stood before Pastor Sandy only hours before.

She pulled him closer.

He looked up at her so seriously now—and then he asked one more time, "You're sure?"

"Absolutely."

And at last, he grinned that killer grin of his. "That's what I needed to hear." He took her in his arms and rolled her beneath him.

She was ready—so ready. She wrapped her legs around him. Lifting her body toward him, she urged him on. He groaned as he filled her.

And then they were moving together, rolling so sweet and slow, holding on tight. Macy and Joe, best friends forever, taking it to the next level on their wedding night.

Chapter Six

Joe woke at 4:00 a.m. as usual. He was spooned around a warm sweet-smelling woman.

It took him about two seconds to remember.

Macy. He pulled her closer and buried his nose in her hair. She always smelled good. And right now, this morning, she smelled like his wife and that made her sweet scent all the better.

The day before came to him. Every moment of it had been good. Especially what had happened when they were finally alone. Sometimes life could be so damn cruel—but it could also surprise a man in beautiful ways.

Rosie whined from directly behind him. He glanced over his shoulder. She was up, her nose on the bed, her tail wagging hopefully.

With care, he eased his arm from around Macy, rolled to his other side and slid out from under the covers.

In two minutes flat, he was dressed in work jeans, a heavy flannel shirt and winter socks.

Rosie bumped out the bedroom door first. Joe paused on the threshold to look back at the bed. Macy slept on. Silently, he shut the door behind him.

Outside, the inch or so of snow from yesterday glittered on the grass. It wouldn't last the morning. The sky was clear now, the gray humps of the Bighorns dusted with white visible in the distance. He stood on the porch in his stocking feet waiting for Rosie to finish her business, feeling like he should pull on his boots and meet his brother at the barn to pitch in with morning chores.

But no one expected him to work today. And hanging out with Macy beat shoveling horse manure hands down—especially after last night.

As Rosie trotted back up the porch steps, the door behind him opened. Rosie kept coming. When she reached him, she swerved around him, intent on heading back into the house. A second later, he heard her paws retreating across the wood floor inside.

Joe turned. Macy stood in the open doorway wearing nothing but that throw blanket he kept at the foot of the bed. Her hair was smashed flat on one side and she was still half asleep, her eyes squinty, her lips pressed together. She looked absolutely beautiful.

"You going out to do chores?" she asked, covering a yawn.

"Nope. Just got up to let Rosie out."

"Well, Rosie's in now. You better get in here, too." She reached out from under the blanket, grabbed his wrist and pulled him through the door. He went happily. In the house with Macy was exactly where he wanted to be.

"Come on." She led him back to the bedroom, where she dropped that blanket on the floor at the foot of the bed. That was all the encouragement he needed to scoop her up in his arms, carry her around to the side of the mattress and gently lay her down.

Married life.

He loved it already.

When he woke up at a little after nine o'clock, she was

lying there on her side, her hand tucked under her cheek, watching him.

"What?" he asked on a yawn.

"I was just listening to you snore."

He wanted to grab her and kiss her, make love to her all over again, but instead, he settled on tugging at a tangled lock of her hair. "Is snoring a deal-breaker for you, then?"

"No. It's not very loud, more of a rumble. And it's not all the time. It's kind of cute, really."

"Cute?" He put on a stern face. "My snoring is far from cute."

She giggled. It was the sweetest little sound. "Don't get your manly panties in a twist. Just consider it a compliment."

Hiding a grin, he asked, "So then, you think you can live with a man who snores?"

Her smooth bare shoulder lifted in a shrug. "Hey. We're married now. Compromises must be made." She sat up. The covers fell to her waist. Her skin was so smooth. And her breasts were sweet and rounded, just begging for his hands.

For another half hour, they rolled around in bed. If he had his way, he would have kept her there longer.

But today was move-in day for her and Ana. They needed to haul enough stuff over from the house in town so that they could get by for a few days, at least. The plan was to accomplish the move in stages during the next week or two, packing things up and bringing them home a little at a time.

When they arrived at the Oberholzer house, Ana ran down the steps to greet them. She wore all black except for a little white collar that made her look even more like Wednesday Addams than usual. The first words out of her mouth were, "Are we moving to the ranch today?"

When Macy confirmed that they were, Ana shot her little fist skyward and shouted, "Yass!"

They spent a few minutes checking in with Curtis and Betty. Then they loaded Ana, her overnight bag, her giant cat and a bunch of cat gear into the crew cab and headed for Macy's place. When they drove up, Josh and Riley were already there, sitting in the cab of a big truck with Bravo Construction printed on each of the cab doors and a trailer hitched on the back.

In the house, Macy had several stacks of boxes ready to go—though when she'd found the time to pack in the past week, Joe had no clue. But she insisted she knew what she needed to bring and if she'd forgotten anything, she would simply get it later. They loaded the boxes into the back of his truck. Pretty much everything in Ana's room would be going with them, so they all pitched in on that next.

They were back at the ranch by a little after three o'clock. Jason showed up as they began carrying stuff into the house. Joe's brother pitched in and so did Joe's dad and mom, who appeared about a half hour after Jason. Once everything from the two trucks was inside, Riley and Josh went on back to town. Meggie and Ana put Ana's clothes away while Joe and Jason reassembled the little girl's bed.

Voodoo and Rosie were something to watch. Rosie wanted to play. Voodoo did not. He hissed at the dog more than once, chittered at her in a warning way every time she came close. At one point, he even bopped her on the nose with a hard flick of his big paw, causing Rosie to let out a yowl and then start barking. Oddly, the barking didn't bother Voodoo at all. He simply dropped to a sit and began grooming himself.

By then, it seemed wise to separate the two. At least for now. So Meggie and Ana took the cat with them to Ana's room and shut the door while they worked to get things put away.

Overall, the afternoon zipped right by. At five o'clock, they trooped over to Jason's where Piper had stew ready for them.

Joe sat next to his bride with Ana on his other side. There was lots of laughter and stories about the wedding the night before, about Curtis and his camera. About sweet Pastor Sandy who had a kind word and a big smile for everyone.

It was great to sit there between his two girls. And they really were his now—his family, to look out for and protect. These past few years, he really had spent a lot of time worrying he would never have a family of his own. Now he didn't have to worry anymore.

Under the table, he felt for Macy's hand. She sent him a private smile as she laced her fingers with his.

Damn. Macy. Who knew?

He thought of last night and couldn't wait to get home and be alone with her again.

After dinner, the Bravo men did the dishes. Then they all sat around for a while, drinking coffee, talking horses and cattle and the necessity to put a new roof on the barn when summer came around.

By seven o'clock, Ana's big brown eyes were drooping shut.

They put on their coats, thanked Piper for dinner, and his folks and Jason for all the help. Then off they went back to his house.

Our house, Joe mentally corrected himself.

Because he didn't live alone anymore.

Macy followed Joe in the front door. He was carrying Ana, who had dropped off to sleep in the short ride from the other house.

"Look at that," Joe whispered, with a nod toward the fireplace.

Macy did look—at Rosie and Voodoo sleeping together on the hearth. Rosie was sprawled on her side. Voodoo had curled up against her, his striped head on Rosie's cheek.

"Bengals are good with dogs," she said. "The two of them just needed a little time to get to know each other, that's all."

He seemed puzzled. "But we corralled the cat in Ana's room."

"Yeah, well. I thought I told you that Voodoo can open doors. He's pretty tall when he's up on his hind legs and he can turn a door handle using both paws."

"Right…" The look on his face told her everything.

"You thought I was making that up."

"Yes, I did. Amazing…"

In his arms, Ana stirred. "Are we home yet?" She yawned.

"We are home." Macy was still surprised at the reality of that. She and her little girl lived on the Double-K Ranch now. With Joe… She shook herself and added briskly, "And you have school tomorrow."

Ana squinted up at Joe. "I guess I better get ready for bed now…"

He set her on the floor. She spotted her cat, who was still sleeping on Rosie. "Huh. I guess they'll be friends, after all."

"Wash up," Macy said, "and brush your teeth."

"Mom." Ana tossed her head. "I'm six years old. I know how to get ready for bed."

"You're right, you do." Macy put up both hands. "Better get after it."

"I'm going, I'm going…" Ana headed for her new room.

As soon as she started up the stairs, Voodoo startled awake, let out a chirp—and jumped up to follow her.

"Well," said Joe an hour and a half later. "We need to do that again..."

Macy watched the muscles of his arm flex as he braced up on an elbow. He really was a very handsome man. She felt a little breathless, just looking at him lying there, close enough to reach out and touch in the most intimate ways—which was exactly what she'd been doing for the past hour or so.

And also what she wouldn't mind doing again.

Just possibly, she had a mad sex crush on her BFF-turned-husband. Which was very convenient, given that they were trying for a baby.

Two and a half weeks since he'd come up with his wild idea that they should get married and here she was, married to him, sleeping in his bed, hoping to make a baby and loving every minute of it.

"What are you staring at?" he asked.

Why lie? "You. I was just thinking that you make an excellent husband. You work hard, you rush around to fulfill my daughter's every wish. And you're not all that bad to look at, either."

He touched her shoulder. "Come here."

She didn't have to be told twice. She rolled to her other side and backed up until he was spooning her.

"That's better." He pulled her even closer.

She felt him stirring against her. "Don't go getting ideas."

"Hey. Baby-making is a high priority for us now."

"True, but doesn't morning come early around here?"

He nuzzled her shoulder, his breath warm on her skin. "You've got a point. I need to be up at four as usual."

"Ranch life. That'll take a little getting used to."

He bit down—so gently—on the spot he'd just nuzzled. "I'll be quiet when I get up. You can sleep in till six."

"But what about you? You need your rest..."

"I'll be the judge of that," he muttered. And then he kissed her.

She wriggled around until she was facing him again, wrapped her arms around his neck and forgot about everything but the feel of his lips pressed to hers.

The following week flew by at warp speed. As October gave way to November, Macy spent every minute she could spare finishing up the move from her place to the ranch. By Friday, the job was pretty much finished.

There was still furniture to be put in storage or sold. Or maybe she'd rent the house furnished. She hadn't decided yet whether to sell or use it for extra income.

Later, she thought. In the spring, she would either put the house on the market or advertise it for lease. Right now, she was plenty busy handling both her jobs, taking care of her daughter and enjoying every minute as Joe Bravo's bride. The man was a miracle—as good a husband as he was a best friend.

Unlike the first guy she'd married...

Caleb's enormous monthly child support payment arrived in Macy's bank account like clockwork on November first. The sight of it just plain pissed her off. Why couldn't he at least give his daughter a call? How hard could that be?

She considered reaching out to him again.

But fat lot of good that would do. He made it a point of pride to let all calls go to voicemail. And he took his sweet time answering a text. When he did get in touch, his brief text or terse call would only make the situation all the more frustrating—and all the sadder.

Sometimes Macy thought she ought to just let it be. She needed to find a way to stop obsessing over the fact that Ana's dad couldn't be bothered to give his daughter a call now and then.

Really, Ana didn't seem to care that her dad had no time for her. She had a full life, grandparents who doted on her, lots of friends—and Joe, who was more of a dad to her than Caleb had ever been. She hardly seemed to remember her biological father anymore.

On the first Monday in November, Macy met Riley for lunch in the newly opened Basement Bar, which was right there in the hotel Riley ran and co-owned with her mother-in-law.

"Hey!" Riley appeared just as the hostess seated Macy at a small table in a quiet corner. Macy rose and hugged her friend. The waitress came by and they ordered club sandwiches.

"This is nice," Macy said. "Cozy, but with a speakeasy vibe."

Riley's face lit up at the compliment. "Exactly what we were going for. We get the lunch crowd and we get most of the hotel visitors—and lots of people from town come for happy hour."

They chatted about nothing in particular until their sandwiches arrived.

Then Riley asked, "So how's married life treating you?"

"It's good." Macy tried to play it cool but failed utterly. She was loving being married to Joe. "Oh, Riley. It's better than good."

"You're happy." It wasn't a question.

Macy nodded. "Marrying Joe was the best move I've ever made."

"Whoa, honey." Riley's grin was slow and knowing. "Look at you. I do believe you're glowing."

Glowing? Macy wouldn't go that far. She was so happy with Joe. But no, she did not *glow* over Joe. Carefully, she folded her hands in her lap to keep herself from pressing her palms to her cheeks. She wasn't blushing and there was no need to check on that.

"Seriously?" she grumbled. "How many times do I have to say it?" She kept her voice low, just between the two of them. "I love Joe, but I'm not *in* love with him. He's one of my two best friends in the whole world. Of course I'm happy to be with him. We make a great team, Joe and me."

Riley fiddled with the straw in her glass of raspberry sparkling water. "The team reference?"

"What about it?"

"It's getting old."

"But we *are* a—"

"Yes, you are. You are also very happy with him."

"Didn't I just say that?"

"Yes, you did. But you seem to think that you're happy in a good-buddies sort of way."

"Yeah?" Macy ate a french fry. Slowly. "So?"

"I think there's more than friendship going on between you two."

"What?" Macy dropped the sandwich she'd been about to bite into. "No. Uh-uh. You've got it all wrong."

Riley sat back with a heavy sigh. "You know what? I'm sorry."

"For what?"

"I'm being overbearing, pushing you about Joe when

you've already told me I'm on the wrong track. I won't do that again. Forgive me?"

Macy slid her hand across the table. Riley took it. "Of course, you're forgiven. And to be perfectly honest…"

"What?"

Macy blew out her cheeks with a hard breath. "Well, on second thought…"

"What? Say it."

"Okay, fine. You're not completely wrong."

Riley stifled a gasp. Then two adorable dimples appeared at the corners of her mouth. "I knew it!"

"Shh!" Macy reminded her. "I don't need the whole world knowing my private business."

Now they were both leaning in, their sandwiches ignored between them.

Riley whispered, "So, you are, um, gone on Joe, then? At least, just a little?"

Macy laughed. It came out low, husky. And she confessed, "I just never had a clue. I mean, *Joe*? My best buddy, *Joe*?"

"You're saying it's good with him, am I right?"

Macy made a show of fanning herself. "Oh, yeah. So good. The best."

Riley couldn't leave it at that. She was having way too much fun digging for details. "So when you say *it*, what you really mean is…"

"You know what I mean."

Being Riley, she just *had* to confirm. "The sex."

"Exactly. What can I tell you? There are no words big or dramatic enough. I'm captivated, enamored, besotted, obsessed…"

"Well, all right then, Mace. Whatever you call it, I would like some of that."

Now they were both laughing.

Riley raised her glass of fizzy water. "Here's to a nice, hot obsession—just between friends."

Macy tapped her glass to Riley's. They both drank. Then she said, "So anyway, I love everything about being Joe's wife. I think our marriage was a really good choice for me, for Joe and for Ana, too."

"I totally agree," said Riley. "Excellent move on your part."

"Thank you. Now, if I could just get Caleb to act like a dad now and then…"

"Not happening, huh?"

"Uh-uh."

"What about Ana? Is she asking about him?"

"No. Never. She hasn't mentioned him in forever. When his name comes up, she takes no interest. She knows who he is but… It's like he's some distant relative who has nothing to do with her or her life."

Riley said, "You know, given the circumstances, that she never asks about him doesn't seem like such a bad thing."

"That's what I keep trying to tell myself."

"Well, that she's happy is what really matters. My boy's a happy boy. And he doesn't have his dad, either."

"Because you are an amazing mom."

"High praise." Riley beamed and picked up her sandwich again. "I'll take it."

"But…" Macy hesitated.

Riley waved a hand. "Just go ahead. Say it. Please."

"Well, don't you think that, as Dillon gets older, there are bound to be issues?"

"That's more than possible, yeah. But I'm not about to create an issue when I really don't see one. Dillon never had any questions about his dad until the past couple of months."

"Since he started preschool and spends lots of time with other kids who do have a dad in their lives, maybe?"

"Yeah. Lately, he's asked about TJ a few times."

"So...what did you tell him?"

"That his dad loved him a lot. I...tell him stories of how TJ used to rock him and sing to him, of how thrilled TJ was when Dillon took his first step."

"I wish I had stories like that about Caleb. Looking back, he was always rushing off somewhere, even when Ana was a baby. He inevitably had some high-priority meeting or trip he just couldn't get out of."

Riley set down her sandwich and straightened her shoulders. "I am not going to say bad things about your ex—but I just might be thinking them. He was there for Ana's birth, though, right?"

"More or less. He kept leaving the birthing room to take calls and make arrangements via text for a trip to Colorado the next day."

"Oh, I can't even..."

Macy shrugged. "My point is that Dillon's only three and you have lots of good things to say to him about his dad, lots of great memories to share. It's not that way for me and Ana. When Ana does start asking about Caleb, I just don't know what I'll say."

"You'll figure it out. I know you will. Remember the good things about him—tell Ana all the reasons you loved him and married him."

"That's excellent advice and I will do exactly that. I'll remember the good times and talk about them. What I'm getting at, though, is that Dillon's always going to know that his dad would be here if he could. Caleb, not so much.

Caleb *could* be making the time to spend with Ana. And he's not. And in the end, I will have to be honest with my daughter that Caleb Storm is not a hands-on kind of dad."

"And that is so not your fault, Macy. That's on him. On a positive note—because you do need to look on the bright side—Caleb Storm is a good provider."

"Oh, yes he is. It's ironic. The courts will go after him if he's a deadbeat, but as long as he pays child support, he's in the clear to be totally absent in every other way. I mean, yeah. Money matters. But love and attention count for a lot, too."

"So you do what you can. You love Ana and so does Joe and you both show her you'll always be there for her. And when she asks questions, you sit down and talk with her honestly in words she can understand."

"Well, yeah. If she ever actually asks any questions."

"She will," Riley said confidently. "But don't push her too hard to face things she doesn't want or even need to deal with right now. From what I see, she's a happy, well-adjusted six-year-old. Don't try to fix what isn't broken, you know?"

Macy studied her friend across their small table. Riley's red hair was a riot of soft curls around her heart-shaped face and her eyes were blue as a cloudless summer sky. To Macy, she looked like the heroine in some lush, sweeping historical saga. And yet Riley Thompson was the most practical, down-to-earth person Macy had ever known. And so insightful, too.

"I think you missed your calling," Macy said. "You should have been a therapist."

"No way. I'm a businesswoman through and through."

Macy glanced around them at the cozy underground bar

and restaurant. Every table was taken. "And you are really good at what you do."

"Why, thank you. My mother-in-law is no slouch, either."

"You're right. Tell Annette that I *love* the Basement Bar."

"Will do. Now, how about dessert?"

"I shouldn't..."

"Guinness Chocolate Cake with White Knight Frosting?"

"Only if we split a slice."

"I'm in."

"You okay?" Joe pulled Macy in nice and close, tucked the covers up around her silky shoulders and smoothed a lock of golden brown hair back off her flushed cheek.

"As if you even need to ask." He wrapped his arm around her again. She laid her hand over his and turned her head back over her shoulder so they could share a quick kiss. "I am spectacular," she added.

"You certainly are." He was already feeling the urge to make love to her again.

"Down, boy," she instructed with a low husky laugh.

He laughed, too. And then he kissed her and she kissed him and the pleasure started all over again.

They didn't get to sleep until after eleven o'clock.

The next morning when he came in from feeding horses and mucking out stalls, the first glow of daylight could be seen on the eastern horizon. In the backyard, he clicked his tongue for Rosie to come on through the gate and then shut it behind her. He stopped before climbing the steps to the deck. Looking up at the fading stars in the still-dark sky, he thought, as he often did, that there was no place on earth he would rather be. At his feet, Rosie let out a questioning whine and nuzzled his pant leg.

He dipped to a crouch, gave her some love and told her what a great gal she was.

In the house, he left his dirty boots in the mudroom and took a few minutes to wipe off Rosie's paws and wash his face and hands in the laundry-area sink. Rosie followed him into the kitchen, where Ana sat at the island. Already dressed for school, she was eating scrambled eggs and munching a slice of toast liberally slathered with blackberry jam.

"Steak and eggs?" Macy asked him from over at the stove as Rosie lapped water from her bowl in the corner.

This was the life, no doubt about it. "Yes, please." He poured himself some coffee and wandered over to the stove where he resisted the urge to pat Macy's fine backside. Best not to, with their daughter right there. Instead, he gave her a quick light peck on the cheek. "Looks good."

She sent him one of those smiles that could light up the darkest night. "Almost ready."

A few minutes later, they joined Ana at the island. Rosie plopped down nearby and Voodoo strutted over, rolled to his back and began batting at Rosie's wagging tail.

Too soon, it was time to clear off their empty plates and get on with the day. Ordinarily, he'd go back out to work on the land for a few hours. But this morning he had a meeting with Josh and Josh's older brother, Ty.

Like Ana, Macy was already dressed for the day. Joe helped with the dishes and then had a quick shower.

He was just tucking his shirt into his jeans when Macy came in from the front room. "Ana?" he asked.

"I took her out to the bus stop and waited with her. The bus came right on time."

"We could take turns driving her, you know."

"Yeah, but she seems fine with the bus. More than one

of her friends takes it. Besides, most of the time I'll be driving her home. For now, hopping on the bus in the morning is a new experience, an adventure for her. Let's see how it goes."

He wanted to touch her, pull her close, claim a long sweet kiss. But if he did that, he would want more and that would mean he wouldn't make his meeting. "Ride into town with me?" he asked.

"Can't. I have errands to run and some stuff to deal with at the house in town. Don't forget, Ana has a group playdate at Lily's after school. It's for two hours. We'll be home around five. I put a pot roast in the slow cooker so dinner's handled."

Damn. She was something special, always one step ahead of most everyone else. "You're way too damned efficient."

"Ha, I try."

All this everyday married-people stuff they had to talk about. He loved it. The ordinariness of it. Two people working together, making a good life for themselves and their kid—and maybe more than one kid if things went as planned.

And to hell with not touching her. He moved in closer. "Anytime you need me to pick her up, you let me know."

"Of course I will…"

Pulling her into his arms, he kissed her, loving the feel of the slim, strong length of her pressed close against him.

Once Macy left, he clicked his tongue for Rosie and let her out into the fenced backyard for the day. Then he climbed into his crew cab and drove to town. At the hardware store, he waited on early customers until a little before nine o'clock when Myron came in.

With the store in good hands, Joe went to Bravo Construction for his meeting with Josh and Ty.

Ty had three new reno projects for Josh and they needed to order various materials—everything from finish lumber and shiplap siding to flooring, drywall, plywood, plumbing and electrical. After the endless meeting, Ty insisted on taking Josh and Joe to lunch.

They went to Arlington's Steakhouse, which was pretty much everybody's first choice there in town for a nice business lunch—or a night out with a special someone, for that matter. Ty had news to share.

"Sadie's going to make me a dad—again," he announced right after the server had delivered them each a top-shelf whiskey. Ty's wife, Sadie, owned Henry's, everybody's favorite local diner. Sadie and Ty already had four kids—two from Ty's marriage to Nicole and two more of their own.

"Congratulations," Joe and Josh said in unison. They toasted to the great news.

Their food came and Ty asked, "So, Joe, how's married life treating you?"

"It's good," Joe replied sincerely. "Real good." Good enough that he couldn't wait to get home to his new wife, though it had only been four hours or so since Macy had headed out the door that morning.

"Excellent," said Ty with a knowing grin. "And about time, too."

Joe scoffed. "I'm twenty-eight, Ty. That's not exactly ancient. Not everybody gets married at eighteen." Ty and his first wife, Nicole, had married right after they graduated from high school. They'd never been happy together and had eventually divorced.

Ty shrugged. "Not talking about your age, cousin. I'm talking about you and Macy."

"What about us?" Joe could hear the defensiveness in his own voice. As a rule, he and Ty got along great. But sometimes Ty could be such a wiseass.

"Oh, come on. It's like Sadie and me with you two. You and Macy were always meant to be but you were blind to the truth for way too long. I'm just happy for you that you figured it out."

There was absolutely no reason for Joe to argue about that. He loved being married to Macy. But the whole meant-to-be thing sounded like something out of a romance novel. He and Macy were not that, no way.

In the chair to his left, Josh shifted uncomfortably. "Ty..."

"What?" Ty seemed surprised at the look on Josh's face, a look that clearly said, *Back off, big brother.* "Oh, come on. It's a good thing, that's all I'm saying. Joe and Macy are a perfect match and they always have been."

What could Joe do then but wholeheartedly agree? "You're right, Ty. Macy is everything to me and I'm a very lucky man."

"Exactly." Ty raised his glass again. "Here's to choosing the right woman and making it legal."

Joe had no problem at all with toasting to that.

Macy was at the flower shop reconciling accounts when the phone rang. Eloise, the hosting mom for Ana's afternoon playdate had a nine-month-old baby boy with a fever.

"I'm so sorry," said Eloise. "He was fine this morning, but now he's running a fever. I need to cancel the playdate."

"I understand. Do you want me to pick up Lily and bring her home?"

"Thanks, but I called her dad. He'll be there to get her after school."

"All right, then. If there's anything I can do—"

"Thanks, Macy. I've got this. I can call the other moms. I don't know if my boy's contagious, but there's no reason to take a chance on him passing it on to Ana or one of the other girls. Plus, he's fussy and I need to focus on him."

Macy made a few more sympathetic noises and then said goodbye.

Ana was surprised to find her mom waiting at the curb when school got out. "I thought Lily's mom was coming to get us?" she asked as Macy hooked her into her booster seat.

"The baby's sick. Lily's mom called me to cancel. Sorry you're missing your playdate."

Ana made a sad face. "Me, too. We were going to make monster cookies and play *Miitopia*. What are we going to do now, Mom?"

"Well, I have some boxes to look through at the house here in town to see what we need to keep and what to give away…"

Ana waited until Macy was back behind the wheel to ask, "Can we just go home?" Apparently, an afternoon at the ranch with Rosie and Voodoo was more interesting than looking through dusty boxes at the house in town. Who knew?

Macy turned and smiled at her daughter. "Sure. Let's go home."

"We can?" Ana visibly brightened.

"No problem. There's no rush on anything at the town house, and I've got plenty to do at home, too."

"Yay!"

At the Double-K, Voodoo was sitting two feet inside the front door when Macy pushed it open. He chirped in greeting, a chirp that morphed into a loud purr, which then turned into a slow meow.

Ana went straight for him. Grabbing him up, she cuddled

him close. His long tail hanging down almost to the floor, the cat nuzzled her cheek and chittered in happiness just to have his favorite human home again. Next, Ana let Rosie in from the backyard. Ana asked for a snack and Macy gave her one. When she'd finished, she carried her plate to the sink and then turned to the cat and dog who lay sprawled near her chair. "Come on, you guys," Ana said. "Let's go upstairs."

Rosie and Voodoo followed where she led.

Macy spent a half hour or so taking stuff out of boxes and putting it away. When she ran up to check on Ana, she found the little girl lying on the floor of her bedroom, cat on one side, dog on the other, reading to them from one of her picture books.

"What, Mom?" Ana asked with a yawn.

A nap, Macy thought, was very likely in the offing. "You need anything?"

"I'm good." Ana reached over and patted Rosie on the head.

Macy closed the door behind her as she went out. She was halfway down the stairs, phone in hand, about to check in with Joe, who was probably still at the hardware store, when the doorbell chimed.

Sticking the phone back in her pocket, she hurried the rest of the way to the door, which had a fanlight window at the top. Macy glanced out and saw a blonde woman she didn't recognize.

She hesitated, but only for a second or two. Then she pulled the door wide.

The woman looked about Macy's age—and exhausted. There were shadows beneath her eyes. She wore jeans, boots and an insulated parka with a hood lined in faux fur. She had a car seat in one hand and a big diaper bag hooked on the opposite shoulder. In the car seat, a baby slept.

A neighbor, maybe? The woman had a look Macy remembered seeing in the mirror on more than one occasion back when Ana was a baby. A look of sheer exhaustion with little relief in sight.

The woman asked, "Is, uh, Joe here? Joe Bravo?"

Macy almost said no that he wasn't home right now. But the woman was clearly at the end of her rope. Just the word *no* might send her running, and that wasn't something Macy wanted to do.

Yeah, she knew she ought to be wary. This woman could so easily be trouble. But Macy didn't think so. The woman seemed desperate more than anything. Macy couldn't help but feel sympathy for her.

Whatever was going on here, it felt wrong to run her off.

Macy introduced herself. "I'm Macy, Joe's wife."

The woman blinked. Clearly, she hadn't heard about the wedding. "He's *married*?"

Macy looked at the baby and then at the woman and suddenly had a very good idea of what was going on here. The realization that the baby might actually be Joe's almost brought her to her knees.

But she didn't give herself more than a second to dwell on it. The woman really was about to turn and run, and if Macy's suspicions were correct, she couldn't just stand here and watch her drive away.

"Hey," Macy said. "Listen. It's like this. We've been friends forever, Joe and me." She spoke slowly and kept her voice soft and nonthreatening. "We both wanted a family with someone we could trust. So last month, we got married."

"Oh! Well, good. I mean, that he's not a cheater…"

Where to even go with that remark? "He's definitely not. And look. Whatever you need to see Joe about, let's not stand here on the porch in the cold. Why don't you come on in?"

"Oh, I don't know..."

"Come on." Macy stepped forward and took the woman's arm. "Come on in..."

Reluctantly, the woman allowed herself to be coaxed into the house. As soon as they passed the threshold, Macy shut the door.

The woman stood there holding the baby in the car seat, shaking her head. "I... I'm so sorry to bother you, um, Macy. I would have called him, but we didn't exchange numbers. I don't even know where to start here..."

Macy's mouth went dry. So then. Apparently, the baby really was Joe's...

She swallowed hard and focused on staying calm. "It's okay. Honestly. Come this way." Gently, she pulled the woman farther into the living room. "Have a seat. Please."

Slowly, the woman sank into a chair and let the diaper bag drop off her shoulder to the floor.

Macy said, "Let me take your coat."

The woman held the car seat closer. "Uh, no. I'll just..." A hard sigh escaped her. "It was a one-night thing, with Joe—and... Oh, who am I kidding? I don't know if I would have called him even if he'd given me his number. I don't know him. And when I found out I was pregnant, I thought I could manage on my own. I mean, I might never have tried to contact him, but, well, now everything's gone wrong..."

It seemed like a good idea to keep the woman talking. "I'm sorry to hear that. What happened?"

"Recently, my boss decided to retire and she closed down the business. Yesterday, I got evicted. I just didn't know where to turn." Now she looked on the verge of tears. "And I... Oh, what am I doing? You don't need to hear all this..."

The baby, who was wrapped in a fluffy turquoise blanket and wore a pink fleece sleeper printed with seahorses, yawned hugely and then, with a soft sigh, settled back into slumber.

"You're welcome here," Macy said. "Honestly. Just take off your coat. I'll get you some hot tea and I'll call Joe. He'll come right home and you two can talk."

The woman closed her eyes and let out a soft moan. "Oh, I really didn't think this through. And now, I realize that I..." A single tear glided down her cheek. She swiped at it angrily with the back of her free hand. "This isn't right. You seem like a nice person. And this is not how I meant for things to be. I had a plan. I kept meaning to come back here, to get hold of Joe, to tell him there was a baby coming. But somehow I never quite got up the nerve. And I waffled. I didn't want to face a man I barely knew and tell him his safe and simple one-night-stand had turned into a whole lot more.

"I started thinking I could do this myself, be a single mom, work and raise my baby, do it all on my own. But everything's gone all wrong and now I just... I don't know what to do."

Macy eased in behind the coffee table and perched on the end of the sofa. "As I said, I'm Macy. And you are...?"

"Tia," she replied with a soft, strangled sound. "Tia Fortier."

"Tia, you did the right thing to come here." Macy held up her phone. "I'm just going to call Joe. He'll come right home and we'll work this out. What do you say?"

Tia drew a slow, shuddering breath. "Yes. All right. I guess you'd better call Joe."

Chapter Seven

Tia Fortier...

Joe was driving too fast. For the third time since he left the hardware store, he reminded himself to ease his foot off the gas. No matter how bad he needed to get home, the last thing he could afford to do was to drive recklessly enough to get into an accident.

Tia Fortier...

This couldn't be happening.

But somehow, it was. Macy had been so calm on the phone. But when she put Tia on, well, that was a whole other story. The woman had sounded seriously stressed.

How could this have happened? He'd been responsible that one night with Tia. He'd used condoms, as always. And they'd agreed—mutually—that it was just one time and that was how they both wanted it.

He turned off the county road and onto the unpaved road that led to the ranch. The truck went into a slight skid, tires spitting gravel because he'd picked up speed again without realizing it.

From the far sides of the barbwire fences that ran along the road on either side, cows and their calves lifted their heads at the sound. They stared as though vaguely offended that men in their pickup trucks so often drove faster than they should.

Slowing yet again, he breathed deep. It had started to rain, a flood of fat drops pouring down from the gunmetal-gray sky.

Five minutes later, he was pulling to a stop behind a white Mazda SUV. He was out of the car and halfway up the steps when the front door opened.

"Hey, Joe." Macy gave him a careful smile.

He couldn't get to her fast enough. "You okay?"

"I am."

He hated that he'd put her in this position. "You sure?"

She stepped out onto the porch and pulled the door shut behind her. "It's okay," she said. "*I'm* okay, honestly. Tia and the baby are in the kitchen."

He raked his hand back through his rain-wet hair. "I'm wrecked."

"I hear you, I do. And that's completely understandable. Just…please don't beat yourself up. I know you. I know you were always careful. Stuff happens. Contraception is never a hundred percent foolproof. That's just a plain fact."

"Still. You didn't sign on for this and I wouldn't blame you if you wanted to punch me in the face."

"Well, I don't. I'm not judging you. It's going to work out. Wait and see. It's going to work out and I'm going to help. What matters is that baby. And that poor woman inside. I know she messed up in a big way, not telling you about this sooner, but still. I feel for her. She seems…sincere, Joe. She really does."

A wave of sheer relief swept through him that Macy could be so completely amazing at a moment like this. He, on the other hand, had no idea what to do next. "I don't even know where to start. She said on the phone that it's a girl."

Macy nodded. "That's right. A sweet little baby girl."

"Mace, I just..." He couldn't remember what he'd been about to say.

"Hey. We will get through this." She took a step closer.

He reached for her. She went into his arms. It was so good to hold her. The world had suddenly fallen out from under him—and here she was, ready and willing to help him find his way back to solid ground.

She flat-out astonished him, that she could be so calm, so focused on doing the right thing. He was lucky she hadn't just packed up Ana and the cat and burnt rubber back to town the minute Tia broke the news that her baby was his.

He believed in Macy, he did. Always had. She said that somehow they would work this out. And he needed to go with that, to believe her.

"Tia's the office manager at a real estate agency up in Sheridan," he said, pulling back enough to look into his wife's big brown eyes. "The night we, uh, hooked up, she mentioned that she knew Nicole." Nicole Stahl, Ty's first wife, owned Bravo Real Estate in town.

Macy said, "Tia *was* the office manager. She lost her job recently when the owner retired. And yesterday, she was evicted from her apartment."

"That's tough."

"Yes, it is. We need to help her out."

"You're right—and what about Ana? Does she know what's going on?"

"Not yet. She has Rosie and Voodoo up in her room with her. I checked on them a minute ago. She's napping. If she comes wandering down, just give her a hug and I'll herd her and the cat and the dog back upstairs. We're going to have to play this by ear, do the best that we can."

He let his arms drop to his sides. "A baby... I just can't believe it."

She took his hand and laced her fingers with his. He pressed his palm to hers and held on tight.

"Right now," she said, "we're going to go inside. We're going to talk to Tia and start figuring stuff out. You ready?"

Hell, no, he thought. "Yeah, I'm ready," he said.

Inside, Joe held Macy's hand good and tight as they crossed the living room and went on into the kitchen.

Tia sat at the table. "Uh. Hi, Joe," she said. She looked exhausted, thinner than he remembered from that night last year, with dark shadows like bruises beneath her eyes. The baby was right there, in her arms—a bundle in a blanket. Joe couldn't see the baby's face.

What in the hell does a man say at a time like this? "Tia. Hello."

She gave him a grim smile and fiddled with the blanket.

He pulled out a chair and dropped into it.

Macy offered him coffee. "Or there's tea, too, if you want."

He said, "Coffee, thanks."

Tia shook her head. Macy put a full mug in front of him and then took the chair to his right.

"Go ahead, Tia," Macy said gently. "Tell Joe what's going on."

Tia started talking. She said what he'd expected her to say—that he was the baby's father. Even knowing she would say that, the words still hit him like a fist to the gut. For a moment, he could hardly draw breath.

But then he managed to ask, "How are you so sure?"

She said there hadn't been anyone else since she and her boyfriend broke up two years ago. "But of course," she added in a tiny voice, "you'll want a paternity test."

"What I want," he said in a voice that hardly sounded like his own, "is to see her face, to hold her myself..."

Tia looked stricken. She cradled the sleeping baby a fraction closer. "Right now?"

"Yeah. Right now."

"Okay..." Tia stood and he rose with her. She bent her head to the baby and whispered something. Then she laid the baby in his arms.

She was warm, the baby. And now that he was looking down at her, he could finally see her face. She was sound asleep, her pale barely-there eyelashes like tiny translucent fans against her round velvety cheeks. "What's her name?" he whispered.

"Camryn—spelled C-a-m-r-y-n."

"You gave her a guy's name?" He dared to touch that perfect cheek. Undisturbed, the baby slept on.

Tia straightened her shoulders. "Girls *are* named Camryn."

"Camryn," he whispered. It was a strong name. He liked that. Slowly, he sank back into his chair.

Tia sat down, too.

He had questions. So many questions. "Why didn't you let me know when you found out you were pregnant?"

"I really did keep meaning to."

"Right..." He adjusted the blanket around the small perfect face and then pinned Tia with a hard look. "But you *didn't* contact me. You didn't let me know that you were having my baby."

Her silence said it all. Finally, she managed, "I'm sorry," in a broken whisper. "And I'm here now," she tried hopefully.

It wasn't enough. He said tightly, "I know we didn't exchange numbers, but you spent the night here. And you got here today, when you finally decided to tell me that I'm a dad—that I've been a dad for...what? Three months now. And for several months before that, you knew that I was going to be a dad."

"Look," she said. "I can't go back and redo the past."

He kept his mouth shut. Anything he said right now would be in anger.

Tia drew a shaky breath. "Listen, Joe. I'm on my own. I have no family—not here in Wyoming, anyway. My parents are no longer living. I have an aunt in Peoria, but that's about all and I'm not close with her. I take care of myself and I like it that way. And I, well, I was afraid to take a chance on you. Even though I thought you were an okay guy after the, uh, night we had, I didn't know you and I didn't know what you'd do when you found out that I was pregnant."

"Doesn't matter." For the sake of the baby in his arms, he kept his voice low. "You knew and you didn't reach out to me." Did that come out hard and mean? Maybe. He reminded himself to back off a bit.

"You're right. I'm not arguing with you. I am very much aware of how wrong it was not to let you know that you were going to be a dad. I just..." She seemed to run out of steam.

Macy caught his eye and gave a quick tight shake of her head. He got the message. He knew he needed to ease off. "Go on," he said, his voice carefully measured.

Tia drew another ragged breath. "Look. I meant to do right, but I just didn't. The truth is, until today, all I did was name you as her father on her birth certificate."

His breath caught when she said that. Every new fact made this miracle in his arms all the more real.

Tia grabbed the diaper bag at her feet and hoisted it

into her lap. She unzipped a side pocket and pulled out an official-looking document. "I have a copy for you. Here."

Carefully, so as not to wake the baby, he reached out and took it.

And there it was on the bottom line: *Father: Joseph Nathan Bravo*

For a moment, he wondered how the hell she knew his middle name. And then he remembered.

It was early in the evening, on that night he met her. They'd struck up a conversation during happy hour at the bar at Arlington's. He'd bought her a drink and they started talking, playing the getting-to-know-you game, sharing enough basic information so that they would each feel comfortable going somewhere private and taking off their clothes.

"I'm Tia," she'd said. "No middle name. Just Tia Fortier, plain and simple. You?"

"Joseph Nathan Bravo," he'd replied. "But call me Joe."

Now, a year later, he glanced up from the angel in his arms. "I do want a paternity test. I want to get that taken care of right away."

"Of course," she said in a voice so small he barely heard it. "I understand."

The main thing right now was not to let her take this baby out of his house until he could be sure she wouldn't vanish into thin air.

Macy was watching him. He met her eyes, saw nothing but compassion in them—for him. And for Tia as well.

He wanted to feel sympathy for Tia, too, but he didn't. Tia Fortier just wasn't all that trustworthy, not from his perspective. She'd had his baby and not bothered to let him know he was the father until she had no other choice—if this miracle in his arms really was his baby, after all.

He looked down at Camryn again, seeking a family resemblance. He saw only a beautiful little girl with hardly any hair and round pink cheeks. She didn't look like him, particularly. Or like his mom or dad or anyone in the Bravo family.

Still, he wanted desperately to believe this baby was his. That he had a daughter—two daughters, really. Because he considered Ana to be his in all the ways that mattered.

He almost smiled, then. Two daughters. Who knew? A month ago he'd wondered if he would ever get to be someone's dad.

"We've got a little girl upstairs," he said. "Ana is six. She's going to come down here soon and want to know what's going on."

"I understand," Tia said again. Her eyes glittered with unshed tears.

He looked at Macy, who nodded at him, letting him know she was right there for him, whatever he needed, however she could help. Then he turned to Tia again. "We're going to need some time with you tonight. It will take a while to come to an agreement as to what happens next. Will you stay until we've talked it out?"

Tia stared. But then she shook herself. "Of course I will."

"All right, then. You'll have dinner with us. And then, after Ana's in bed, we will talk about what to do next."

"Yes. All right." She sounded kind of frantic, suddenly. "That's good. That works." Popping to her feet, she pulled an electronic key fob from her pocket. "I've got pictures on a thumb drive in the car, pictures I thought you might want. Pictures of the day she was born, and a bunch more of her that show how much she's grown already. I'll just run out and get the drive."

What was she up to? All he knew was that he wasn't letting her take Camryn outside to her car. Not yet. Not until she'd shared a whole lot more information than she had so far. Not until they'd come to the beginnings of an understanding as to where they were going from here.

But she didn't reach for the baby. "I'll be right back."

He relaxed. "Thanks. I would love to have those pictures."

"Okay, then," she said. "I'll..."

There were footsteps on the stairs. Ana came toward them and stopped in the arch to the living area. She had Rosie at her heels and Voodoo in her arms.

"I was sleeping," Ana said with a big yawn as she looked up at Tia. "Hi. I'm Ana." Voodoo slipped free of her grip. He landed on all four paws and strutted toward his water bowl.

Tia offered a quick tight smile. "Good to meet you, Ana." She turned to Joe and Macy again. "I'll be right back," she promised, and headed for the door.

Ana watched her go, then turned to frown at Joe. "Is that a baby you've got?"

He couldn't help grinning. "It is. She's three months old and her name is Camryn. Come look."

As the front door opened and then clicked shut, Ana moved close. "Wow." She stuck her face right down to an inch from Camryn's and then she looked up again. Those big dark eyes met his. "Can I hold her?"

"Soon."

Ana wrinkled her nose in disapproval. "Joe. I know what you really mean and you mean not right now."

"Pretty much, yeah. But soon."

With a sigh, Ana leaned her head on Joe's shoulder. He thought, *My girls*, and glanced up to find Macy watching them through misty eyes. It was a good moment—a moment he needed right now when he was reeling from the impossible reality of the baby in his arms.

And then he heard the faint sound of a car starting up and driving away out in front. It had to be Tia. The woman was taking off.

Macy stifled a gasp and met Joe's eyes.

An entire conversation occurred in that shared glance. Of utmost importance right now was not to alarm either the baby or Ana.

Joe did his part. He said, "Ana, if you'll sit down, you can hold Camryn."

Ana's face lit up. "Really? Now?"

"Now." To Macy, he said, "Why don't you…check on Tia?"

"Will do." Rising, she turned for the front door.

As she passed through the arch to the living room, she heard a kitchen chair scrape the floor behind her. "I'm ready," Ana announced.

"Let's try the sofa," Joe suggested. "It's softer and more comfortable…"

"'Kay!" Ana gleefully agreed.

Macy pulled open the front door and slipped through, easing it quietly shut behind her.

The rain had stopped. And the Mazda was nowhere in sight. Two tubs of baby formula, a big bag of disposable diapers and a large suitcase waited a few feet away at the top of the porch steps.

Tia was definitely running away.

Macy took off. Dodging all the baby stuff, she raced down the steps and along the stone walk to the dirt ranch road just beyond the patch of front-yard grass. No sign of the white car.

For several awful seconds, Macy just stood there, staring off down the narrow road, feeling awful for everyone—the baby, the mother. Joe. Should she have guessed that Tia was about to run?

Probably. What should she do now? She had no idea. Mindlessly, she kept going, kept trudging along. She was hoping against hope that...

What? Tia was gone. There was no way Macy would catch up with her on foot.

She was just about to turn and slog back through the mud to the house, when lights appeared up ahead on the road—taillights, backing toward her through the gloom.

Macy took off running toward the car. When she came even with the driver's door of the Mazda, she slapped at it with the flat of her hand.

Wide-eyed and crying, Tia looked over as she braked. Breathless, Macy braced her hands on her knees and sucked in air.

The driver's side window hummed down. Tia stuck her head out. "I'm an idiot," she said. Tears streamed down her face.

Macy nodded. "Yeah. Pretty much."

They stared at each other. Then Tia said, "Get in." She leaned away to open the passenger door.

Macy ran around and got in. "Sorry, my shoes are—"

"Don't worry about the mud."

"Fair enough."

Tia said, "There are tissues in the glove box."

Macy realized right then that she was crying, too. She took a tissue and held out the box. They both wiped their eyes and blew their noses.

And then Macy said, "Just go forward, follow this road in a circle. It will take you back to the house."

Tia shifted into Drive and took her foot off the brake.

They circled past the main house and then drove by Jason and Piper's place. When they got back to where they'd started, Tia stopped the car and turned off the engine.

She looked out her window at the baby gear on the porch. "I've run away a lot. When you don't have much and things are falling apart, starting over can seem like the only choice."

"So...that was your plan, to leave the baby with Joe and run off?"

"Pretty much. I told you I got kicked out of my apartment yesterday. Last night, Camryn and me, we slept in this car. I'm a twenty-seven-year-old single mother with no job and not-quite-two-hundred dollars in my pocket. My bank balance is zip. I remembered Joe as a good guy, you know? The way he talked that night we were together, how considerate he was, how honest he seemed... I just knew he would be a good dad. I thought I would come back here, talk to him, make sure he was the way I remembered him..."

"And then leave your baby and just drive away?"

"Yeah." Tia met her eyes across the console. "You were kind of a surprise."

"I noticed."

"But then, well, it turns out you're perfect. You're the mom I could never be."

"I am far from perfect. And you shouldn't put yourself down. Tia, it's obvious you love your baby and want the best for her."

"I do. And I'm not the best. I'm just not."

"Please don't say that."

"It's the truth. I want her to have what *I* never did, a real family. A mom and dad who love her and would do anything for her."

"Tia. *You* love her. I believe that you would do anything for her."

"I would. I really would. And I tried, to do this on my own. I just messed it all up. Leaving her here with you and Joe... I can tell from the short time I've spent with you that it would be the best thing for her."

"I don't think so, Tia. Not for her, not for you, either."

"It's not about me. Like I said, I'm used to leaving, used to starting over."

"But it's clear you really don't want to leave her." Macy handed her another tissue. "You did the right thing, to come here, to tell Joe at last. You were right about Joe. He's a good man, the best. And we'll figure this out together—you, Joe and me—just wait and see."

"I don't see how."

"One step at a time," Macy said. "Don't think about all the things you should have done, all the stuff you need to do. Just take it one day, one hour, one minute at a time..."

"I'm not sure about this," Joe said when he and Macy were finally alone in bed. It was almost eleven o'clock. They'd put Tia and Camryn in the spare room upstairs. Tia had agreed that she and the baby would stay with them for a while, at least. Until they had time to figure out the next step.

Right now, Joe was thinking he would get zero sleep tonight. He'd be listening for the sound of footsteps on the stairs, of the Mazda driving away outside. "You think she'll take off again?"

"No." Macy had her head on his shoulder. She tipped her head back enough to look up at him. Her big eyes gleamed at him through the dark. "I think she's a good person, Joe.

I really do. She's in a tough place and this, having to turn to her baby daddy for help—it's a lot."

"Baby daddy?" He brushed his hand down her arm in a slow caress. "Seriously?"

She snuggled in closer. "Hey. Own it."

"I'm just so damn pissed at her, you know? She should have come to me in the first place. I should have been there for Camryn."

"You are there for Camryn now." Her gaze was steady, locked with his. "And you will continue to be from now on."

He bent his head and kissed her. "I'm calling Ethan tomorrow." Ethan Bravo was Joe's second cousin and also a lawyer. He and his law partner, Gavin Stahl, had an office right there in town. "We need that paternity test ASAP. I'll ask Ethan to set it up."

"I think that's a good idea. Though I honestly believe the baby is yours. And remember, Tia did put your name on the birth certificate."

He thought of Camryn's rosebud mouth, her bright eyes and barely-there wisps of pale blonde hair. She was one of the two most beautiful babies he'd ever seen—Ana having been the other.

Macy said, "We need to take care of Tia, find her a place to live in town—and a job in town, too."

He was really putting in the effort not to be hard-hearted about Tia. Too bad the woman was a sore spot for him. All this time, she'd been living twenty miles from him. All she'd had to do was reach out and he would have helped her through the pregnancy. He could have been there to see his little girl born...

Yeah, he wanted to trust Camryn's mother, but so far he just didn't. "What? Tia can't find her own damn job?"

"Joe." Macy pressed her soft hand to the side of his face

and looked up at him steadily. Those soulful eyes of hers were full of patience—and a flicker of annoyance, too. "Try having your kid's other birth parent a thousand miles away and a pain in the ass to get a hold of. I think you might change your tune then."

"Caleb," he said glumly.

"Yeah. He's not here for Ana the way he should be. Tia, though, she's trying. She loves Camryn and she wants to be a good mom."

"But, Mace, she's been so far from straight with me. I just don't trust her."

"Well, I do. I trust her love for that baby. I trust her good heart. And even if I'm wrong about that, I still think we want Tia close. We want to be able to be right there for her because being there for her is being there for Camryn. We want to work with Tia, we *need* to work with her."

"*We* do, huh?"

She pinned him with a steely glare. "Yes. We do."

He let out a tired breath. "Aw, Mace..."

"Take a page out of your cousin Ty's book. He and Nicole fought like a pair of honey badgers all through their disaster of a marriage. But now he's married to her best friend, Sadie, and Nicole's happily remarried, too. And it works. It works like gangbusters. The kids go back and forth between Ty's place and Nicole's. They all get along. They're family. That's what we want with Tia."

"We don't even know Tia."

She pressed her lips together. He read her so well. She was bound and determined to make him see her side of this argument and she was choosing her words with care. "The point is, we will *get* to know her. And she's going to learn that she can trust us. Just as we will come to trust her. She needs a family, Joe. Her mom and dad are dead. There's just that aunt in Illinois and they're not close. As she said, she's always starting over..."

"Mace, you are not reassuring me that she's someone we can rely on."

"What I'm doing is begging you to give the poor woman a break. She's alone. You and me, we grew up with parents who would do anything for us. She didn't. She needs a family and we're going to be her family, you just wait and see."

What could he say? "Give me time, okay?" He kept his tone mild and tried to think trusting thoughts. "Eventually, I'll get over how long it took her to let me meet my daughter. I'll get over tonight, when she walked out the front door and almost didn't come back."

"But she *did* come back. And not because I went after her. She realized she was making a big mistake and she put the car in reverse."

"Okay."

"What does *okay* mean?"

"It means I see your point and I will make more of an effort to, uh, be there for her."

Macy laughed. Even at a time like this when he would rather have a root canal than continue beating this subject to death—even when she insisted on taking Tia's side, he loved the sound of Macy's laugh.

"Spoken like a man who is ready for this conversation to end," she said.

"Yeah, well. Can you just take my word that I'm trying?"

"Absolutely." She lifted up enough to press her sweet lips to his. "Thank you for agreeing to try." She cuddled in close with her head under his chin. He breathed in the scent of her hair and felt the tension start to flow out of him. She sighed. "Now I will allow you to go to sleep."

"Sleep?" He pulled her even closer, ran his hand down

the silky skin of her back all the way to the perfect curve of her beautiful ass. "In a little while…" He kissed her again, more deeply this time.

She wrapped her arms around his neck and made a hungry little sound low in her throat. "Married life. There are definitely challenges."

"Yeah. Big ones."

"And yet…" A low moan escaped her. "It has its perks."

The next day, Joe went to see his cousin Ethan at Stahl and Bravo, Attorneys at Law. Ethan sent Joe to a DNA lab in Casper to get his cheek swabbed. Joe called Tia and she brought Camryn to the lab so they could swab her cheek, too.

Two days later, on Friday at 1:00 p.m., Joe logged on to the lab's secure online portal and found confirmation of what he already knew—Camryn was his child.

Rising from his battered metal desk in his cubicle of an office there at Bravo Hardware, he went through the inner door to Macy's office and pulled her up out of her chair.

She let out a shriek and faked a sex-kitten voice. "Oh, Mr. Bravo! This is so unprofessional…"

"It's official." He kissed her. She wrapped her arms around his neck and kissed him back. That went on long enough that he seriously considered the idea of having his way with her right there on her desk.

She pulled back enough to meet his eyes. "Not at our place of business, you naughty man—and *what's* official?"

"The DNA results are in. You are looking at Camryn's biological dad."

Her eyes got all dewy. "Joe. Congratulations."

"Thank you."

"I'm so glad. I had no doubt that she was yours, but still. It's such a relief to know for sure."

"Yeah. Yeah it is." Now that there was no doubt his claim was a real one, he felt better about everything. He was Camryn's father and he could take that to court if he had to. "We need to start spreading the news." They'd already explained the situation to Josh, Riley and the family, but now everyone needed to know that the DNA results confirmed what they'd already believed.

She nodded. "Let's get after it."

"You think they'll be okay with hearing the news over the phone?"

She considered the question. "I think we want to get the word out and this is the quickest way, you know?"

What she said made sense to him. "You're right. Let's go for it. I'll start with Josh. And Jason."

They began making calls.

An hour later, everyone important had heard the big news that Joe was now officially Camryn's dad.

Joe hung up from talking to his parents as Macy said goodbye to Betty and Curtis.

"Well?" Macy asked.

Joe grinned. "My dad said, 'You sound happy.' And I said, 'I am, Dad. I truly am.' After that, they both laughed and congratulated me—how about Betty and Curtis?"

Macy made a thoughtful sound. "My mom wanted to know how we were handling it, how I felt about it."

"Look at me." When she met his eyes, he asked flatly, "Your mom's pissed at me, right?"

"I wouldn't use the word *pissed*, exactly."

"So what word *would* you use?"

"Well, Joe..." Her voice trailed off.

"Macy, you said that when you told her the other day about Tia showing up with Camryn, she seemed a little shocked."

"Yeah. Because she was. Think about it, Joe. My mom and dad have been together since high school, you know that. They're conservative and traditional. I honestly believe they were both virgins on their wedding night. They're not like your parents. I mean, your dad was a total bad boy who had a very difficult childhood, a guy who swore he'd never settle down. Your mom had to chase him all the way to LA, keep after him relentlessly until he finally—"

"Macy. I do know their story. I'm the one who told it to you, remember?"

"Yes, I do. And what I'm trying to say is that, yes, your parents are a real love match. But they also know how hard the world is, how sometimes a person might only be ready to get together with another person just for a night. But my parents don't really get why anyone would spend a night with a stranger. Frankly, my mom and dad were disappointed in me when they found out I was three months' pregnant with Ana and still single—and that Caleb had such a busy schedule he wouldn't be marrying me until several months later."

Joe closed his eyes and took a breath through his nose. "Now you're making me want to track him down and rearrange that irritating face of his…"

She actually laughed. "He is who he is—and I did have a point I was making."

"Sorry," he said, and meant it. "Continue."

"Okay, then. What I was getting at is that my mom and dad got over the shock that their precious only daughter had sex before marriage—and ended up pregnant, too. Then later, they were freaked out when I told them I'd filed for divorce. But that's behind us and has been for quite some time. And now they've learned that you had sex with a stranger and made a baby with her…"

"Damn. It sounds completely irresponsible when you put it that way. I used a condom, I promise you."

"I get it. I do—and I never said that what happened between you and Tia was irresponsible and neither did my mom."

"So she said something the other day, then, when you first told her that Tia and Camryn were staying with us, right? Something you didn't tell me then."

Macy shrugged. "All right, yes. Two days ago, she asked why you hadn't called Tia the next morning after the night you spent together. She couldn't understand why you wouldn't be concerned about how she was doing after what had 'happened' between you. Then I explained that the point of a hook up is that you don't have to call the next morning."

He groaned. "And then she was even more disappointed in me, right?"

"No. She was fine two days ago and she's fine now. She still thinks the world of you. You're a hero to her."

"You're just saying that to make me feel better." And right now, he felt about two inches tall.

"Please. My mom said that it wasn't her place to judge and she knows you and I are going to do the right thing in a tough situation. She said that she and my dad will help in any way they can—whatever you need or I need or the baby needs, we only have to call and they will be there."

He knew what to do then. "I'll go see her tomorrow, try to make it right with her."

"Joe, you don't have to make anything right. It's going to be fine."

"I'll go see Betty anyway."

Those big brown eyes regarded him steadily. And then, finally, she said, "All right. If you really think you need to."

"I do—and I think we should get together right away with my folks, too. I mean, they have a grandbaby they haven't even met." He'd gone to his mom's house the other day to tell her the situation. Since then, he'd kept expecting her or his dad to drop by. But they hadn't.

"They're probably waiting for us to lead the way," Macy said. "Call them. Invite them to our place for dinner tonight. They can meet Camryn."

"And they'll get to meet Tia, too." It came out sounding more than a little bit sarcastic.

Macy sympathized. "I know this is not easy. Would it be better if Tia had her own place?"

"Yeah." They needed to work on that. "I guess we'll be helping her find something."

"How about if I offer her the house in town? Rent-free, for now. I haven't decided yet what I want to do with it, so I'm happy to let her and Camryn move in there for a while."

The problem was he didn't want Camryn living in town. He wanted his newfound daughter at the ranch with him. But it wasn't like he was going to be able to hang around the house taking care of a baby all day.

And come to think of it, what about Tia? The woman needed a job. And once she found one, who would take care of Camryn when her mom was at work? This was all a lot more complicated than it had seemed a few days ago.

"What?" Macy asked. "You look seriously stressed. Take a deep breath."

"Fine." He made a show of breathing deep and then he muttered, "It might have been a lot easier if she'd just kept on going instead of coming back the other night."

"Nobody promised it was going to be easy, Joe."

He knew she was right—as usual. "Look. What I just said? That was wrong. It's just that I want to have Camryn close. If she's living in town, I probably won't see her every day. But then, I don't love the idea of having Tia as a permanent houseguest, either."

"I know what you mean. It *is* complicated." The stern look was gone. She gave him her sweetest smile. "Because you're definitely a hands-on kind of dad. And I really, really like that about you."

"You're hot when you say nice things about me." He was only half joking. And then he grumbled, "I really get why people end up letting judges make their custody arrangements for them."

"Please." She gave him another of those disapproving looks. "It's always better if co-parents can work together and come to an agreement that everyone is happy with."

"Sorry," he said sincerely. "On a more positive note, I talked to Nicole."

She brightened. "About a job for Tia at Bravo Real Estate?"

"Yeah. Nicole already has an office manager, but she knows and likes Tia from Tia's last job up in Sheridan. Nicole said she would be happy to give her a recommendation, at least. And then I remembered that Josh has been looking for an office manager at Bravo Construction. He says he'll talk to her, see if she might be a good fit for that job."

"Okay, then. Tia's got a place to live and a job interview, too. Things could be worse."

Joe still felt on edge. He had to talk to Betty and he wasn't looking forward to it. He needed to do it and get it over with.

Macy had already left Bravo Hardware for the day when he told Myron to close up and went over to Betty's Blooms.

Betty was standing behind the cash register when he entered the store. "Joe! Is everything all right?"

"Everything's fine." He saw that the part-time clerk, Maria, was waiting on a customer. "I was wondering if you have a minute to talk?"

"About...?"

"Could we go somewhere private?"

"Well, of course." She bustled out from behind the counter. "Maria? We'll be in back." The clerk nodded and turned to the customer again. Joe fell in step behind Betty as she ducked through the door to the back room.

She had a single-serve Keurig machine back there. Six minutes later, they each had a cup. She cleared them a space at a large worktable next to a shelving unit full of different-sized vases.

"Now," she said, settling into her chair and then sipping from her cup. "What's going on?"

He launched into his...whatever it was. Apology? Explanation? "So then, you know that it's official. I have a baby girl."

Betty lifted the cup and knocked back another gulp of coffee. "Oh, Joe. It's going to work out. It's all going to be fine, you'll see."

He almost smiled then. "That is exactly what Macy said."

"And she's right."

"Well, thank you for the encouragement. We're, uh, figuring things out. Little by little, I guess you might say."

"Of course you are." She patted his arm.

"Macy said you were shocked, that I would, you know, meet a woman at a bar and—"

"Joe!" She cut him off. "I was surprised, yes. But believe it or not, I do understand that young people have always found ways to, er, get together. I know that you and Macy are doing the right thing, that you are helping the mother of your child. I admire you for that."

He'd expected more pushback—at the very least, a judgmental glance or a disappointed frown. "You do?"

"I do," she replied strongly. "Children are God's greatest gift. And I am one lucky grandma. Thanks to you and my daughter, I not only have Ana to be grateful for, but your baby daughter as well."

"Aw, Betty." She really was the sweetest woman. "I just would hate it if you lost respect for me, that's all."

"Joe! What? Never." She really seemed to mean it. "The more babies, the better as far as I'm concerned."

Five minutes later, she was hugging him goodbye at the door.

"I'll be happy to look after her during the day," Joe's mom said that evening when they sat down to eat. "The more the merrier." Meggie Bravo had Jason's kids over at the main house all the time and she'd offered more than once to take Ana. "Anytime," Meggie said. "Just give me a call."

The meet-the-surprise-baby dinner was going pretty well, Macy thought. Joe's folks had taken the situation in stride.

Tia was quiet, though—quiet and a little bit withdrawn. Macy sympathized. It couldn't be all that easy to stay in the spare room of the virtual stranger who had fathered your child. Tia had to be wondering what life was going to throw at her next.

But she did put on a smile for Meggie. "Thank you," she said. "I will definitely take you up on your offer."

And she did.

The following Monday, Tia dropped off Camryn at Meggie's and went into town to talk to Josh about working for him.

He hired her. She agreed to start the next day.

Tuesday morning, she left Camryn at Meggie's again and headed for her new job. By Friday, Josh was singing her praises.

Over the weekend, Joe, Josh, Riley and Macy helped Tia get settled in at the house in town. Macy had left enough furniture and kitchen stuff behind for Tia to manage pretty well. She already had a collapsible crib. The nursery room would come later. For now, Camryn would be sleeping in Tia's room.

Sunday, Tia cooked spaghetti for all of them—including the kids. Besides Ana and Camryn, Josh brought his three-year-old son, Shane, and Riley came with Dillon. Ana took charge of the two boys. She sat them down and read them stories, acting out the voices of the different characters, putting on a real show. The boys were enthralled.

Before the evening ended, Tia took Macy aside. "Thank you," she said. "For so much, for everything…"

"No problem. I mean that. I'm so glad you came back that first night."

"Me, too. I mean, it's hectic. I can barely keep up. But it's so much better for me here. It really is. I don't feel so completely alone."

"That's good. Because you're not alone. You and Camryn are family to us."

"Well. Camryn is, anyway."

"Stop leaving yourself out. You're Camryn's mom and that means you're family, too."

Tia put up both hands. "Fine. I give up. I'm family."

"Say that with a smile."

Tia actually laughed. "I'm family."

"That's better."

"And Macy, I'm glad. I mean, it's probably too soon to say this, but I'm starting to think that I really might be able to make a life here."

"You *are* making a life here," Macy reassured her. "And you're doing a great job of it, too."

"It means so much, how helpful you've all been. I'm not used to people trying so hard to help me. I've always been kind of a loner and mostly, I'm okay with that. But it's not so great being alone when you have a baby. In fact, it turned out to be pretty much impossible."

"Oh, I do hear you."

"I know you do. And I appreciate that you do. It's good to be included, to feel like you guys have my back."

"We do. We're here anytime you need us."

"Thank you—I know I keep saying that, but I'm so grateful and I want to be sure you know that."

"I know you are."

Tia guided a swatch of blond hair behind her ear. "I've been thinking and I wanted to ask your opinion about something."

"Sure..."

"There's a single mom's group up in Sheridan. They have weekly meetings Tuesday evenings and an active Facebook group where you can get encouragement and support whenever you need it. I kept meaning to look into it when I was living there. But I felt like I never had a spare moment, you know, not while my life was burning down around me."

"A support group sounds really good."

"You think?"

"Yeah. Maybe go to a meeting, see what the group's about?"

"Okay, I think I'll check it out."

"What did Tia say when she got you alone?" Joe asked that night in bed.

"She's grateful. She wanted to thank us for helping her."

He slid an arm around Macy's shoulders and pulled her closer. "She wanted to thank *us*?" he teased in her ear.

Macy elbowed him lightly in the ribs. "Have it your way. She thanked me, especially."

He bit her ear, sending a tiny flare of heat racing over her skin.

"She thanked *you*, period."

"No, she made it clear she's just generally grateful to all of us. And she meant it, too."

He started tickling her. She laughed and batted his hand away, but that didn't stop him. "Admit it, Mace. She's most grateful to you."

With a snort-laugh, she gave in. "Fine. She thanked *me*."

"Good. Because you deserve it..." And then he kissed her.

After that, it was all about his hands on her body and his mouth pressed to hers. As he rose up above her, she stared into those fine blue eyes of his and almost said, *Oh, Joe. I love you, I do.*

But she held those words back. He might think she meant that she was *in* love with him. And saying that out loud would be dangerous.

Even if, lately, she'd started to realize it was true.

Chapter Eight

At four thirty in the afternoon the next day, while Meggie looked after Camryn and Ana, Joe and Macy met Tia at Stahl and Bravo, Attorneys at Law. They were there to construct a workable parenting plan.

Joe thought it went pretty well. He and Tia agreed on joint legal and physical custody of Camryn. They also put together a flexible custody schedule, one they could all live with. No, the schedule wasn't ideal. He wanted his baby to live with him all the time. But he wasn't going to get that and he'd reconciled himself to it. Because Macy was right. Camryn needed her mom, too.

As they hashed out the details, he reminded himself often that his little girl deserved to grow up with both her birth parents actively involved in her life. He was kind of getting into the idea that his baby would have a mom and a dad, and Macy and Ana—and a whole town full of Bravos to help her get her start in life. Camryn was a gift—and he intended to treasure her and make sure she had everything any little girl could ever need.

After the meeting, Joe and Macy returned to the ranch. They stopped at the main house to pick up both Ana and Camryn.

When they went inside, Meggie had the kids in the living room. She sat in a rocker with Camryn. Both Ana and Jason's four-year-old, Emmy, were lying on the floor drawing pictures on typing paper. Emmy's one-year-old brother, Miles, sat nearby alternately drooling on a blue teething ring and stacking colored blocks in the bed of a toy dump truck.

Ana glanced up. "Hi, Mom. Hi, Joe." And then she went right back to her art project.

Emmy lifted a hand and waved at them, but she never looked up from her work.

"How'd the meeting go?" Meggie asked as she smoothed a cloth diaper on her shoulder, gently lifted Camryn up onto it and rose from the rocker.

"Really well," Joe said. "Camryn will be here with us Monday through Thursday most weeks. Tia gets her on weekends. We agreed that makes the most sense given that she works all week for Josh and it isn't practical for her to take the baby to work with her."

"Sounds fair—here you go." Meggie offered him the sleeping baby.

He took her and cradled her close. "Thanks, Mom. For everything."

"Anytime. You know that."

Ana looked up from her coloring again. "Mom, come see my dragon."

Macy crouched to admire the scaly green monster who appeared to be smiling. "Excellent. But shouldn't he be breathing fire?"

Ana wrinkled her nose. "He's a pet dragon, Mom. He only breathes fire to *protect* people from the evil wizards."

"Ah. Clearly a pet dragon is the best kind to have—you ready to go?"

"Hmm. Yeah…" Ana was focused on her dragon again. Her tongue stuck out of the side of her mouth as she gave the friendly monster oversized green scales.

"Well, come on, then," Macy coaxed. "Put away your crayons, get your coat. And bring your dragon. He deserves a spot on the fridge."

Joe came down the stairs at a little after nine o'clock to find Macy stretched out on the sofa fiddling with her phone.

"Ana is out for the night," he announced. His favorite six-year-old was asleep upstairs, her cat beside her and Rosie taking up most of the space at the foot of the bed. "What about Camryn?"

"She's asleep." Camryn had a soft-sided crib in Joe and Macy's room.

Joe wasn't exactly thrilled about bringing the baby into the bedroom he and Macy shared. He preferred having his wife to himself at night. But both Macy and Tia had informed him that this was the doctor-recommended way of things. Babies slept in their parents' room until six months of age. Supposedly sleeping in the same room with the adults reduced the risk of Sudden Infant Death Syndrome by 50 percent.

No way Joe could argue with that.

And he would get Macy to himself on Tia's nights with Camryn. Surprisingly, it was all working out. He had never been happier. And he kind of wanted to celebrate.

"How about we break out the Jim Beam?" he suggested.

Macy sat up and set the phone on the coffee table. She looked so good, he thought, in a big green sweater that drooped off one silky shoulder, a pair of faded skinny jeans and thick red socks. He couldn't wait to undress her…

But Camryn was sound asleep in the bedroom. They would need to get creative.

A quickie in the guest room, maybe? Or somehow managing to be very, very quiet in their own bed…

Macy was watching him. He couldn't read the look on her face. She folded her arms across her chest and said, "Uh-uh. No drinks."

Was there something wrong? Was she sick? If so, he damn well should have noticed. "Are you feeling okay?"

She rested her elbow on the sofa arm and braced her chin on her fist. "I'm fine, just…late."

"Late for…?"

She gave him a look that was both patient and possibly a little bit smug. Apparently, she thought he ought to be able to figure it out.

He had no idea what was up with her—or did he? His heart slammed against his rib cage as the light finally dawned. "Macy…?" Words deserted him.

"Joe…?" She laughed. "You should see your face. Your mouth is hanging open."

He shut it. She grasped his fingers and he pulled her up into his arms. "Damn," he whispered as he gathered her close.

For a moment, she clung to him. He took pleasure in the feel of her slim body pressed to his. Then she pulled back enough to look up at him. "Eight days late," she said. "And I'm never late."

He touched the side of her beautiful face. "It must have been on our wedding night."

"Looks that way, yeah."

"Is this really happening?"

Her dark eyes were misty. "What's that they say? Be careful what you wish for…"

He did not agree. "Oh, hell no. This—you, Ana, Camryn. And now another baby... I've got no regrets. None. We're a family. What we have together is all I ever wanted, you know that it is."

"I do. But it's a lot, Joe."

"It's everything. It honestly is."

She reached up and pressed her hand to the side of his face. "It's just... I keep thinking we should have stuck with the original plan, should have waited for a year or so to start trying. It's not going to be easy. I mean, as it turns out, we've already got a baby."

"We'll manage. I'll be there for whatever you need." He meant that from the bottom of his heart. "You know you can count on me, I swear it."

Her smile was tender now. "I don't doubt you, Joe. Honestly, I trust you and I know I can always depend on you."

"Always," he vowed. "No matter what." Then he caught her face between his hands and claimed a long sweet kiss. When he finally lifted his head, his excitement took over. "Damn. I have to tell you. This might be the happiest day of my life—so far." She glanced away. "Hey," he said. "Look at me." Reluctantly, she met his eyes. "What's the matter? Talk to me. Please."

"Well, this is all happening really fast, don't you think?"

He wanted to understand her concerns. But all he felt was happiness. "Sorry, but no. This is great news. The best."

"I'm glad you feel that way. I am. For me, though, it does feel a bit overwhelming. And we might be getting ahead of ourselves here. I'm a week late, but I haven't even taken a home test yet."

"Shh." He pressed a finger to her lips. "This is real. We're having a baby. I just know it."

"Oh, Joe." She laughed. "Of course, you do. But I think I'll stop at State Street Drugs tomorrow and pick up a test, just to be sure."

"Go for it."

"I'll do that." She rested her hand against his heart. It felt good there. It felt right.

Marrying his best friend? Smartest move he'd ever made.

That night, Camryn fussed a lot, probably missing her mom, not used to this house or the crib she was sleeping in. Joe and Macy took turns getting up to soothe her.

"I'll get her," he whispered in Macy's ear when it was her turn to check Camryn's diaper and walk her or rock her or feed her until she dropped off to sleep again. Macy said no, she would do it.

The second time he volunteered to take her turn for her, she kissed his scruffy chin and said, "Joe. In case you haven't noticed, she wakes me up every time, too. Since I'm already up, I might as well do my part."

"If you're sure," he said groggily.

She kissed him again. "Sleep."

And he did. Twenty minutes later, when she silently crawled back in beside him, he was already off in dreamland, completely oblivious. Lucky man. He didn't stir as she settled the covers over herself and closed her eyes.

The next time Camryn cried, Joe slept on. Macy considered just taking his turn for him. But then again, no way. She'd done the night shift alone when Ana was a baby. Caleb had never once dragged himself out of bed to change Ana's diaper or walk the floor with her.

Macy and Joe, though, they were a real team. They were in this together.

And dear Lord in Heaven, with Ana and Camryn and possibly a new baby come summer, Macy was going to need her teammate on the job, night after night.

Camryn let out a shriek.

Joe shot bolt upright in bed. "Okay, okay. I'm coming, okay…"

Macy sat up beside him. He leaned his head on her shoulder and sighed. Her heart just melted.

"Go back to sleep," he instructed, and slid out of the bed. She snuggled down under the covers and closed her eyes.

Sometime later, she woke to Camryn fussing and Joe wrapped around her spoon-style snoring softly in her ear. Reluctantly, she eased herself free of his warm embrace and slid from the bed…

Before dawn, when Joe's phone alarm started playing an upbeat country tune, Macy groaned and wished she could sleep the whole day away. Miraculously, the alarm didn't seem to bother Camryn.

Joe rolled away from her and turned it off. The silence was beautiful. She almost went to sleep again.

"Tired?" he asked quietly. He was watching her from his pillow, his hair sleep-mussed, dark smudges beneath those sky-blue eyes.

"Kids," she whispered. "What were we thinking?"

He reached out, eased his warm fingers under her hair and curled them around the back of her neck. Pulling her closer, he pressed his forehead to hers. "We got through it," he said.

"Barely," she replied. "And that was just our first night."

But then he smiled and she smiled and pretty soon they were both laughing while trying hard not to make a sound. Every moment Camryn slept was a blessing meant to be cherished and enjoyed.

Her heart felt so full. It had been a rough night. But still, she'd kind of loved every minute of it. "Oh, Joe, I..." She stopped herself just in time.

"What?" he asked, super-quietly.

I love you, she thought. "What a night," she said, because *I love you* was too dangerous. They were friends. They were lovers. They were husband and wife.

But if she said she loved him now, he would know the kind of love she meant. It was the kind of love he'd sworn he didn't want. Not ever again.

Lately, as she'd begun to understand the true depth of her devotion to him, she'd found herself hoping his opinion on love would change as time went by. After all, he already trusted her—to back him up no matter what, to be there to help whenever he needed a hand. She kept telling herself he would learn to trust her love. She wouldn't cheat on him and then dump him like Lindsay. Or make him a promise she couldn't keep the way Becca had.

It all seemed so blatantly obvious to her now. It had always been Joe for her. She just hadn't put it together—not for years and years of being his best friend. Eventually Joe would see the truth, too. He would realize he was in love with her and he would know that he could trust her to treat him right.

And when he finally did see the light, she would be right there for him. She would be ready, willing and able to give him all her love every day for the rest of their lives.

It would all work out. There was no reason to get all twisted up about it. She was in love with her husband. What could be more natural than that?

From her crib, Camryn let out a single soft cry.

Macy sighed. "Go on," she said to Joe. "Morning chores won't do themselves."

"You sure?"

"You've got eggs to gather and horses to tend to. I'll take care of the baby."

He pulled her close for a quick kiss before rolling out of bed. Two minutes later, he was gone. By then, Camryn was working up a real head of steam.

Macy rolled out of bed, yanked on her clothes and went to the crib where Camryn was kicking at her blankets and waving her tiny fists in a full-on fury.

"Hey, now. Come on, now…." Macy gathered her up. Camryn wriggled and cried all the harder. She smelled like a full diaper.

Cradling her close, gently rubbing her back, Macy carried her to the portable changing table Joe had set up in the bedroom the night before.

By afternoon, Macy was running on fumes. After she picked up Ana at school, she dropped her off for an hour at a friend's house, made a quick trip to the grocery store and then stopped at State Street Drugs for that test she would take tomorrow morning. She bought a few of them, just in case the result was inconclusive and she needed to test again.

She kept thinking of Tia. Tomorrow was Thanksgiving. It just seemed wrong for Tia to be alone for the holiday. She should have talked to Joe about that before she left the hardware store.

Back in her Subaru, she texted him.

Can you talk?

The phone rang in her hand.

"What's up?" Joe asked.

"I've been thinking about Tia, that she's on her own and we've got Camryn. What would you say to inviting her for Thanksgiving?" Most years, every Bravo for miles around assembled at The Rising Sun Ranch, which was owned jointly by Joe's dad, Nate, and Nate's cousins, Zach and Cash.

But the families kept growing and Thanksgiving had become a giant undertaking. This year, the Bravos had decided to gather in smaller groups. Tomorrow, Nate and Meggie were hosting Thanksgiving for the immediate family right there on the Double-K. Macy's parents were coming, too, as was Piper Bravo's flamboyant mom, Emmaline Stokely.

He was too quiet. "Joe?" she prompted. "You still there?"

"Yeah."

"So...that's a no?"

"No. That's not a no. It's me being stubborn and a little resentful."

She couldn't help smiling. "Resentful of Tia?"

"That's right."

She knew him so well. In the end, he would say yes. "So, then, want to vent?"

He scoffed. "It's nothing you haven't heard before—and yeah. I get it. Tia shouldn't be alone on Thanksgiving. Go ahead and invite her."

Macy said nothing. She waited for him to figure it out.

And he did. "You think *I* should do it?"

"Yes, I do. She's very well aware that you're, uh, not her biggest fan. If I invite her, she's probably going to assume that you don't really want her there."

"Well, I—"

"Don't say it. Please. That woman is doing her best and

you need to step up, to show her that you're putting any bad feelings aside because that's the best thing for Camryn."

He muttered a bad word, but then he said, "You're right."

She wanted to reach through the phone and hug him. "Okay, then. Call her and invite her right away. If she says no, I'll call her next."

"So we're tag-teaming her?"

"Of course. I mean, we want her to come."

"Right…"

"Joe," she said sternly, and realized she sounded like just about every nagging wife in the history of wifedom. "Be nice. Convince her to come."

He was silent, no doubt running through all the objections he wanted to offer even though he knew he shouldn't. Finally, he said gently, "I will be nice. I promise."

She almost declared her love for him right then and there. Somehow, she managed to control herself. "Terrific. Call me back after you talk to her?"

"Will do." And then he was gone.

Five minutes later, just as she pulled up in front of the house where Ana was hanging out with her friends, he called.

She hit the phone icon. "How'd it go?"

"It went fine. She'll be there tomorrow."

"Excellent."

"Yeah. She started in with how she was good on her own, that she has some new support group up in Sheridan and she'd been invited to a Thanksgiving dinner with a few women she'd met there."

"She mentioned to me that she might join a single mom's group. I'm glad to hear she did. But anyway, you kept after her?"

"Yeah, I kept trying. I said, 'Come on. Join us. Say yes. Be at my folks' house at two.'"

"That's perfect. And she said...?"

"She got all concerned about what to bring and I told her she didn't need to bring anything."

"Let me guess. She insisted she *had* to bring something."

"That's right. So I told her to call my mom about that. And then she said, 'Thanks, Joe. I'll be there.'"

"I'm so glad." Macy was tearing up. Just a little.

Joe said, "Yeah, well. You're the one who said that we want her close, that we need to make it work with her. And I'm realizing you're right about that. We need to include her—at least until she's got a solid support system of her own nearby."

"Good job," she said. She was thinking, *I love you, Joe.* The unsaid words echoed inside her head.

"I'll be home in an hour."

"See you then." She dropped the phone on the empty seat beside her and swiped at the tears trailing down her face.

For a few minutes more, she just sat there in front of Ana's friend's house dabbing at her eyes with a tissue, waiting for her tears to dry and reminding herself that there was nothing to cry about.

That night was a definite improvement over the night before. Camryn only woke them up three times and Joe was grateful.

When his alarm went off at four, he grabbed his phone and silenced it immediately. He and Macy stared at each other, waiting. He could see in her soft brown eyes that she was doing the same thing he was—willing the baby in the nearby crib to sleep on.

And she did.

Macy whispered, "I need to take the test first thing."

And he very much wanted to be there for that. "So then you'll do it now, before I head out?"

"Yeah." She pushed back the covers and rose from the bed.

He got out on his side. As he pulled on faded jeans, she grabbed her robe off the chair beneath the window. Belting it, she circled the end of the bed and tiptoed around the silent crib. He zipped up his jeans and followed her through the open door to the bathroom, closing it behind him.

She turned. "Joe. Come on. I'm not peeing on a stick with you standing there watching."

He wanted to ask why not. After all, he'd seen every inch of her fine body already, hadn't he?

But he'd lived long enough to know that when a woman wanted her privacy, a man had damn well better make sure she got it. "Okay." He put up both hands in surrender—but then just had to ask, "Can I come back in as soon as you finish, er, collecting the sample?"

She was chuckling as she rolled her eyes. "Sure. Now go."

He went, silently closing the door behind him and then waiting right there with his heart pounding in his ears for her to let him back in.

It seemed to take forever. But in reality it had only been a couple of minutes at most when she opened the bathroom door, pulled him inside and shut the door again.

"You can come in now." Her face was flushed the sweetest shade of pink as she led him to the counter by the sink where the test stick waited.

A lifetime passed as they stared at it together—well, okay, maybe more like sixty seconds. But it sure as hell felt like a lifetime.

Two hot-pink lines materialized in the result window.

His heart slammed against his rib cage. "Doesn't that mean yes, we're having a baby?"

Laughing, she let go of his hand and threw both arms around his neck. "Yes, Joe. That means yes, we are having a baby!"

Chapter Nine

Joe picked her up and spun her around right there by the bathroom sink. "We can share the news today!" he whisper-shouted. He could not wait to tell the family—and everyone else he knew, for that matter.

She pushed gently at his shoulders. "Joe..."

Carefully, he set her down. "What'd I do? What's the matter?"

"It's a little early to tell people, that's all."

"What? Why?"

"Well, most people wait for three months, because most miscarriages happened in the first trimester."

"Oh, come on. Nothing's going to go wrong. But if it did, the people who love us would want to be there for us—for you. And you wouldn't have to explain how you lost a baby when you hadn't even told them yet that you were pregnant."

"Hmm." Macy frowned as she thought it over. "You know. When you put it that way, I kind of think you're right."

He let out a sigh of relief. "Great. We'll tell everyone today."

But her face had *I'm not going for that* written all over it. "What?"

"Can we please just wait till after I get a confirmation from my doctor?"

"How long will that take?"

"It depends on how soon I can get in to see him. He'll take a blood sample and send it to a lab and we should get the results within a couple of days of the appointment—and then we can tell everyone. How about that?"

"Damn." He'd been fantasizing about telling everyone today. But apparently, that wasn't going to happen. "When will the appointment be?"

"I'll call Dr. Hayes's office when it opens Monday morning and I'll take the first available appointment."

What could he say but, "Okay. I'll wait."

Joe still wanted to blurt out the news to everyone at Thanksgiving dinner. But somehow he managed to keep his mouth shut. And even though he had to corral his own excitement, it was still the best Thanksgiving ever as far as Joe was concerned.

He went through the day in a golden haze of sheer happiness, hugging anyone who got near him, pounding his brother, his dad and Macy's dad on the back, laughing too loud, announcing that his mom's turkey dinner was the best he'd ever had.

Because it was. Today, everything was the best he'd ever had. He had Macy and Ana and a beautiful baby daughter and another baby on the way. Life just didn't get any better than this.

He even approached Tia, who had Camryn in her arms. She cradled the baby close as Joe babbled on about how much he appreciated that she'd finally showed up at the Double-K with their daughter. He told her he was so glad to have Camryn in his life, that it meant everything that he could be there to help his daughter grow up.

Tia looked up at him and gulped. "Thank you for saying that, Joe. I'm grateful, too, I really am. You've been so... good and helpful, you and Macy."

"Mostly Macy," he corrected with a smile. "You can say it. I can take it."

"Well, yeah. She is a lifesaver. But you've helped, too. I can't tell you how much I appreciate all you've done to help me get a fresh start here in Medicine Creek."

He almost argued some more on Macy's behalf—because Tia really was giving him way too much credit. However, the poor woman looked so uncomfortable. She probably thought he'd had one too many hot ciders.

But he hadn't. He was drunk on happiness, high on life. He wanted everyone to know about the two pink lines on the pregnancy test stick. He couldn't wait to shout the news from the rooftops.

"Glad to help, really," he said lamely. She nodded and blinked up at him, at a loss as to what to say next.

Macy's mom rescued the two of them from the strained conversation by moving close to admire the baby. Tia turned to her. Joe left the two of them to coo over the adorableness of Camryn.

For the rest of the afternoon, he tried to keep his excitement under control. It wasn't easy. But he did his best.

First thing on Monday, Macy called Dr. Hayes, who fit her in that morning. She went right over there.

That day and the next dragged by at the speed of a dying snail. But finally, on Wednesday afternoon, Macy got the call confirming what they already knew. She was pregnant and in good health. The baby was due August 3.

They told Ana first. Ana said she couldn't wait for a new

baby sister. "Or a brother," she added. "A brother would be okay, too."

"You sure now?" Joe teased her.

"Yeah," she replied. "A baby brother would be just fine."

By Friday, Joe had spread the big news far and wide. Everyone was happy for them.

But no one could possibly be happier than Joe himself. He had it all, really.

As she had the day after Thanksgiving, Tia picked up Camryn that afternoon to take her to the town house for the weekend. When Joe got home from work, the baby was already gone. He missed her, but he had big plans for Saturday.

The next morning, once he'd done his chores, he cooked breakfast for Macy and Ana. Then the three of them piled into his crew cab and headed for BLM land. He'd gotten a permit for a tree online.

They cut down a nice Douglas fir, strapped it into the pickup bed and headed back home, where all three of them made more than one trip to the attic area above the garage to bring down the boxes of Christmas decorations collected by both Joe and Macy over the years.

As Voodoo darted around chasing shadows and Rosie snoozed by the fireplace, Ana, Macy and Joe decorated their first tree as a family. It was a great day. The best. The house smelled of evergreen and the tree looked so beautiful all lit up, standing tall by the big window that faced the front porch.

The cat, surprisingly to Joe, left the tree alone. When he mentioned that, Ana said, "The tree makes him sneeze."

"He was a kitten when he saw his first Christmas tree," Macy explained. "He sniffed it, shook his head and sneezed. And he never went near a Christmas tree again."

After dinner, they played Beetlejuice Uno and then Ana read them two chapters of *How to Twist a Dragon's Tale*. She begged to read more, but she couldn't stop yawning and her eyes kept drooping shut.

Macy herded her upstairs. Joe went up a little later to kiss her good-night. She was already in bed with Voodoo beside her and Rosie at her feet.

"Joe," she said groggily. "There you are."

He sat on the edge of the bed and smoothed the covers up nice and snug around her, disturbing the cat. Voodoo batted at his hand, got up, stretched and stalked down the bed to join Rosie.

Joe said, "'Night, Anabanana."

"Ew. I'm not a banana."

"Anafofana?"

"Joe…"

"Anazarcana?"

"Stop it."

He put on a sad face. "So then… Just Ana?"

"Yes!" She gave him a smile then—a slightly shy one, it seemed to him. "Can I ask you a question?"

"Anything."

"Well, Joe. Are you my dad now?"

Terror grabbed him by the throat and tried to strangle him. It was a big question. Huge. And if he didn't watch out, he was pretty much guaranteed to screw it up.

"Well." He turned his head to the side and gave a quick cough to clear his locked-up throat. "Ahem. I love you like a dad would. I will always take care of you like a dad should. I will be there whenever you need me, the way a dad is meant to do. But what I'm called is your stepdad. That means I'm the one who gets to help take care of you because I married your mom."

Her eyes did not leave his face. "But you always took care of me, Joe."

"Yeah." Should he elaborate? Maybe not. But then he did it anyway. "I always took care of you. And I always will."

"So then, why can't I just call you Dad?"

His heart seized up—and then went racing. Why not, indeed? How could Ana calling him dad be a bad thing? He didn't think it could. Those big eyes looked up at him, all trusting and serious. She wanted what he wanted. For him to be her dad.

She asked again, "Can I, Joe?"

Why should he hesitate? There was only one answer to that question. He gave it gladly. "You bet you can. I would love it if you did. Please, Ana. Call me Dad."

She reached up her little arms. He bent close and she wrapped those arms around his neck. She smelled like toothpaste and watermelon shampoo and he loved her every bit as much as any biological dad ever could.

Her soft lips touched his cheek. "Good night, Dad."

Downstairs, he found Macy in the kitchen putting dishes away. He came up behind her and wrapped his arms around her.

She let herself lean back against him. "Hey."

He pressed his mouth to the side of her throat and whispered, "Come to bed." She turned her head and he kissed her, a slow one, endlessly sweet. "Bed," he said again.

She didn't argue, so he scooped her up in his arms, carried her through the living room and into the short hall to their bedroom, where he let her feet slide to the floor. He shut the door and turned the privacy lock. And then he walked her backward to the bed.

Clothes flew every which way. In two minutes flat, he

had everything off her. She did her part, too, undressing him as he stripped her bare.

They fell to the bed in a tangle of arms and legs and eager kisses. It was sloppy and fast and so very good. He rolled her beneath him and she laughed, a low husky, sexy sound as she braced a bare foot on the comforter and gave a little push. He got the message and let her guide him over onto his back.

She rose up above him, folding those slim legs to either side of him, pressing in close. "Joe..."

He captured her face between his hands and pulled her down until their lips met and she opened to him. He breathed her in as she eased a hand down between them.

When she took him inside, he almost lost it right there. But somehow, he maintained just enough control to move with her, slow, easy. Agonizingly sweet. She was a wave on top of him, her body holding him, claiming him. He was drowning in her and he could not think of a better way to go.

When she came, she threw her head back and cried out his name. Then she collapsed on top of him, her breath coming fast. He pulled her closer.

She started to move again, guiding him, urging him over and on top of her. After that, he took control—or she gave it to him.

However it happened, he rocked into her and everything went white as his climax barreled through him.

Joe waited to go into what had happened with Ana.

He waited until he and Macy were under the covers, holding each other, talking about the day just past, agreeing that it had been pretty much perfect, a great beginning to their first Christmas as a family. That seemed like the ideal opening to him, so he shared what he and Ana had talked about when he tucked her into bed.

Macy rested her head on his shoulder and ran her soft hand over his chest. "You handled that moment beautifully, Joe."

He caught her hand. "I was afraid I might blow it."

"No way," Macy said. "You did good, really good."

He brought her fingers to his lips and kissed them. "Have you heard from Caleb lately?"

A low sound of frustration escaped her. "No. He still pays child support like clockwork. But outside of that, crickets. Ana hasn't seen or spoken to him since... I don't even know. Never, not since the divorce."

He stroked a hand down her silky hair, brushed a slow caress along her arm. "Macy, I've been thinking..."

Something in his voice must have alerted her, because she raised her head from his shoulder and looked in his eyes. "About...?"

"Look, I know he provides for her financially and at least he does that well. But you just said he hasn't spoken with her in at least three years. He doesn't even reach out to you to see how she's doing, does he?"

"No, he doesn't. And it's a problem—one I have no idea how to solve. He won't pick up when I call. Once in a blue moon, I get a text from him. A short text. The last one was on the day you and I got married. Two sentences. 'Congratulations, Macy. Will call when I have the time.' He must not have had time yet, because it's been radio silence ever since."

He tipped up her chin so that he could see those big brown eyes. "He didn't deserve you."

"I completely agree. That's why he and I are divorced."

"He doesn't deserve Ana, either."

"Please never tell her that."

"Never. I swear it."

"Look." Joe chose his words carefully. "What does he offer her but money?"

"Nothing."

"Does she really need his money?"

Macy shrugged. "Not now, but maybe she will someday. And she's entitled to the money he sends."

Money did matter. Joe knew that. But there were things that mattered even more. "Just answer the question."

"Fine. She is happy and well provided for. And I've saved every penny he's paid so far. It's a lot and it's gathering interest until she's old enough to take control of it. So, no. As of right now, anyway, she doesn't *need* any more of his money. But hey, he agreed to pay it and he owes it to her."

"Because he's her father."

"Exactly."

"What if he wasn't? What if I adopted her?"

"Oh, Joe…" Her eyes told him everything. She loved that he wanted to claim Ana as his own—at the same time as she hesitated to think of cutting the only real remaining tie between Ana and her birth father.

"I know," he said. "Money matters, and Ana's entitled to payments until she's eighteen. But I don't trust that guy. I don't want him hurting her any more than he already has through sheer neglect. I don't want him to have any claim on her. The way it is now, he could lurch to life and decide he wants her with him—and then take us to court and fight us to get his way. The courts are big on the rights of biological parents, so yeah. He would probably get shared custody. If that happened, how would it be for her? Would he even be there for her when she's living with him?"

"I've worried about the same things. But he is her father. It feels wrong to try to cut him out completely."

"If he agrees to let her go, that's his choice."

"I don't think he will agree."

"You said yourself he never calls, never asks about her, hasn't seen her or spoken to her in three years."

"Caleb has a lot of pride. I think he'd be worried about how it would look if he gave up his rights as a father."

"He's a dick, plain and simple."

"I'm not arguing that point."

"Because you know you'll lose." He softened that with a shrug and a grin.

"Joe." She said his name so patiently. "From Caleb's point of view, he's leaving Ana in my care and he doesn't see anything wrong with that. To him, she's still his daughter and that's not going to change."

Joe was losing this battle and he knew it. Caleb Storm *was* Ana's father and that counted for a lot. More carefully, he suggested, "Could we just go talk to Ethan about it, see what he says?"

She gave him a sad smile. "Off to the family lawyer to deal with yet another custody dispute?"

"Aw, come on. That's not fair. It was a parenting plan with Tia. That's a completely different thing."

"I know. It's just... I do feel bad about Caleb. I don't know how to reach him. Truth is, I've pretty much given up on him."

"So then let's just talk with Ethan, tell him the situation and see what he says—because he's a lawyer and also because he understands our situation firsthand. Remember I told you that—"

"I remember, Joe. Ethan's in the process of adopting his wife's new baby, Gabrielle."

"You got it. Gabby's birth father voluntarily gave up his rights. It can happen, Mace. It really can."

"I'm not doubting that. I'm reminding you that I was married to Caleb for three years, that I do have some idea of how the man's mind works. Despite his continued resistance to spending time with his daughter, I don't think he'll give her up without a fight—a fight that we're far too likely to lose."

"We won't know if we don't try."

She lifted up enough to drop a sweet soft kiss on his lips. He wanted to grab hold of her, pull her down on top of him, kiss her until she melted against him and they made love for hours—till morning came, at least. Sometimes it stunned him how much he wanted her now. Even at times like this, when they were dealing with a difficult situation and had conflicting ideas about how to proceed...

He still wanted her.

And that was fine. She was his and he was hers. They trusted each other unconditionally, a trust built on the friendship they shared.

But it's different between us now that we're married...

The thought was a whisper inside his head. Because his feelings for her ran deeper than ever. Too deep, maybe. Too complex. He felt...

Oh, what did it matter? They were friends. They were married. They were solid, as a team. And he liked getting her naked whenever possible. What they had was good. No need to analyze the situation to death.

She gave him that glowing smile of hers. "I do love that you want to adopt her. You are and always will be the father Ana counts on, the one she can turn to. The one who loves her unconditionally and would do anything for her."

Her words meant the world to him. He held her gaze. "I want to be all those things."

"And you are, Joe. You truly are. Some legal document is never going to change that."

"Just say we can go talk to Ethan, get his take on what's possible."

She sighed. But then she gave in. "All right. Let's talk to Ethan."

Macy kind of hoped Joe would take his time getting them that appointment with Ethan Bravo.

But no. He didn't fool around. Early Tuesday afternoon, Ethan ushered them into his office at Stahl and Bravo, Attorneys at Law.

"Have a seat, you two." Ethan gestured at the sofa and chairs arranged across the room from his wide desk.

Macy and Joe sat together on the sofa. Ethan took a club chair. He offered coffee. They declined. There was chitchat. Ethan congratulated them on their marriage. They talked about Ethan's daughter and his wife, Matty.

Eventually, Ethan got down to business. "So then, how can I help?"

Joe explained that he wanted to adopt Ana.

"I see…" Ethan leaned toward them as he explained the ins and outs of stepparent adoption. Then he asked about Ana's birth father.

When Macy said that Caleb showed little interest in his daughter, but always sent the support money right on time, Ethan sat back in his chair again.

He said what Macy already knew. "Given that the birth father has been paying and continues to pay support, you're unlikely to have his parental rights terminated by the court. He would need to give them up voluntarily."

It was exactly what Macy had known the lawyer would say. She said carefully, "I've told Joe that I just don't think my ex-husband will agree to give up his rights as Ana's dad."

"Why is that?" Ethan asked.

"Well, pride is a big thing with Caleb. The way he sees it, that he provides for Ana is what matters. He thinks he's doing his job as a father. He doesn't listen or even seem to care when I point out that he's never there for her. He blows me off when I try to convince him that she needs to know him. The way he sees it, he's sending the support payments in full and on time—and that's enough."

Joe took her hand. When she met his eyes, he said, "Can we just try, serve him papers and see if he signs them? That's all I'm asking."

She understood his insistence. He wanted to do right by Ana. And she loved him for it, she did. So much. She turned to Ethan again. "I was thinking that I could call Caleb and feel him out about the idea of giving up his paternal rights, see if maybe I can convince him to step back."

"From what you've told me so far," Ethan said, "that's probably your best course of action. Child abandonment laws are different in every state. Here in Wyoming, as long as the child is safe and well cared for and the father is financially responsible, you don't have much of a case for abandonment—unless the birth father has ever abused Ana in any way?"

"Not unless you count lack of contact for three years. The real problem is he's just...not there for her."

Ethan said, "But *you're* there."

"Yes. And so is Joe."

"That's good—and ironically, it's also your problem in terms of forcing the issue. Ana is loved and cared for and lacks for nothing. She has not been abandoned, neglected or abused." Ethan turned to Joe. "I know it's not what you want to hear, Joe, but your best approach in this situation is probably Macy's suggestion. Let her try talking to her ex-husband. She can lay out all the positive reasons for him to relinquish his parental rights and let you adopt Ana."

Joe sat back with a hard sigh. "Why can't we just serve him?"

"You can," said Ethan. "But that's a move that's more likely to work on a man who doesn't want the financial responsibility of supporting his child. From everything you've told me so far, Caleb Storm is not that guy."

"He's not," Macy said. "He's fine sending money. It's what he does."

"I just want to try," said Joe, his voice rough with emotion.

Macy leaned closer to him. She wrapped her free hand around their joined ones. "I know. I get it. I just don't want to end up making things worse than they already are."

All Joe could think about the rest of that afternoon was the discouraging meeting with Ethan.

When he and Macy left Stahl and Bravo, she went to pick up Ana from school. He returned to Bravo Hardware, where he tried to keep a smile on his face and be helpful to his employees and customers. It wasn't easy, not when his chances of becoming more than Ana's stepdad now seemed minimal at best.

He felt instantly better when he walked in the door at home. The house smelled like dinner. The Christmas tree was all lit up in the front window, a bunch of brightly wrapped packages already piled beneath it.

In the kitchen, the dog and cat snoozed in the corner,

Rosie on her side with her tongue hanging out and Voodoo curled up against Rosie's back. Ana sat at the table cutting brightly colored construction paper into strips. As for Camryn, she cooed in her bouncy seat on the floor near the kitchen counter where Macy was busy putting the evening meal together.

Macy sent him a smile over her shoulder as Ana called, "Dad! Come look."

Dad. He loved the sound of that. "What's up?" He went to her and bent close.

Ana beamed up at him. "I'm making more Christmas garland to hang on the tree." She held up a chain of red and green construction paper.

"Looks good," he said.

"I know. Here." She offered him the scissors. "You cut the paper, I'll glue the chain."

Macy said, "Dinner in ten minutes..."

He looked around at his family, breathed in the homey smells of cooking and Christmas and realized he felt pretty good, after all.

Joe's upbeat attitude lasted until he came back downstairs after tucking Ana in bed. He found Macy sitting on the sofa with the baby monitor in her hand.

"I fed Camryn and she's snoozing in her crib." Macy set the monitor on the coffee table. "We should probably talk," she added. Now her voice sounded cautious.

He was instantly wary. And that happy family feeling? Not so happy anymore. "I'm just going to get a drink," he said.

"Go for it."

He almost offered her one—and then he remembered. No drinks for Macy. They were having a baby.

Gratitude swept through him, humbling him. He reminded himself to keep a check on his attitude. Really, he had so much now. And that was mostly thanks to the woman on the sofa looking up at him with a forced smile on her lips and worry in her eyes.

The thing was...he wanted to fix the situation with Caleb Storm. But both his wife and his cousin Ethan were telling him that he most likely couldn't. He hated that. He truly did.

He'd hated the situation with Caleb for a long time now. Caleb had hurt Macy. And he was far from a father to the little girl sleeping upstairs with her pets cuddled close.

Yeah, Macy seemed to be over Caleb now. And she was willing to tolerate the man's refusal to be anything resembling a dad. Joe knew he should respect her assessment of the situation with her ex and follow her lead.

But damn it, he still thought they should at least try. She'd said more than once that she would call the guy and talk to him about giving up his rights. If that was the only approach that might have a chance of working, Joe wanted her to go through with it, and the sooner the better.

"Joe?"

He realized he'd been standing there, staring at nothing. "Uh, sorry—be right back." He turned for the kitchen.

A few minutes later, he was setting his drink near the baby monitor and dropping down next to Macy on the sofa.

She drew her feet up to the side and leaned into him. Her shoulder brushed his arm. He felt that now-familiar surge of desire for her. She was hot, beautiful, funny and so damn smart—the whole package. She also happened to be the best human being he knew.

He didn't want to hurt her, didn't want to give her grief...

"So," she said. "I've been thinking about Caleb—about how to handle this thing with him..."

He should let her talk, say all she had to say. But he burst right in with, "Will you call him, then?"

She inched away from him and folded her arms across her middle. "I will, yeah." Her reluctance to do that was written all over her face.

"But...?"

"Joe, you know how I feel. I don't really think Caleb will give up his rights, but I'll call him and talk to him about it because I know how much it means to you—how much Ana means to you. I'll give it a try. I'll be calm and reasonable. I'll say that you would like to adopt Ana and that I would like that, too. I'll say..." Her voice trailed off.

"What?" he prompted, after several seconds of silence.

She blinked and drew a deep breath. "Joe, I'm just trying to get you to understand that he's not going to like it. That if I do it, things might get worse."

"Worse, how?"

"He could sue *us* for custody."

"You really think he would do that?"

She thought the question over for a moment. And then she sighed. "You're right. It's doubtful that he would sue. Once I finally get to talk to him, he'll just be a jerk on the phone and then be impossible to get a hold of."

"So then, nothing changes."

"That's right. It will all stay the same. He's not going to say yes and I already know that. But I said I would call him and try to get through to him. And I will."

"Can I be there when you do?"

He knew the answer to that when she just stared at him, a world of patience in those brown eyes.

He said, "So I'm guessing that's a no?"

"Yes. That's a no."

"Why not?"

"Joe, it's a matter of respect."

"Yeah, well. I don't respect that man."

"And I get why you don't. But right now, he is Ana's biological and legal father. As her mother, it's my job to start this conversation with him alone."

Was she right? She usually was. But damn it, he wanted to be there in case she needed him. "I just want to support you."

"Do you really think that you can just sit there while I talk to him and not cut in if things get heated?"

He closed his eyes and pulled in a long slow breath. The truth was not convenient. He admitted to it, anyway. "Yeah, well. Probably not."

"Okay, then. I'll call him tomorrow from the flower shop."

Chapter Ten

Macy wasn't the least surprised that her call to Caleb the next morning went straight to voicemail. As always, she left a message.

"Caleb, I need to talk with you. And I mean soon. It's about Ana's care and it's not something I'm comfortable writing in a text or sending in an email. Please call me back as soon as you can."

"Well, did you talk to him?" Joe asked that afternoon when they were alone in her office at the hardware store.

"I called, but he didn't pick up. I left a message."

"You think he'll call back?"

"If he doesn't I'll reach out again tomorrow."

"Macy. He's going to blow you off indefinitely and we both know it. It's what he does. We need to take action."

"Joe. We agreed that I would handle this," she reminded him for the umpteenth time.

He made a low sound of pure frustration, but he left it at that.

Caleb didn't call that night.

The next day, she tried a text.

Please call me, Caleb. We need to talk.

Surprise, surprise. He failed to respond. Somehow, she needed to motivate him to get back to her.

On Thursday morning, when she called again, she just went ahead and said what was on her mind. "Caleb, Joe and I have been talking. He wants to adopt Ana. Would that work for you?"

Twenty minutes later, as she was selling two dozen red roses to dear old Mr. Petrov for his wife of fifty years, her cell rang in her pocket. She fished it out, saw that Caleb was calling and signaled her mom to ring up the sale.

"Caleb, hello," she said as she headed for the back room. "Thank you for calling back."

"What in the hell is going on?"

"Hey. Settle down. Take a breath." She shut the backroom door for privacy and sat down at her computer between the walk-in cooler and the rows of shelves lined with vases. "Listen, I—"

"Out of the blue, you hit me with *this*?"

"Caleb, if you'll only let me—"

"No. You don't get to talk first. Uh-uh. Wrong. Unacceptable. I'll have you know that I just walked out of an important meeting because of this crap you laid on me—in a text, no less."

"Caleb, I've reached out more than once. You haven't responded. I decided I needed to be more specific about my reason for calling. Joe is a wonderful father to Ana. He loves her and she loves him. You are busy with so many—"

"Ana is my daughter. That is not going to change. Forget it. You want to take me to court, you go right ahead. It will be bad. It will be brutal for you and that cowhand you married, just wait and see."

Had she ever really loved this man? Right now, she felt nothing but frustration mixed with bewilderment and more than a touch of righteous fury. How had she ever managed to carry on anything resembling an actual conversation with him—let alone a relationship? "Caleb. Threats are not called for here. This can be a reasonable conversation if you'll only allow it to be."

There was silence on his end. She hoped that was a good sign.

He said, "It's not going to happen." At least his voice was calmer now. "She is *my* daughter. Don't mess with me, Macy. I mean that. If you do, you will regret it."

"Really, Caleb? Threats?"

"Listen to me. I've got enough trouble with Jaquel. I don't need you piling on." Macy read the subtext in that remark. His second wife was getting tired of the Caleb show, too. Imagine that. "You women," he muttered, "always coming up with completely unreasonable demands..."

"Oh, please. Get over yourself. I'm not making demands. I only want to discuss the possibility of—"

"That. Right there. There *is* no possibility that I'm giving up my rights as a father. Period. Full stop. Are we clear on that?"

She closed her eyes and counted to five. "I understand." She should probably leave it there—for now, anyway. He wasn't the least bit receptive and she was getting nowhere. She opened her mouth to say goodbye.

But Caleb wasn't finished. "And don't even start on me about how I never see Ana. I take care of my end and we both know it, too. Get this through your head, Macy. No other guy is going to be adopting my kid. That's a hard line and you need to accept it." There was more in that vein. Macy tuned him out. Finally, he said, "I can't talk anymore. I have to go."

And he disconnected the call.

She stuck her phone in her pocket and then just sat there at her desk in the backroom of her mom's shop thinking about what a self-absorbed jerk Caleb could be—and how very grateful she was not to be married to him anymore.

Right then, the door to the front of the store swung open and her mom stuck her head in. "You okay in here?"

Macy put on a smile. "Never better."

Betty wasn't buying. "I *am* your mother and I know when you're lying."

"Yeah, well." Macy stood. "It's a long story. Let me just say you're the best, and I'm handling it."

Out in front, the bell over the door jingled. Betty turned to go, but then paused and turned back to add, "You need me, I'm right here."

"I know, Mom. And I love you for it."

That evening, Macy was waiting for Joe when he came down from tucking Ana in bed. He crossed the living room and came to sit beside her on the sofa. She slid in even closer. He put his arm around her and she leaned her head on his shoulder.

"Go ahead," she said softly. "Ask me."

"Did you...talk to Caleb today?"

"Yeah." She tipped her head back to meet his eyes. He looked so serious, even as he tried to smile. She wished with all her heart that she had better news for him.

Joe was such a great dad. And she loved him so much. She was *in* love with him. And one of these days very soon, she would need to work up the courage to say her love out loud.

I love you, Joe, she thought. *I think that I always have, even when life and other people got in the way...*

He pressed his warm lips to her temple. "Come on," he

said as he eased his arm out from around her. Rising, he offered his hand.

She took it and followed him to their room where Camryn's crib was empty. The baby had gone home with Tia that evening.

They sat together on the bed.

"So what happened?" Joe asked. "What did Caleb say?"

"It's not what we were hoping for."

"Just tell me what he said."

"Well, there was ranting and a big dose of outrage from him that I would dare to ask him to give up his rights. Bottom line, he says no. Absolutely not."

"Damn. I knew that fool would behave that way. So, all right, then. We take him to court."

She waited until he looked at her. "No," she said gently.

He narrowed his eyes. "Why not?"

"Joe, I was married to him. I was too young to understand what I was getting into, I see that now. He was never the kind of man a woman could count on. But I was dazzled at first, head over heels. It took me until six months after the wedding to start seeing the truth…"

"And the truth is?"

"Caleb is big on new things, on grand gestures. But making it work day-to-day? He's nothing like you, Joe. The man has no clue. Believe me, over the years I was with him, I got to know him pretty well—and by that I mean the *real* Caleb Storm. He's thoroughly self-absorbed and emotionally unavailable. It's like he never really grew up."

Joe stared off toward the dark windows on the far wall for several seconds. Finally, he spoke. "None of what you just said is news to me—but I really appreciate that part about how your ex and I are nothing alike."

"Good. Because that you're not like Caleb—Joe, I love that about you."

He didn't smile, but he did take her hand. "Go on," he said.

"The thing is, Caleb is all about Caleb. And part of that means never giving up anything he feels entitled to. Including his role as a father. And I don't think it's wise for us to take him to court over it. We won't win and we'll cause a lot of upheaval for Ana. And then, in the end, I'm pretty sure the court will leave things mostly as they are, with a slap on the wrist for Caleb and a warning to him to work with us on a visitation plan that will force him to spend some time with his estranged daughter."

"We don't know for sure that it would end like that."

"You heard what Ethan said the other day. Caleb is an absent dad, but not a deadbeat. His claim on Ana will hold up in court. It is what it is and I want to leave it alone, at least for now."

Joe looked away from her—toward the dark night out there beyond the window. For a long bittersweet moment, they just sat there, together, not looking at each other—but still holding hands.

Finally, he faced her again. "For now—but not forever?"

"I can't predict the future. But we'll be honest with Ana—on Ana's terms. Right now, she calls you dad and she's happy with that, happy with *you*, with our lives as they are now, with our family. When she has questions about Caleb, we'll answer them truthfully, telling her the good things about Caleb as well as the bad."

He let go of her hand and scooted away a fraction. "Well, coming up with good things to say about Caleb is going to be a serious challenge for me."

"For me, too. But somehow, we'll manage it. Because

we want what's best for Ana. And someday, very likely, she will want to know more about Caleb and it will be our responsibility to help her with that."

"Talk about a thankless job..."

She closed the slight distance he'd put between them and bumped his shoulder with hers. He took the hint and put his arm around her. "Ana adores you," she said.

"It's mutual." Pulling her with him, he fell back across the bed. "I still think we should go forward on this. I want to adopt Ana."

"And I love that you do." She turned her head toward him and waited until he looked at her. Then she said, "But, Joe, I don't think that's a fight we can win. I really don't."

He just looked at her for several seconds. Finally, he said, "It's completely unfair that you're the boss in this."

She chuckled then. "Well, I do get the final vote—when it comes to Ana, anyway." Now their noses were almost touching.

Up close, in the light from the bedside lamp, those blue eyes of his were deep enough to drown in. "We'll make it work." His voice was gruff. "Somehow."

"I know we will."

"Come here..." He pulled her closer.

I love you, Joe. I'm in love with you...

It sounded so good inside her head. Someday, she needed to get brave and say it out loud.

But probably not tonight.

I love you, Joe. The unspoken words echoed in her head as she lifted her mouth to welcome his kiss.

"You need to tell him," Riley advised on Monday when they met for lunch at the Stagecoach Grill.

That was right after Macy had gathered all her courage

and confessed to her other best friend that she was deeply in love with Joe.

"But I'm afraid to tell him," Macy said. "The whole deal with us is that we do love each other, we're always there for each other, we are a team and we always will be. But we're not in love."

Riley scoffed. "I don't even know where to start with you. Or him. I mean, didn't I *say* you were in love with him when you were thinking about marrying him back in October?"

"You did. And you were right."

"Humph," said Riley. "Being right really should be more satisfying." The Grill had one of those fancy copper espresso machines now. Macy and Riley were both drinking pumpkin spice lattes. Riley sipped hers and then set down her cup. "How many years have you known the guy?"

"Since kindergarten, same as you."

"Hmm. Let's do the math."

"Do we have to?"

"Oh, you bet we do. We were what, five? So...twenty-three years. You have loved Joe Bravo for twenty-three years?"

"Looking back now? Yeah, pretty much. Not that I realized it then." She sipped her own latte and reminisced. "He was always asking me questions in kindergarten, I remember. Did I like lizards? Did I eat broccoli? I found him annoying, but I still wanted to be around him all the time."

"Macy." Riley dredged a steak fry in ketchup and stuck half of it in her mouth. "You need to tell him."

"Oh, I'm not so sure about that. Lindsay broke his heart and then Becca stomped it to death. He's officially sworn off love forever."

"Yeah, well. He needs to get over that. And he will. With

your help. He's already completely in love with you—even if he's being a lunkhead about it, refusing to admit the truth to you or to himself. You need to get honest, lay it right out there. Tell him you're in love with him so he can get going on realizing that he's in love with you, too."

"Excuse me? You're saying I shouldn't take him at his word? Shouldn't believe him when he tells me that there's a corner of his heart he just can't share with me?"

"I'm saying he's been hurt and he's trying to protect himself. One way or another, you've got to get beyond the barriers he's put up."

"By letting him know I'm in love with him so that he can reject me?"

Riley frowned. "That's not what I meant."

"Okay, then what *did* you mean?"

"I'm only trying to encourage you to be honest, to find a way to shake him up a little, get him to see that…" Riley seemed to run out of words. She pushed her plate away. "Oh, never mind. What do I know? I miss TJ, Mace. Always will. But I wouldn't put *my* heart on the line ever again—and not because the love of my life screwed me over. But because he died and some part of me curled up and died with him."

Macy reached across the table to clasp Riley's hand. "Don't be so hard on yourself. You are the real deal and I love you a lot. And maybe someday, you'll—"

"Nope. Had the man of my dreams, lost him. Let's leave it at that." Riley sat a little straighter. "But that's me." Her voice was brisk now. "Your situation is different. You can still have a beautiful marriage with the love of your life. So don't miss your chance. We all deserve at least one great love. You haven't had yours yet because Caleb sure wasn't it. Try again until you get it right."

"But what if he turns me down?"

"Macy. You're married to him. And I have never seen that man as happy as he is with you. Joe is not letting you go, believe me. Not now, not when he's finally got exactly the life he's always wanted—with you. Take a chance on him, be honest with him about how you feel. I think he's worth it. And I think you deserve to have everything with him, all that he can give, including that stubborn heart of his."

Macy went to Bravo Hardware after lunch. When she arrived, Joe was working the register, making small talk with Minnie Labrecque, who was in her fifties, weighed about ninety pounds soaking wet and ran a cute little bed-and-breakfast in an old Victorian on Mill Street.

When Macy stuck her head in from the warehouse area, he gave her a nod and a slow smile. She almost marched right over to him then and there, grabbed his hand and dragged him back to the office to have her way with him.

But no. If she did that, she could end up betraying her true feelings, crying out that she loved him, *had* loved him practically forever, but just hadn't known it till recently.

Back in her office, there were bills to pay and inventory to track. She went to work. Joe wandered in from out front several times that afternoon. He had questions about plumbing orders and an overdue account. She gave him the information he needed.

Once, as he bent close to look at a spreadsheet, she glanced up at him and he kissed her. It was just a quick peck, affectionate, light as a breath.

She almost grabbed him, yanked him close and started tearing off his clothes right then and there.

Was she ridiculous?

Yeah.

She wondered if she would ever have the nerve to tell him what was in her heart.

After school, she picked up her daughter and two of Ana's friends and drove them out to the ranch for a playdate. The girls seemed to have a great time just hanging out in Ana's room with the dog and the cat. Macy could hear them laughing and chattering together up there.

At four thirty, Macy herded them all back into the Subaru and drove Ana's friends home. On their return to the ranch, Macy and Ana stopped at Meggie's for Camryn.

"She's got a cold," Meggie said as she handed over the fussing baby. "She was sniffling when Tia dropped her off this morning. Tia and I talked about it. There's no fever so Tia and I agreed that she would go on to work. But she asked that we call her if it gets any worse."

"Got it. What else?"

"Well, as of now, Camryn needs the usual. Lots of liquids, a cool mist humidifier and nasal saline. The saline's in the diaper bag. If you need a humidifier—"

"I've got one, don't worry."

Meggie nodded. "Just call if you need me."

"You know I will."

Outside, the baby started wailing when Macy put her in her car seat.

"Aww, Cammy," said Ana from over in her own seat. "Don't cry. It's okay…"

As if in answer, Camryn let out another wail.

"Let's get her home." Macy wiped gently at Camryn's runny nose.

Ana concurred. "She needs to be all comfy in her crib."

At home, Ana went upstairs to work on her weekly

homework packet. Voodoo and Rosie trotted right along behind her.

Macy did her best to comfort poor Camryn. The baby was miserable. When she finally settled down a little, Macy put her in her bouncy seat, dabbed petroleum jelly on her red nose and got dinner started.

For about twenty minutes, there was a lovely silence because Camryn had actually dropped off to sleep. Too bad when she woke up she wailed like the end of the world had come. Macy carried her to the bedroom, changed her diaper, put the crying baby in her crib and got the humidifier going. Camryn was still crying when Macy grabbed the baby monitor and retreated to the kitchen to get dinner started.

Ten minutes of wailing ensued followed by another ten of fitful fussing. And then, at last, silence. Macy returned to the bedroom, silently pushed open the door and tiptoed to the crib. A red-nosed angel with her thumb in her mouth, Camryn was sound asleep.

Macy was back in the kitchen peeling potatoes about ten minutes later when she heard the back door open and close.

Not long after that, Joe's arms slid around her. "Smells good in here," he said as his lips brushed the side of her throat. The light caress made her sigh. "Ana upstairs?"

"Um-hmm." She turned in his embrace. "The dog and the cat are helping her with her homework."

He gave her one of those smiles, a smile like the one earlier that day, when he stood behind the counter at the hardware store chatting with Millie Labrecque. It was a private smile, one for her and her alone. It sent a wave of warmth and good feeling radiating through her.

"And Camryn?" he asked.

"Napping. She's got a cold, but I set up the humidifier in

the bedroom to help clear the congestion. She went to sleep about half an hour ago. As for dinner, it's Swiss steak and I'm on it." She held up the half-peeled potato in her hand.

He sniffed the air. "Suddenly, I'm starving."

"Won't be long now," she promised. *I love you, Joe*, she thought. It sounded just fine inside her head—honest and heartfelt. But her sincerity wasn't going to make him love her back the way she wanted him to. She kept her love to herself and added, "I do feel sorry for poor Camryn. It's no fun having a stuffy nose."

"It's such a tiny nose, after all…" The way he looked at her made a thousand fluttery creatures take flight in her belly.

The look in his eyes said he thought she was the most gorgeous woman on the planet. She tried to take comfort in that, reminding herself that even though he refused to fall in love with her, he prized her—as a friend, as a woman, as a life companion, as a mother to his daughter and her daughter and their unborn baby sleeping within her.

They had everything. She knew that. Did she just *have* to have a heartfelt declaration of romantic love, too?

He touched her cheek and then eased his long fingers around the back of her neck. "Want me to check on her?"

She stared up at him, longing burning through her, urging her to drag him to bed and crawl all over him for the next hour or so. To kiss him and hold him and whisper the truth she was terrified to reveal to him.

I'm in love with you, Joe. I didn't mean for this to happen, but it has. Joe, you're the one for me…

No.

Not now. Not with a cranky baby in the crib next to the bed in question—and a six-year-old upstairs expecting to be called down for dinner soon.

As for Joe, he was waiting for her answer. Now, if she could only remember the question...

Right. Should he go check on Camryn?

"Sure," she replied at last. "But quietly. I'm warning you, do not wake her up if she's sleeping."

"Understood." He cradled her face between his hands and kissed her. It was an unhurried kiss, one that didn't go deep, yet still told her everything—that he was glad to be home. That if they didn't have two kids to deal with, he would be lifting her into his arms and carrying her straight to their bed.

Really, he gave her so much. She should just let herself be happy with the beautiful life they had together. She should stop longing for the one thing he'd made it very clear he couldn't give her.

"I'll be back..." He bent close again for one more quick kiss and then turned to go check on the baby.

In bed that night, Joe pulled his sleeping wife back against his body and curved himself around her. Macy sighed but hardly stirred.

Something was bothering her. All evening she'd seemed distracted—and sad, too. She'd put on a happy face but he wasn't fooled. He'd waited for her to open up about whatever the problem was. But she hadn't come clean, not even after Ana was in bed.

Maybe she was simply exhausted, what with the sick baby and their busy schedules and never getting a moment to herself—oh, and being pregnant, too.

"Joe..." She said his name in her sleep. He remained absolutely still for several seconds, hoping that she might say more. But then she only sighed and slept on.

He ached to wake her, to kiss her and run his greedy hands all over her, make her moan and cry out his name.

But that wouldn't be happening. Not tonight. Not tomorrow night, either. They wouldn't get their bedroom to themselves again until Friday night when Tia would take the baby for the weekend.

"What?" Macy asked groggily, turning her head to look back at him through half-shut eyes. Had he managed to wake her just by stewing over what the hell might be going on with her? "You all right, Joe?"

He smoothed her hair off her cheek. "Never better. What about you? I know things are hectic. You doing okay?"

She took his hand and pressed it to her belly, reassuring him with her touch—and reminding him again of their baby, still so tiny, the size of a raspberry now at eight weeks, sleeping beneath his cradling palm. "I'm all right," she whispered. "Just tired…"

Not exactly an opening—and if they were going to have a talk, they needed to find another room to do it in. "Let's go out to the living room."

"Why?"

"So we can talk."

"About…?"

"Whatever you want to talk about."

She wriggled around in his arms so that they faced each other. "Listen, I'm beat. Let's just try to get some sleep before the baby wakes up again."

He held her eyes through the darkness. "You sure?"

"Sleep, Joe. I need sleep."

"Well, if you…"

In the crib, Camryn stirred and let out a tiny breathy cry. Macy put two fingers to his lips. He got the message.

Neither of them moved or spoke. At least a minute went by during which the baby was blessedly silent.

Finally, Macy whispered, "Sleep…" And then she turned so he was spooning her again. Grasping his hand, she pulled his arm back around her and then laced her fingers with his. "'Night…"

He let it be.

Whatever was going on with her, she would tell him eventually. And when she did, they would work through it, figure it out. Together, same as they always had.

Chapter Eleven

A *letter* Macy thought the next day as she sat at her desk in the back of her mom's shop.

She should write a letter to Joe the way she used to do. Just grab a piece of paper and write down exactly what was in her heart, reveal the secret she was keeping from him. She could take her time, choose each word carefully, lay it all out for him simply. Clearly and honestly.

But then again, no...

A letter wouldn't cut it. If he didn't want to hear about how she'd gone and fallen in love with him, he wasn't going to enjoy reading about it, either.

She should just tell him.

Or not.

Probably not.

Definitely not. Her best move was no move at all. She should just go on loving him and loving their life together and keep her mouth shut about falling for him.

A low whimper of frustration escaped her. Pressing her index and middle fingers to her temples, she rubbed in circles to ease the gathering tension there.

Because love? It gave her a headache.

Blinking, she forced herself to focus on her laptop screen.

A letter...

The social marketing checklist on her laptop blurred before her eyes. Flipping the laptop shut, she pushed it aside and rolled her swivel chair to the printer a few feet away. After stealing several sheets from the paper tray, she rolled back to her desk again and dug around in the drawer for a pen.

Dear Joe,
Guess what? I'm in love with you.
Yours truly,
Your Wife

Well. It was direct and to the point, for sure. But was it going to convince him to give true love with her a chance?

With a whine of frustration, she covered her face with her hands. How many letters had she written to Joe over the years?

Probably a hundred. Seventy-five, at least.

She might never be able to write him the perfect love letter, the kind of letter that would mend his broken heart and have him confessing that he loved her, too—in all the ways.

But she could damn well do better than *Guess what? I'm in love with you.*

After wadding that attempt into a tiny wrinkled ball, she dropped it in the wastebasket beside her desk and tried again.

Dear Joe,
I need to tell you what you don't want to know. And it's hard. Impossible, even. So hard, I can't figure out where to start. I don't know how to say it. I don't know how tell you that the one thing you claim you

don't want from me is the very thing I can't stop myself from giving you.

It doesn't matter what you say. It doesn't matter how you react. I have to tell you. I need for you to know.

Joe, I didn't mean for this to happen. But it has.

I'm in love with you, Joe. Deeply. Passionately. And forever.

You're my best friend and you are also the one for me. It's perfect. Or it should be.

Except that you say you can never be in love with me, too...

With a groan, Macy flopped back in her chair. "Nope," she grumbled aloud to the shelves full of empty vases. "Not working." Wadding that effort into a second ball, she batted it into the wastebasket with the other one.

And then she tried again.

And again.

The balled-up rejected drafts hit the wastebasket one by one, each attempt less satisfactory than the one before it. Clearly, the universe was trying to tell her something—something along the lines of, *He doesn't need a love letter from you. He's in love with you already but he just doesn't know it.*

Won't admit it.

Can't say it.

Or at least, that was what she wanted to believe. But *did* she believe it, really?

She stacked her arms on her desk and dropped her head on them with a frustrated groan. This was going nowhere.

And yet, two minutes later, she picked up the pen and tried again.

I know what I promised—what we promised each other. It was everything, all the love in the world and then some. But not the rest. Not the... What do I even call it?

The passion?

We have that.

The adoration?

That, too. Because Joe, I do adore you. You are everything a man should be and then some.

You are everything to me.

And I don't care if I come off like some cheesy old-time love song. I love you so much in all the ways we agreed on—and here's the thing. I also love you in the way we promised we wouldn't.

I love you so much that

Okay, no. Just no. A letter wasn't going to do it.

She loved him—in *all* the ways. She loved him and he'd made it so painfully clear that he didn't, couldn't or wouldn't return her love. Not fully. Not in the deepest way. And if she needed to tell him that her love for him went all the way down to the core of her—she would do that, *tell* him. She would say, *I'm in love with you, Joe*, while looking him square in the eye.

Letters were lovely. You could share a lot and learn a lot about yourself and about another person by writing letters back and forth. But not this. For this, a letter wasn't going to cut it.

When and if she ever revealed the secret of her heart to her husband, she would do it out loud and face-to-face.

That night was worse than the night before. Camryn fussed constantly. Neither Joe nor Macy got much sleep.

The next morning the house was quiet as Joe dragged himself from bed, pulled on his work clothes and headed out into the icy December darkness for morning chores. Rosie came down the stairs as he was heading for the back door. She whined at him and wagged her tail.

"Well, come on, then," he said. She followed him out.

When they reentered the house at 7:30 a.m., the first thing he heard was the baby crying. Shucking off his boots, he went through into the kitchen on stocking feet with Rosie at his heels.

Camryn wailed louder as Macy walked her back and forth across the kitchen floor. "Shh," Macy soothed. "It's okay, you're all right." She rubbed Camryn's back.

"How's she doing?" Joe asked.

"She's got a fever of a 100.2. I need to call Tia—here." She passed him the yowling baby and he took over trying to soothe her.

"Is Cammy okay?" Ana, in red pajamas and Grinch socks, stood in the arch to the living room, her black hair flat on one side, her eyes low and sleepy. Voodoo dropped to a sit at her side.

"She's not feeling good," Joe said, and kept on walking.

"Poor Cammy." Ana made a sad face. "I'm just going to get my own cereal, 'kay?"

"All right," said Joe.

The baby kept wailing as Joe tried to soothe her and Macy talked to Tia.

A minute later, Macy finished the call and set her phone on the island. "Tia wants to take the baby to her pediatrician up in Sheridan. She's calling Josh to let him know she'll be in late."

Joe pressed his lips to Camryn's too-warm forehead. The baby squirmed and kept crying.

Macy went on, "The plan now is that I'll take Camryn up there, meet Tia for the doctor visit and then bring the baby back home with me. Depending on what the doctor says, I'll either stay home with her or take her to your mom's and then go on into town."

"Got it," he replied as Camryn wailed in his ear. He bounced her gently as he walked. "Drop a text if you need me. I'll be there quick."

Macy gave him a strange little smile—both tender and sad. "I know you will."

That smile stuck with him, kind of nagging at him, through the hectic hour or so of comforting the baby, getting Ana out the door and then a few minutes later, Macy and Camryn, too.

"You sure you don't want me to drive you up there?" he asked as he helped Macy get the baby and the baby gear into the Subaru. "Or I could just take her and you can go to work as usual."

She kissed his cheek. "You can do it next time. It just so happens that today it's not a problem to take the morning off since I'm on top of things at both stores."

"Of course you are." He tipped up her chin and stole a kiss from her soft lips as the baby sniffled and fussed in her car seat.

"Gotta go," she said, and bustled around to the driver's door.

He followed, stepping in to open her door for her and shutting it as she hooked up her seat belt. In no time, he was waving as she drove away.

Macy called him an hour later. "Camryn's pediatrician has informed us that Camryn has a cold."

Joe laughed. "No kidding."

"The doctor prescribed children's acetaminophen, plenty of rest, lots of liquids and the continued use of the humidifier. I got the go-ahead to take Camryn to your mom's for the day—and yeah, I called Meggie to make sure she was up for that."

"Let me guess. Mom said yes."

"That's right. Your mom's a rock and it's all good. Are you already at the hardware store?"

"Yep." Fall work, weaning and shipping were done. In the winter, they put out feed for the cattle, but feeding wouldn't start until January. That meant he could spend more time at the store.

"Tia's already on her way back to work," Macy said. "I'll drop Cammy off with Meggie and head for the flower shop. I should be at the hardware store around one o'clock."

"You know, you could just go on home after you check in at your mom's shop. We've got it under control here, I promise you."

"You're sweet, but I like to stay on top of things."

He thought of her sad smile earlier that morning. "Everything...okay?"

There was a beat of silence on her end. "Why?"

He realized that now probably wasn't the time to explore whatever might or might not be bothering her. "Well, if it's not one thing, it's another around here," he said. "And it seems to me like you're always the one picking up the slack."

"I'm not the only one. You work hard, too."

"And I can work harder, no problem. Understand?"

"Thanks, Joe. But don't worry about me. I'm fine and I will let you know if things get to be too much for me. They're not, though. Yes, our lives are busy, but I like it that way. So far, it's all completely manageable."

That made him feel marginally better. "You're sure?"

"Positive." Camryn chose that moment to let out a whine followed by a wail. "Hear that?" Macy asked. "I've got to start up this car and get going. I'm praying she'll settle down once we're on the move."

"All right, then. Later…"

Tonight, he thought as they ended the call. Once the kids were in bed they could talk some more, hopefully without being interrupted. He still had a sense that things weren't quite right with her but he couldn't figure out what might be wrong.

He needed to know what the problem was. And then to do whatever he could to fix it.

"Acetaminophen is a miracle drug, no doubt about it," Macy put the baby monitor on the coffee table and joined him on the sofa. It was eight thirty that night. Both the kids were in bed and no one was crying.

He put his arm around her and pulled her close enough to press a kiss to her temple. "It's so nice when they're quiet."

"Pure heaven, and that's no lie." She pulled away, but only to kick off her fleece-lined house shoes. Then she scooted back against the padded sofa arm and plunked her stocking feet in his lap. He began rubbing them, using his thumbs to press and stroke along her instep. She sighed and closed her eyes. "That feels good…"

Joe watched her face. She had a sort of dreamy look, with her eyes shut and her mouth softly parted. He thought about happiness. Because this was it. Just him and Macy, here by the fire at the end of the day with the kids safe in bed.

Convincing her to marry him?

Best move he'd ever made.

She asked, "Do you recall what we were talking about this morning on the phone—before Camryn interrupted us?"

He was pleased that she'd brought the subject up again herself. But that was Macy, always ready to tackle any issue or question head-on.

Back in the day—with Lindsay and then later with Becca—he used to have to practically beg to find out what was going on with either of them. Lindsay would go quiet. When he asked her what was wrong, she would say she didn't want to talk about it. And Becca always said she was fine. Just fine. She'd put on that glowing smile—and pour herself another drink.

"Joe?"

"Yeah?"

"You with me?"

He blinked and nodded. "Sorry. Just kind of lost in thought there for a minute—but yeah. I remember what we talked about this morning. I reminded you how hard you work and promised to pick up the slack anywhere you need me to."

"Yes, you did. And thank you." She let her head drop back with a sigh as he pressed his knuckles to the pad of her heel. "I am definitely staying married to you."

"Whew. Had me worried for a minute or two there."

She was watching him again. "I'm your ride or die, remember? And you are mine. You are the best, Joe. I mean that sincerely."

And there it was again, the smile that tried to be bright and yet somehow came across as slightly forlorn. She seemed to be studying his face.

Something was definitely going on with her. He was certain of that now. "What is it? What's wrong?"

She frowned. "What do you mean?"

This evasion was a little too much like Lindsay and he didn't like it. "Come on, Macy. Tell me what's bothering you."

"Joe, I..." That was as far as she got. And then she just looked at him, eyes wary—and that sad look? It was back.

He didn't get it. What was there to be sad about? "Mace, whatever's on your mind, it can't be that bad." He took her hand and tugged her closer. "Come on. Come here."

She came to him, swinging her feet to the side, snuggling in beside him.

He wrapped his arm around her and pressed a light kiss to the top of her head. When she lifted her sweet face to him, her eyes were deep enough to drown in. "Talk to me, Mace. I'm here. I'm listening."

For a moment, he thought she would do it, tell him what was wrong so he could fix it. But in the end, she looked away with a sigh.

He tried again. "Please..."

That brought another heavy sigh from her. He kept his mouth shut and waited.

Finally, she nodded. "All right, Joe. The thing is, the way I feel about you..." The words trailed away.

About then, it hit him—like a blinding light bursting on in a darkened room. He *knew* what she was trying to say.

And he didn't want to hear it.

He felt relieved that she'd hesitated. He would do anything for her and he wanted her happy—but not that. He just couldn't bring himself to go *there*.

Now he hoped she would give up, let it be. And then he

could back off, reassure her in a generalized way. They could go on as they had been.

It was so good with her. They didn't need this. She didn't need to make it into the one thing he could not do again.

But then she drew a breath—and out it came. "I'm in love with you, Joe. It's real and it's deep. Truthfully, I've come to realize that I've been in love with you forever, since we were kids. But I denied it. I hid my love away from you—and from myself, too. I don't really know why. Maybe I just wasn't ready. Maybe I needed the time to grow up."

"Macy, I—"

"No." She touched her fingertips to his lips. "Please. You asked me and now I'm telling you. Just let me finish." And she went right on. "I left, went to college, met Caleb, had Ana, all without realizing who you really were to me. I probably never would have figured it out. But then Ana and I came home again and you and me, we..." She seemed not to know how to go on. With a little laugh that was more like a moan, she said, "I just can't deny it anymore. I just can't pretend we are everything *but* in love..."

He hardly knew what to say, so he said nothing.

She stared past him, toward the Christmas tree over by the front window. "What can I tell you?" She seemed to be asking herself as much as him. "I still wouldn't have realized what I really wanted. Not until this...marriage plan of yours. Not until it was you and me, making a life together. Living together. Sleeping together. Raising our kids together, having a baby. Joe, I can be thick-headed, but this life we've built has finally made me see that you are it for me and you always have been."

No! The denial echoed inside his head.

They'd had an understanding, after all. They knew where they stood with each other. What they had was so good.

But this, what she wanted now? It was not part of the deal. He couldn't give the words back to her, not honestly. And he refused to lie to her.

However...

He didn't want to lose her, either.

No. Losing her. That would be the worst. He couldn't bear that. They were a team and he loved what they had. And he would do just about anything to keep her at his side.

Maybe if he just said it. Maybe that would be enough for her. "I love you, too." It was true. He did love her, always had, for so many years now. At least since freshman year of high school when she made him write letters and he was so sure he would hate it and yet it turned out to be fun, to be something he looked forward to—another smart-ass, bossy, funny letter from brainy Macy Oberholzer.

She looked at him for the longest time, searching his face, seeking something she wasn't going to find. "I know that you love me," she said mildly. "But you're not *in* love with me, are you, Joe?"

How the hell was he supposed to answer that one? She was the best thing that had ever happened to him and he wasn't going to lose her by being a fool.

So what, then? Make himself do it, just say what she needed to hear? *Yes, I am, Macy. I'm in love with you...*

Would that even work with her? She knew him so well. She would see the lie coming before he got the words out of his mouth.

No, lying was out. Really, he had nothing, nowhere to go with this, not a hopeful word to say. He could lose her over this and that angered and terrified him equally.

She said, "Whatever happened—with Lindsay, with Becca... Joe, that's not going to happen with me. I am not either of those women. I'm your best friend. I always will be. I'm not going to leave you. I'm not going to cheat on you. And I'm not going to die on you, either."

"You say that. But stuff happens." His voice sounded strange to his own ears. Rough. Impatient. Pissed off.

"Okay, then." She touched his arm. He stiffened and she dropped her hand. "Let's focus on the cheating. Cheating does not just happen. Cheating is a choice and it's one that I'm never going to make. Believe me."

"I know that," he muttered, and knew damn well that he sounded like some sulky kid.

"As for death," she went on. "You're right. Death comes for everyone. I could die tomorrow."

"Damn it." He shut his eyes, shook his head. "Don't say that."

"It's just the truth. But the good news is, it's not likely I'll die anytime soon. I've got every reason to believe I have a lot of good years ahead of me. Years I fully intend to spend with you."

He looked at her then, a hard look through narrowed eyes—a look he should have softened. But the nerve she'd hit was just too damn raw. It wasn't supposed to be like this. He demanded gruffly, "You mean that? You're not... calling it quits with me?"

She took his hand and he let her, because she was everything and he would do anything for her.

Except this damn falling-in-love thing. He couldn't do that. Because he didn't believe in it. Not anymore.

Yeah, his parents were in love. His brother, Jason, and his wife, Piper, were in love. His sister was in love and blissfully happy with her much-older big-city, wheeler-dealer husband. And Joe was happy for them.

But for him, being "in love" had never given him a damn

thing but heartbreak. He'd tried it twice. Both times the outcome had been unbearable.

He wanted something better than being in love. He wanted something real. Something he could count on—and he had that at last. With Macy. But suddenly that wasn't enough for her. Now she wanted to up the stakes, change the rules.

Uh-uh. No, thank you. Not going there. No way.

"Okay," she said cautiously.

He had no idea what she meant by that. "Okay, what?"

"Joe, you are suddenly locked up tight. Are you even willing to talk about this?"

"What's there to talk about?"

She drew in a slow careful breath and let it out on a hard sigh. "I'll take that as a no."

He should apologize. He was being a jerk and he knew it.

But this subject was the one he avoided at all costs. He'd thought she understood that. He had nothing to give her in this conversation.

But for her sake, he made himself try anyway. "You are mine," he said. "And I'm yours. You are the most important person in my life. I would do anything for you—except this. I'm not screwing up what we have with hearts and flowers. That only leads to lies and demands and promises that won't be kept. Sorry. No can do."

She just sat there. Her eyes were sadder than before.

He'd done that to her. He'd hurt her and he despised himself for that. But what she wanted, he couldn't give her. What she wanted, he just didn't have in him to provide.

And as for parroting the right words to her—no. She wouldn't buy that. She would see the lie written right there on his face.

"Okay, then." Her voice was kind. She even tried a shaky smile. "We should get some sleep."

"You go ahead," he said. "I'll be there in a minute."

With a nod, she picked up her slippers and the baby monitor and left him there. He refused to watch her go. But the house was so quiet that he heard the click when she shut the bedroom door. After that, for a while, he just sat there, staring into the middle distance.

Rosie's tags jingled as she got up and stretched.

"Want to go outside, girl?"

She let out a soft whine and ambled over to the door. He rose, followed her out and waited on the porch until she came trotting back up the front steps. Together, they reentered the silent house.

Rosie headed for the doggy bed by the fire. Joe turned into the short hall—and stopped at the shut bedroom door.

Was Macy lying awake in there, waiting for him? Would she expect to talk some more?

Well, too bad. He couldn't face her. Not tonight.

Back in the living room, he took the quilt from the shelf under the coffee table and stretched out on the sofa.

The night crawled by. He heard Camryn crying around two. He didn't get up, just laid there waiting like the damn coward he was. He didn't want to go in there if he didn't have to, didn't want to face his wife after the way he'd let her down.

It wasn't long before the crying stopped.

He closed his eyes and waited for sleep. It didn't happen for the longest time. As the night crawled by, he thought of things he usually didn't allow himself to remember.

Of Lindsay staring up at him, eyes bright with tears, begging him to forgive her, to give her just one more chance…

Of Becca, solemn and sober, promising that she would

go to her meetings regularly, that she would never take another drink, that she loved him and she needed him and she couldn't live without him to lean on...

He didn't remember falling asleep.

But he woke to the smell of coffee brewing and the sight of Ana standing over him with Voodoo in her arms.

"Morning," he said, trying to play it cool and easy.

"Dad, why are you sleeping on the sofa?"

"I, uh, must have dropped off."

Voodoo made one of those chittering sounds and squirmed in Ana's arms. She let him slide to the floor. "Mom says it's after six and there's coffee in the kitchen."

"Great." Not only could he smell the coffee, he also got a whiff of bacon frying.

Ana clambered up on the sofa and got right in his face. "Did you skip your morning chores?"

The knot in his gut loosened a fraction. This kid. Nothing got by her. "Nah, I'm on it. This morning, I'll be getting a late start, though."

"Well, you better get up, then."

"Yes, ma'am."

She wrinkled her nose at him. "Don't call me ma'am, Dad. I'm only six."

"Got it."

"Okay, then." She slid back down to the floor. When he didn't immediately jump to his feet, she braced her small fists on her hips. "Are you getting up or not?"

"I'm up, I'm up." He pushed back the quilt and stood. "Let's go."

Ana led him to the kitchen where Camryn cooed in her BabyBjörn and Macy was transferring the bacon from the frying pan to a paper-towel-covered plate.

"Hungry?" Macy asked. Her eyes had dark smudges beneath them but still, she managed a smile.

"Nah. I need to get out to the barn. I'll just grab some coffee for now." He took his steel thermos from a cabinet and filled it from the pot. "Camryn seems better."

Macy nodded. "Yes, much better. She only woke up once last night."

"Excellent." They stared at each other. Even with the baby cooing and Ana laughing at Voodoo as he smacked a toy mouse around under the table, the silence was deafening. "Well, better get going." He put the lid on the steaming thermos and got the hell out of there.

"You feeling okay, sweetheart?"

It was 9:00 a.m. and Macy was sitting at her desk in the backroom of Betty's Blooms. Stifling a sigh, she closed her eyes for a minute before turning in her swivel chair. "I'm fine, Mom. Why?"

Her mom frowned down at her. "You look tired."

"I'm good, honestly."

"Those bags under your eyes tell a whole different story." Betty sat in the folding chair next to Macy's desk. "You need to take it a little easier now, with the baby on the way. You have a lot on your plate. Think about cutting back a bit, not pushing yourself constantly."

"I promise you, Mom, I'm not pushing myself." She thought of Joe last night, the wrecked look in those blue eyes. Lucky for Lindsay, she lived in Cheyenne now—far enough away that Macy never had to see that woman's face and be tempted to slap her silly. As for Becca, it was hard to be furious with a dead woman. And yet, somehow Macy was managing it. Joe had the biggest heart in the world. And those women had broken it.

"Something's really bothering you," her mom said.

Macy put on a smile. "You know how it is. Kids. Christmas. Work. All of it. It's life, Mom." *Well, and Joe not loving me—at least, not the way I want him to. Joe not loving me is the worst.*

He'd turned away from her. And it hurt. A lot. More than it should, probably. It was so obvious that Joe wanted her, was true to her, *loved* her deeply. And she wasn't really sure why she needed him to say the words and mean it.

Probably because, after the wrecking ball Caleb had taken to her heart and her confidence as a woman, Macy had issues, too. Issues and insecurities as to her own—what? Lovableness, maybe.

Her mom was watching her, waiting for her to open up and share what was bothering her. Macy trusted her mom. She wanted to go ahead, tell all and get her mom's take on the situation.

But Betty Oberholzer was action-oriented, a can-do kind of mom. Macy cringed at the thought of her mom wading in to help "fix" the problem with Joe.

Betty got up again and braced her fists on her ample hips. "Take some time off. Maria and I can manage fine through the holidays. Anything you just have to do, you can do remotely. You hardly need to be here in the shop to deal with the accounts, tweak the upcoming Valentine's Day promotion or update the website…"

"Mom. I have a routine and I like my routine. There is nothing the matter with me."

"At least take a couple of days off."

"But I still have to come into town to work at the hardware store and Ana likes it when I pick her up from school."

"It's almost Christmas break. Ana can take the bus for

a few days and if I can do without you right here in person for a bit, so can Joe."

"Mom."

"What?"

"Stop. I love you and I'm grateful for you—but no. I'm perfectly fine and I'm not taking time off right now."

"You're as stubborn as your father."

"So I've been told—by you, and frequently."

"If you change your mind—"

"You'll be the first to know."

"Come up here," Betty briskly commanded as she held down a hand. "Give me a hug."

Macy rose, let herself be engulfed in her mom's loving embrace and fervently hoped Betty would leave it at that. She got her wish, too. Her mom let it be.

That afternoon at the hardware store, Macy avoided Joe. Surprise, surprise, he steered clear of her, too. They went about their separate tasks and shared very little conversation beyond twin nods of greeting when he arrived. And then, as she left to pick up Ana from school, she gave him a wave goodbye.

"See you later," he said—bringing the sum total of their communication that afternoon to those three words, a pair of nods and a wave.

Macy tried not to get depressed about the emotional chasm that now yawned between them. It was what it was. She had no idea what to do to make things better—not unless Joe suddenly came to his senses and decided to actually communicate with her.

She reminded herself to be patient, to trust in her husband and the goodness of his heart. To believe in his love, even if he was having trouble expressing it.

When she stopped off at Meggie's to pick up the baby,

it was snowing—not enough to stick for long, but enough that a thin sparkling blanket of white covered the ground. Ana came inside with her.

"Grandma Meggie," Ana said, "Are you coming to the Christmas pageant at my school? It's tomorrow in the afternoon. I get to be a shepherd and an elf."

"Wouldn't miss it," Meggie replied.

"Bring Grandpa Nate."

"You bet I will—and how about dinner here at our house on Sunday?" Meggie offered. "Five o'clock? Jason, Piper and their kids are coming, too."

Macy put on a big smile. "That would be great, Meggie. What should I bring?"

"Just yourselves. I've got it handled."

"We'll be there."

Back at their house, Ana said she wanted to play in the snow. She took Rosie into the backyard with her.

Inside on the living room floor, Macy spread out the play mat she'd bought the week before and set up the baby gym that went with it. When she put the baby on the mat, Camryn stared dreamily up at the dangling monkeys and bright-colored plush chains and bells while trying to chew on her toes, which were covered by her footed onesie.

And then, after a few minutes of chewing and random kicking, the baby actually reached out for one of the chains and even managed to bat it so it swung from the frame. Camryn's face lit up and a sound exactly like a giggle escaped her.

Macy clapped her hands. "Look at you! Go for it, girl!"

About then, Macy heard a *splat*. It had come from the window over the sink. She glanced up just in time to see a second mushy snowball hit the glass.

Macy bent close to Camryn. "What's that? Let's go

check." She scooped up the little one and carried her into the kitchen and over to the window.

Out in the backyard, Ana had created a small lopsided snowman with sticks for arms and pebbles for the eyes, nose and crooked smile. As for Rosie, she circled the soggy snowman, wagging her tail, even barking once, as though in appreciation.

Macy knocked on the window and gave her daughter an enthusiastic thumbs-up. Ana beamed her proud gap-toothed smile.

"What's going on in here?"

Joe...

Macy's poor heart went haywire and her knees turned to rubber. *Pitiful*, she thought. *Here I am going into cardiac arrest at the sound of his voice while the man sleeps on the sofa and refuses to talk about what's gone wrong between us.*

Turning, she saw him standing at the end of the short hallway that led to the mudroom. He looked so good, so tall, strong and handsome. Just the sight of him made her heart ache with longing.

She forced a smile. "Ana made a snowman in the backyard."

His stocking feet soundless on the wood floor, he came to join her at the window, close enough that his arm brushed hers. The barely-there touch sent sparks shooting through her.

Ana spotted him through the glass. Smiling proudly, she swept out a hand toward her lopsided snowman and then executed a slow graceful bow. He raised both hands high so that she could see him clapping.

In Macy's arms, the baby cooed. It was such a sweet moment—bittersweet, really. For Macy, anyway.

They had a beautiful family together—a beautiful *life* together. She loved him and he loved her. It should be enough for her.

But still, she wanted more. Her greedy heart just wouldn't settle. She wanted that battered part of him, the deepest heart of him. But he'd given that heart away twice before—and had it shattered both times.

Logically, she understood that he refused to risk his heart again. But her love denied logic. Her love wanted all of him.

And she wasn't going to be satisfied until he gave her what she craved.

Chapter Twelve

That night, she put in real effort to keep things light and easy. It didn't help. He still looked at her with wariness, as though waiting for her to start an argument or make some weepy, off-the-wall demand.

Macy did no such thing. She kept her attitude in check and a smile on her face. At bedtime, she expected him to make some weak excuse for why she should go on in before him—so that he could avoid coming to bed with her and spend a second night on the sofa.

As a result, she was not surprised or even all that hurt when he hung back.

"Got a few things I should check out in the barn," he said.

She didn't know whether to laugh or burst into tears. Because seriously? What just had to be done in the barn at ten o'clock at night?

But she held it together. "All right, then." Going on tiptoe, she kissed his beard-scruffy cheek. "See you in a bit."

"'Night, Macy."

'Night, Macy'? That sounded pretty final. Feeling certain that she wouldn't be seeing him again until she got up the next morning, she left him alone.

* * *

In the barn, Joe sat on a hay bale with Maysie, the one-eyed barn cat, in his lap. Maysie had a loud purr and an independent spirit. She could be affectionate when the mood struck, but she'd always rejected his attempts to bring her to the house to live. Inevitably, she managed to escape back to her home in the barn.

Outside, an owl hooted. The two horses in the occupied stalls shifted at the sound. Maysie jumped to the hay-strewn floor and strutted away.

Joe braced his forearms on his spread knees, stared into the hay-scented darkness and thought about the past. About Lindsay and the first time she cheated—or at least, the first time he found out about it.

It was summer. They'd been exclusive since Easter. They were seventeen and he took her to the last day of the Wyoming State Fair down in Buffalo. He'd had no clue that she'd already been to the fair at least once before.

They visited the midway and he'd caught her with some carny—a wiry guy with a narrow face who was running the ring toss. That was after she'd batted her pretty green eyes at Joe and begged him to get her some cotton candy while she tried her luck at winning a red teddy bear.

Joe came back to find her leaning into the ring-toss booth, whispering with the ring-toss guy.

"Come on, babe." The guy lifted his hand and ran a finger down the side of her throat. "I'm done at midnight. Meet me again. You know you loved it."

"I can't, Dirk. Please. I'm here with my..." Right then, she sent a furtive glance over her shoulder and spotted Joe standing fifteen feet away holding her giant wad of pink spun sugar on a paper cone. "Joe!" Her pretty lips

stretched in a trembling smile. "Hey!" She darted away from Dirk's booth and came at him, throwing her arms around him, laughing like there was something hysterically funny going on.

"Lindsay," he said flatly. "Here's your cotton candy." And he held out his arm and dropped it on the ground.

She gasped—and let go of him. He headed for Dirk, who'd turned away the moment Joe came toward him. Jumping over the barrier and landing in Dirk's domain, he grabbed the guy by the shoulder, spun him around and punched him in the jaw.

Dirk staggered and fell back but managed to stay on his feet.

"Joe!" Lindsay was already crying.

He pretended not to hear her as Dirk looked him up and down. "Fair enough," the carny sneered, working his jaw to judge the damage. "I don't want no trouble with you. Get the hell out of my booth."

"No problem." Joe jumped the low booth wall again and headed for the exit to the lot where he'd left his truck.

Sobbing, Lindsay fell in step behind him, "Joe, please don't be mad at me."

People were staring. He tried not to see them, just kept on walking, out through the turnstile gate, and on to his battered blue ranch truck.

As for Lindsay, she trotted right along in his wake, bawling, begging him, "Please Joe. Just let me tell you about it, just let me explain..."

"I don't want to hear it, no way." He jerked his arm free when she grabbed it as they reached the truck.

"Don't just leave me here." Tears ran down her cheeks and dripped off her chin. "I love you, I do! I'm just messed

up, Joe! You know that. I told you that. I told you everything. You know what happened to me..."

He didn't have the heart to drive off and leave her there. "Get in," he said. "I'll take you home."

The tears kept falling and her nose was running, too. They got in.

He popped open the glove box and shoved a packet of tissues at her. "Here."

"Thank you," she said in a tiny voice of total defeat.

He glanced over at her as he started up the truck. And he tried to stay strong, to hold firm against her. But something was wrong with him. He had a heart made of mush.

She turned those beautiful green eyes on him and he knew that eventually he would forgive her.

And he had forgiven her. Both that time at the fair and another time in the middle of senior year when some guy she'd once been in foster care with showed up in town. That guy had crawled in her bedroom window at her adoptive parents' house.

Joe knew because Lindsay told him all about it. That guy's name was Roger and she swore she hadn't slept with him—just kissed him and fooled around with him a bit. Joe hadn't known what to believe. But when she looked at him like she'd die if he left her...

Well, just like with the ring-toss guy, he forgave her again.

Were there more betrayals—other than the guy she'd finally dumped Joe for? Hell if he knew.

When he decided to go into the service, she'd begged him not to leave her, said she couldn't live without him, that she wasn't that strong, that she couldn't stand to be alone. Turned out, his departure hadn't killed her. She'd strung him along for a while and then dumped him for the guy from Cheyenne.

Stepping in and out of shafts of moonlight from the two high windows on either end of the barn, Maysie wandered back over. When she got to him, she plunked her butt at his feet and stared up at him through her good eye.

"I knew you'd be back," he said and patted his thighs.

She leaped to his lap, curled up and started purring. He sat there petting her for a while. When she jumped down again, he returned to the house.

Rosie greeted him inside in the mudroom door. He took off his boots and knelt to scratch her ruff and tell her what a good girl she was.

From there, he went on to the kitchen, where he considered pouring himself a drink. But then he just kept on going to the empty living room where embers still glowed in the fireplace.

It was past midnight. He'd sat out there in the barn for two hours, just him and Maysie and the two horses in their stalls. Was that sad? Yep.

He took the quilt from the low coffee table shelf and shook it open. And then he just stood there, staring at the sofa, longing for his bed. And his wife.

It was hard keeping his distance from her. The last couple of months had been nothing short of a revelation for him. He had everything he'd ever dreamed of—a wife he trusted and adored, two daughters and a baby on the way.

And now it was all blown to hell. Because he just couldn't bear to answer the questions he saw in Macy's eyes.

Was it only last night that it had all gone to hell?

Already, it felt like a decade to him—a decade of loneliness, an empty sad little world where he couldn't let his guard down with the one person he trusted absolutely.

"Oh, hell no," he whispered to no one at all.

And then he dropped the blanket on the sofa and turned for the short hall that led to their bedroom.

When he tried the doorknob, he found it unlocked. Slowly he turned the knob and carefully pushed the door inward.

The room beyond was dark and silent. He slipped in and shut the door without making a sound. And then he tiptoed to Camryn's crib.

The aching tightness in his chest eased a little when he stared down at this miracle who was his daughter. She slept on her back, both arms up and bent at the elbows, her perfect little starfish hands by her head. Her mouth was moving. She seemed to be dreaming—and sucking at a nonexistent bottle.

He dared to bend down and brush a kiss on her forehead. She smelled of milk and baby lotion. And she didn't stir, just went on sleeping, sucking a bottle that wasn't there.

When he straightened, his gaze went to the bed. Through the shadows, he could make out Macy curled on her side, the covers drawn up to her chin.

He shouldn't go to her. He should leave this room now and spend another night on the sofa. Still stalling, putting off the decision as to where to lie down, he tiptoed to the bathroom, shut the door, splashed water on his face and brushed his teeth. When he turned off the light and entered the dark bedroom again, he went to the bed, shed his clothes and tossed them on a chair.

Carefully, he lifted the covers—just enough to crawl in between the sheets.

Macy stirred, made a soft sleepy sound.

He wrapped his arm around her and pulled her back against his body.

"Joe?"

"Shh. Sleep..."

She didn't argue. Instead, with a sigh, she went loose and easy in his arms.

He breathed in the scent of her hair, reveled in the feel of her body touching his. Nothing was settled. Nothing was right.

And yet he tumbled into sleep like a man falling off a cliff.

When Macy woke in the morning, Joe was gone. She pushed back the covers and went to the crib. The baby was still sleeping.

Returning to the bed, Macy perched on the edge of it. She remembered waking up with Joe wrapped around her. The memory made her smile. He must have missed her. That was something, at least.

But it wasn't enough, no way. She wanted his whole heart.

Shoving her tangled hair back out of her eyes, she grabbed her phone from the nightstand. It was 6:15 a.m. She could probably manage a quick shower before Camryn started fussing.

Yawning, she rose again and tiptoed to the bathroom.

A half an hour later, she was dressed and ready for the day. Camryn was awake by then, waving her hands and feet, making small questioning sounds.

Macy put a cloth diaper on her shoulder, scooped the baby into her arms and kissed the top of her almost-bald head. "Getting hungry?"

Camryn let out a fussy cry.

"Well, all right, then. Let's see what we can do about that."

Following the delicious scent of frying sausage and fresh-brewed coffee, Macy carried the whining baby through the living room to the kitchen, where Joe stood at the stove and Ana was busy setting the table.

"Mom! We're having scrambled eggs and sausage."

"Perfect." Macy bounced Cammy lightly, trying to soothe the baby until she could get a bottle ready.

Joe was one step ahead of her. "Here you go." He held up a full bottle. Macy took it and found it was just the right temperature.

She met his eyes for a second and wasn't sure what she saw in them. Resistance, maybe? Longing? Evasion? All of the above? "Thank you." At his quick nod, she looked away and settled into her usual seat at the table.

Camryn was hungry. With a tiny grunt of satisfaction, she latched right on.

"Coffee?" Joe asked.

She shook her head. "I'll get it in a minute." Their gazes locked. Her chest felt suddenly tight. It was hard, having all these feelings when he couldn't seem to accept them from her. It hurt.

A lot.

He turned back to the stove.

The morning passed quickly as they bustled around getting ready for the last school day before Christmas vacation. Joe walked Ana to the bus stop before heading out to meet his dad in the tractor shed. Macy took Camryn to the main house and reluctantly kissed her goodbye for the weekend. Tia would pick her up after work.

Macy played Christmas tunes all the way to town. She turned the sound up extra loud, trying to drown out the sadness in her heart. She kept thinking it shouldn't be possible to miss another person so acutely—not when you lived in the same house with him.

Betty's Blooms was a Christmas fantasy scented of flowers and evergreen. Her mom had put up three trees, each with a different color scheme and theme. They were beautiful, those trees, the ornaments sparkling, the programmed lights twinkling. The shop's smart speaker played holiday tunes one after another.

Business was brisk. People came in to place Christmas orders—things like wreaths, table centerpieces and festive flower arrangements to be presented as hostess gifts.

More than once, Macy caught her mom watching her with a look of concern in her eyes. But Betty kept her thoughts to herself and Macy decided to be grateful for that.

That afternoon at the hardware store, Macy kept busy at her desk. Joe never once came near her. Maybe that was for the best. Yes, she longed to break the silence between them, to do whatever was required to get their old intimacy back. But she had no desire to tackle a conversation like that at work.

At three o'clock, she and Joe headed for Medicine Creek Elementary School to attend the annual Christmas pageant. They would be going home after the show, so Joe took his pickup and she had the Subaru. Which was fine. Driving herself saved her the misery of being stuck in a vehicle with him when he apparently had nothing to say to her—at least nothing she wanted to hear.

The multiuse room was packed with parents, grandparents, relatives and friends. Macy had her mom and dad on one side, Joe on the other. Meggie sat next to Joe with Nate on her other side.

The show was great. Ana was an adorable elf and wore

a long gray beard as a wise man. She had four lines total and spoke them slowly and clearly with only a hint of lisp.

Afterward, the guests, school staff and students visited together while munching Christmas cookies and drinking holiday punch. Everyone agreed it was the best Christmas show ever.

What wasn't so great? That night when Joe once again came to bed late and was gone when she woke in the morning.

Macy honestly had no idea what to do about him—about *them*. About their wonderful marriage that had lately started feeling like a long slog down a rutted road to nowhere.

No, Joe hadn't left her. He would never do that. But what about that promise he'd made on their wedding day— the one where he said he would love and cherish her? He couldn't do either of those while he was constantly avoiding her. Macy needed to break through to him, get him to talk to her the way he used to. But he was a million miles away from her now and she had no idea how to close the vast distance between them.

Somehow, they made it through the weekend.

Dinner at the main house on Sunday felt pretty stiff and awkward to Macy, but only between her and her emotionally unavailable husband. Everyone else—Ana, Nate and Meggie, Joe's brother, Jason, and his family—all seemed to have a great time.

Once or twice during the visit, Macy thought she caught Joe's mom watching her, and she wondered if her mother-in-law knew what was going on. But then Meggie smiled. It was a warm, relaxed smile.

Nope, Macy decided. Meggie had no clue that her younger son was just going through the motions when it came to his relationship with his wife.

Monday, Macy texted Riley from the flower shop.

Help! Got time for lunch?

For you, always. Dillon's at day care. What about Ana and the baby?

The kids are with Meggie.

Come to my place?

You got it. I'll bring the food. Chicken tacos from Carmelita's?

Perfect.

Macy got to Riley's at 11:30 a.m. She was halfway up the steps when Riley pulled open the front door.

"You're a lifesaver," Macy said.

Riley put her hand to her heart and sighed dramatically. "*You* brought chicken tacos and that is everything to me." She gestured Macy inside. "Right this way."

They sat at the kitchen table. Riley poured them both coffee and they dug right in. "Now tell me," Riley commanded, "what's going on?"

Macy didn't even know where to begin. So she just laid it right out there. "I told Joe that I'm in love with him."

Riley's green eyes went wide—and then she grinned in a smug and thoroughly annoying way. "About time. How'd it go?"

Macy winced. "Not well."

"Oh, honey." Riley's grin disappeared. She sagged in her chair. "Why not?"

"Because he's sworn never to fall in love again."

"Oh, please. Too late for that. The man is already in love with you."

"Riley, he really did have a bad time—with Lindsay *and* with Becca…"

"I remember." Riley was slowly shaking her head. "It was horrible, what happened to Becca. As for Lindsay, we all knew she had issues. Both of those women were messed up, plain and simple. It should be obvious to Joe that you are not them. It's a whole other situation, you and Joe. You are a rock and there is no way you'll be messing him over. He knows you and somewhere deep down he has to know that you would never do him wrong."

"Yeah, well. I went into this marriage knowing the score. He told me from the start what he could and couldn't give me. My falling in love with him wasn't supposed to happen."

"Ugh. I can't even… As if you can make a deal about something like falling in love."

"Riley, the way he sees it, we had an agreement and I've broken it."

"That makes zero sense. The whole point of getting married is that you get to be *in* love with your best friend."

"He just doesn't see it that way."

"He should get over himself."

"Oh, come on. He's been burned twice and that's two times too many."

Riley scoffed. "He's wrong, plain and simple. He needs to appreciate how lucky he is to have you as his wife."

"He does appreciate me."

"Not nearly enough."

Macy still had no clue where to go from here. "So…are you saying I should leave him?"

Riley blinked. "Whoa. Do you *want* to leave him?"

"No. Never. Not a chance!"

"So you're not giving up?"

"Well, I am discouraged, I have to admit. Falling in love with him wasn't my plan, either."

Riley pressed her lips together and offered a tight smile.

Macy rolled her eyes. "Just go ahead and say it. I can take it."

"Never mind. You don't need to hear that I told you so."

"You're so noble." Macy laid on the sarcasm.

"You bet I am." Riley pushed back her chair and held out her arms. Macy went into them. They both held on tight.

"Thank you," Macy whispered, "for being here, for letting me vent."

"Always," Riley replied. And then she took Macy by the shoulders and held her away so she could look her in the eye. "Give him time, Mace. That guy is gone on you. Eventually, he'll come around."

Macy blinked away unwanted tears. "Do you really believe that?"

Riley took way too long to answer. Finally, she shrugged. "I wish I were wiser. Too bad I'm not. I don't know what will happen in the end, but I can't believe that Joe would ever be fool enough to let you get away."

Macy didn't know whether to laugh or cry. "Caleb did."

"Honey. Joe is no Caleb."

"I know that. Joe's a good guy, the best. But he's been hurt—and hurt bad. He may never be able to give me what I want from him."

"You love him," Riley reminded her. "You're *in* love with him. Don't give up on him. Give him some time to admit to himself that you're the one for him."

Chapter Thirteen

That afternoon, Joe had a meeting with Josh and Ty Bravo at Bravo Construction. Macy hardly saw him. At home, he was pleasant. And distant.

Nothing had changed. She went to bed alone. In the middle of the night, he joined her. When he slid under the covers beside her, she almost scooted away.

But her love was stronger than her pride. He wrapped his arms around her and she let him. She had missed him so. She ached for him. His touch eased her wounded heart. She fell asleep within minutes.

And when she woke, he was gone.

Tuesday morning, as Macy worked on the accounts receivable at Betty's Blooms, her cell rang. It was Tia. "I was wondering," Tia said kind of shyly, "if you could maybe meet me for lunch. I was thinking the Stagecoach Grill."

"Sure. What time?"

"Half an hour?"

"I'll be there."

At the restaurant, they ordered Chef's salads. Tia talked about how much she loved her job with Josh and how glad she was that she'd knocked on Joe's door that day in early November.

"I'm glad, too, Tia. And so is Joe."

"I know he is," said Tia. "But what I'm really happy about is that *you* answered the door that day." She seemed to be carefully choosing her words. "Joe's a good man. He loves Camryn and clearly wants her. I have no doubt he would've stepped up even if he didn't have you in his corner. I know he would've helped me that day. But you..." She hesitated. Her eyes shone with unshed tears.

Macy said, "Hey. Tia, I only did what I thought was right."

"Exactly. That's it. You did what was right and you did it with an open heart. And that made all the difference. I just want you to know that lately, when I'm not sure what my next move is or how to handle whatever's going on, I think 'what would Macy do?' and it helps, it really does. It kind of clears out all the mental garbage and allows me decide what to do next." She sniffled.

Macy was also blinking away tears. "Oh, Tia. Thank you..."

They both took a minute to pull travel packs of tissue from their shoulder bags.

Dabbing the moisture from her eyes, Tia said, "I'm the one who will always be grateful. Thank *you*."

"You are so welcome. And I am so glad I've helped."

"You have."

"And Tia, I'm not going anywhere. If you need me—or Joe—we're there for you. Count on it."

"I believe you. And it means so much. And that leads me to my news. I've been so grateful that you let me stay in your house."

"Stay as long as you need to."

"Well, that's what I'm getting at. I've found a little place on Summit Street. The rent is very reasonable. My credit is crap and it's going to take a while to fix that, but Josh vouched for me with the landlady. I've signed a lease and I can move in right away."

"Wow." Macy leaned closer across their small table. "It's a big step."

"Yeah." A glowing smile lit up Tia's pretty face. "I'm excited."

"I'm glad. How can we help?"

"As of now, I'm on it. But I'll let you know if there's anything. I've made some friends in my single mom's group—which it turns out is not just for moms. There are single dads in the group, too. My new friends are pitching in."

"So when's the move?"

"Tomorrow and Thursday. Josh gave me the time off so I can get settled before Christmas."

"Congratulations."

"I'm excited—and I do know that I owe you rent for the last month and a half and…"

Macy stopped her with an upraised hand. "No. We're family. Forget it. That house would be sitting vacant right now if you hadn't needed it. I'm just glad it was available for you."

"You sure?"

"Absolutely."

"Thank you—yet again." Tia gave a nervous little cough and asked, "So then, you'll tell Joe?"

"About your move?"

"Yeah."

"I think he would appreciate hearing the news from you." Not to mention that lately communicating with Joe was almost as difficult for Macy as it seemed to be for Tia.

Tia groaned. "Now how did I know you would say that?"

Macy set down her fork. "You and Joe have an important relationship as Camryn's parents. I want to be there for Cammy and for you. But I never want to be the go-between. And look at it this way. The more you deal with Joe directly, the easier it will be."

"Thanks, *Mom*," Tia replied.

"Oh, please. I'm what? A year older than you?"

Tia's expression had softened. "I know I said that sarcastically but really, it's a compliment. I hardly knew my own mom, but you are teaching me what a good mom should be. You always say the thing I really need to hear."

They stared at each other. And then they both smiled.

Macy said gently, "Call Joe. Tell him your news."

"I will. Promise."

Joe was moving stock in the warehouse area behind the store that afternoon when Tia called. She said she'd been to lunch with Macy.

He was instantly, nonsensically jealous. Because he would damn well like to go to lunch with Macy. He missed her. A lot—even though they lived in the same house together.

It was bad, this distance that yawned between them. He wanted to be with her in the old way, the good, easy, close way, but he didn't want to deal with the whole love issue. Talking about love made his gut churn and his head ache.

Why couldn't they just go on as they had been? Things had been great between them until she suddenly had to tell him that she was in love with him.

If she had *feelings*, well, fine. She could have them. He didn't get why they had to talk about them, to *share* them. To come to some meaningful understanding of what they *had* together.

He hated that stuff. He didn't trust it. Both Lindsay and Becca had been real big on the importance of feelings. On the great gift they were giving him by trusting him, by being *in love* with him. What had being *in love* ever given him but misery?

Did he need a little counseling? Probably.

But more than that, he needed Macy to let it go, to just... be with him, not look at him like she was waiting for him to admit that they were soulmates forever.

"Joe? You still there?"

He realized he'd kind of lost track of what Tia was saying. "Right here, yeah."

"Ah, good. As I said, I'm moving."

"Right. Got that."

"I'll text you my new address."

"That'll work. Need help with the move?"

"Nope. I appreciate the offer, but I've got it handled."

"Good enough, then," he said. "Thanks for keeping me in the loop."

"Of course. Thanks for..."

"Yeah?"

"Thanks for being there, Joe. And for being a great dad to our daughter. Bye, now." She ended the call.

He stood beside the loading dock with the phone in his hand, humbled that Tia could be so gracious to him, even after he'd started out so defensive and suspicious of her that day she first showed up out of nowhere with Camryn in her arms. Now, he could see how wrong he'd been to be so distrustful of her. Tia had grit and a lot of heart.

And thank God for Macy. She'd kept him focused on what mattered, made sure that Tia had whatever she needed to make a life here in town.

Macy...

As he thought her name, she emerged from her office. He watched her come toward him, thinking that she looked beautiful—and tired, too. Because of him. She obviously wasn't sleeping well. But then, neither was he.

He did want to get past this rough patch they'd hit, to get back on solid ground with her. He just didn't know how to make that happen when he couldn't tell her what she needed to hear and do it sincerely.

"Hey." She came to a stop a good three feet from the toes of his work boots.

"Hey." This was their level of communication now. Short and not so sweet.

"My mom just called," she said, all business, expression neutral. "She's had a toothache since last night. The dentist is willing to fit her in half an hour from now. I need to go relieve her."

"No problem. Myron can close up. I'll pick up the kids." School was out until after the New Year, so both Ana and Cammy were spending the day with Joe's mom.

"You have your car seat and a booster?" They had two sets of seats for the girls, one for the Subaru and one for his crew cab.

"I've got them with me."

She nodded. "Dinner's in the Crock-Pot. I should be home by six at the latest."

"See you then."

"Bye, Joe."

Feeling like the worst husband ever, he watched her walk away.

Okay, fine. It was all his fault and he knew it. She needed what he wasn't giving her—and he was bitter that she'd gone and changed the rules on him. In the end, even he knew that his bitterness wasn't going to win her back.

He would have to get his act together, do *something* to

put their marriage back on track. But so far, he hadn't made a whole lot of progress on that front.

At a little after three o'clock, he pulled up in front of his mom's house.

Inside, the Christmas tree twinkled in the corner near the door to the kitchen. His mom sat in the rocker by the sofa feeding Camryn a bottle. Jason's little guy, Miles, was playing with blocks nearby. Rosie had spent the day there. She got right up from her spot in the corner and came to greet him.

Ana and Emmy were lying on the rug by the fire with a book open between them. Emmy glanced up. "Hi, Uncle Joe!"

"Hey there, Emmy."

"We are reading," Emmy informed him.

Glancing his way with a frown, Ana asked, "Where's Mom?"

He explained about Betty's trip to the dentist. "Your mom will be home for dinner."

Ana tipped her head to the side and studied him as though gauging his sincerity. "We need to finish this book," she said.

"Yeah!" Emmy enthusiastically agreed. "It's getting real good."

"Go for it. I can wait." He sat on the sofa.

Ana bent her head to the book again and Emmy leaned in close.

Joe's mom asked, "How's everything?"

He felt instantly guilty as he answered with a bald-faced lie. "Good. Real good."

Meggie just looked at him. How was it his mom always knew when he lied? She had radar when it came to anyone in the family. Most likely she'd noticed something off between him and Macy during dinner on Sunday.

Wonderful. Now he had to watch his back. Meggie would be looking for her chance to feel him out as to what had gone wrong between him and his wife. Lucky for him, this wasn't that chance. She wouldn't be probing him for answers with the kids there.

Twenty-five long minutes later, Joe had a bundled-up Camryn in his arms and the diaper bag slung over one shoulder. He herded Ana and Rosie out the door. It was snowing and raining simultaneously. He buckled Camryn into her car seat and then helped Ana with her booster. Rosie, he took up in front with him.

Shortly after he climbed behind the wheel, he was pulling into his own garage. Camryn instantly started wailing. She liked riding in the truck, but she didn't like it when the vehicle stopped.

As Cammy wailed, he freed Ana from her booster seat. Then he unhooked the baby from her seat and gathered her close. She kept crying, but not quite so hard.

In the mudroom, he shucked off his boots with the still-crying baby in his arms as Ana shed her shoes and took off her coat and hat. Voodoo must have heard the commotion. He appeared in the doorway that led to the kitchen.

"I'm going to put my stuff away and get a juice box," Ana announced.

"That's fine," he said.

Off she went, both the dog and the cat at her heels.

He shifted the baby from one arm to the other and managed to extricate himself from his coat. About then, he smelled a full diaper.

For the next half hour or so, Cammy cried as he changed her, walked her, put her in her BabyBjörn, used every trick in the book to soothe her. Finally, sucking her pacifier for all she was worth, she settled down. Breathing a long sigh of relief, he sank to the sofa with her in his arms.

Now that the dirty diaper was disposed of, he could smell dinner in the slow cooker—Macy's Tuscan chicken. One of his favorites.

He almost smiled. Macy was a good cook, so yeah, he had a lot of favorites.

"Dad?" Ana stood at the foot of the stairs, Voodoo in her arms and Rosie beside her. He patted the cushion next to him. She came right over, climbed up beside him and whispered, "Cammy's nice when she's not screaming."

"Oh, yes she is." He adjusted the blanket around the baby's angelic little face as Ana patted the spot on her other side and Voodoo jumped up to claim it.

"Dad?"

"Hmm?"

"Are you sad?"

He looked down into her big worried eyes and had no idea how to answer. He didn't want to lie to her, but he didn't want to put his grown-up problems on her, either. "I'm okay."

She wrinkled up her nose at him. "Well, whatever you are okay about, I hope it gets better soon."

He shifted the baby so he could hold her on one arm and then put the other around Ana. "I love you," he whispered, bending down a little awkwardly to press a kiss to the top of her head.

"I know," she whispered back, leaning against him. "I love you, too, Dad."

Macy got home at a little after six o'clock.

They had dinner and then streamed *Eloise at Christ-*

mastime on the big screen over the fireplace. When it was bedtime for Ana, Joe tucked her in.

And then, as the evening crawled by, he tried to think what to do to close the distance between him and Macy. It was an exercise in self-deception. Because he knew damn well what to do.

And yet he did nothing.

That night, as he sat up alone staring into the embers of the dying fire, it came to him.

A letter. He would write his wife a letter, the way they used to do. A letter that would somehow explain everything—how much he needed her and…

With a groan, he hung his head.

Who did he think he was kidding? If he couldn't deal with this problem face-to-face, no way was he going to be able to write it all down. He was no poet. He was just a guy who didn't know how to cope with his own damn feelings.

Used to be he could tell Macy almost anything in a letter. But everything was different this time. She was his wife now. They were all wrapped up together—and just lately, at the same time, miles and miles apart.

In the morning after chores, Joe came in for breakfast, which Macy set before him.

"Thanks," he said.

With a nod, she turned away. He became acutely aware for the umpteenth time that he needed to fix things with her.

And then he just sat there, holding Camryn, eating the omelet his wife had prepared. At least his two daughters still liked him. Ana sent him a smile as she munched toast and jam. And Cammy was so sweet, sucking on her pacifier, staring up at him in that dazed way babies had.

Out of nowhere, Macy shoved back her chair. He looked up, alarmed.

"I'm fine," she said tightly. "Morning sickness. I'm okay..." And she ran from the table. He stared after her. She was almost eight weeks along and, until this morning, hadn't been sick once that he knew about. Was she okay?

"Mom!" Ana cried. "Mom...?"

About then, Macy made it to the bedroom. He knew because she slammed the door behind her.

Cammy's eyes popped extra wide and her little mouth dropped open. Joe caught the pacifier as she let out a wail.

"Ana!" he said, raising his voice enough to be heard over Camryn's cries. "Your mom's okay. Leave her be."

Ana still looked scared to death. "Dad, what's going on?"

He put the baby on his shoulder and rubbed her back. "Everything's fine, don't worry..."

"But I *am* worried. What's wrong with Mom?"

He bounced the baby and whispered reassurances into her little pink ear.

"Dad?"

He got up and walked Camryn. Simultaneously, he set about trying to ease Ana's fears. "You remember that your mom's having a baby when the summer comes, right?"

"What's the next baby got to do with it?"

The next baby. He almost laughed. Last year at this time, he was wondering if he would ever have children. Now he had two daughters and a baby on the way.

Camryn let out a loud screech directly into his ear. As she sucked in air to scream some more, Joe stuck the pacifier in.

And he got lucky. The baby went right to work soothing herself with it. He continued to walk her back and forth by the table as he explained to his older daughter that pregnant moms sometimes got tummy upsets.

"Why?" demanded Ana.

"It's called hormone changes and it's really just about the mom's body adjusting to the baby growing inside her."

"Ew," replied Ana.

"Well, it doesn't feel good to throw up, but still, it's all completely safe and natural." Or at least, it had better be.

Ana remained skeptical. "You sure?"

"I am, yes," he said firmly.

Macy emerged from the bedroom right then. "Listen to your father," she said. *Your father.* Joe did like the sound of that.

"Mom!" Ana jumped up and went to her. "Dad says you're okay, but—"

"I am just fine." Macy knelt and gathered her close. "I promise you I am." She met Joe's eyes over Ana's shoulder. The look on her face...

It spoke of longing and tenderness—and of gratitude that he was there, being a father to the little girl they both loved.

Love.

Damn. He did love Ana. And Camryn.

And he loved Macy. So much. What the hell was wrong with him that he just couldn't give her the words in the order that she needed to hear them?

One way or another, he had to get his head on straight about this. Maybe it wouldn't be such a bad idea if his mother tracked him down and gave him a good talking-to, after all.

As it turned out, it wasn't Meggie who came looking for him.

At four thirty the next morning, Nate Bravo appeared in the barn just as Joe was about to start sweeping out stalls.

"Morning, son." He held up a big thermos. "How about some coffee?"

Joe knew from the look on his father's face that something serious was going on. "What's the matter?"

Nate sat on a hay bale. "Come on. Have a seat."

Joe stayed where he was and indicated his thermos, which he'd left on a stool a few feet away. "I've got my own."

"Great. More for me." Nate patted the bale next to the one he sat on. "This won't take long."

The quicker the better, Joe thought as he grabbed his own coffee and approached the offered bale with caution. "Okay, what?" He sat down.

Nate took his time, pouring coffee and screwing the lid back on the thermos, enjoying a long slow sip.

Finally, after what felt like forever to Joe, Nate said, "Son, your life is your business. Your mom's big on giving advice, but I generally like to hang back, let you kids figure things out in your own way…"

Joe didn't get it. "So…you're not planning to tell me what you think I need to hear?"

Nate took a slow sip of coffee and then just sat there, frowning thoughtfully down at the barn floor between his battered boots.

"You know, Dad, those stalls aren't going to clean themselves."

"Give me a minute, let me…gather my thoughts."

Joe tamped down his impatience as Maysie approached, walked in a circle and curled up at his feet. He bent to give her a pat on the head.

Finally, after another endless pause, his dad spoke again. "Son, what's gone wrong between you and Macy?"

Did Joe know he needed help? Definitely. But he got defensive, anyway. "Listen, Dad. What's going on between me and my wife is our business, period."

Nate set down his coffee and put up both hands. "Whoa, there. Don't shoot, I'm unarmed."

"Very funny."

Nate said mildly, "I'm only here to help."

Joe felt the urge to get salty again. But really, why? He might as well face the truth. He'd messed things up pretty bad and he needed to take any help he could get. "Okay, fine. I want it to work with Macy. I want that a lot. She's everything to me. But you know me, Dad. You know that after Becca, some things just *don't* work for me."

Nate said nothing. It was clear from the baffled frown on his face that he had no idea what Joe was talking about. But then finally, he mustered a response. "I'm just going to say it. Yes, what happened to Becca was heartbreaking. I know it was sheer hell for you, losing her. What I don't know is what you mean when you say things don't *work* for you."

Joe let out a grunt of frustration. "Being in love, Dad. That's what doesn't work for me. It never has, not with Lindsay and not with Becca. Being in love has never done anything for me except break my damn heart. And now Macy says *she's* in love with me. She wants me to say it back to her. And I just can't."

Nate's frown was even deeper than before. "Joe, she's your wife. I would be pretty damn worried if she *weren't* in love with you."

Joe groaned and tried again. "Okay, so. Macy and me, we have an understanding. We love each other but it's not all magical and romantic. After Becca, I just can't go there again. I don't want all the passionate, fairy-tale crap that's always so deep and meaningful and beautiful—until it blows up in my face. Being *in love* is not what I want and Macy knew that from the first."

"So you're saying she agreed that you two would have a loving marriage, you just wouldn't be *in* love."

"Finally, you're getting it."

"But now, what you agreed to isn't enough for her."

"Exactly—and look, Dad. I know it's my fault. I know it's not right to let her say she's in love with me and then not say it back. I get it. I'm messing up. But I'm pissed off, too. Because being in love is..." He could not find the word.

Nate tried to help. "Scarier than hell?"

"Damn straight it is. And I just can't go there."

Nate let a long moment pass before he said matter-of-factly, "Son, you can make all the agreements you want and enter into them with honest determination to keep your word, to stay the course. But people change. What they *want* changes. And Macy has a right to decide that what you agreed to before you got married just isn't enough for her now."

Joe hung his head. "Damn it, Dad. I get that. I do."

"Good. Then you have to know that if you want to make your marriage work, you have to be willing to grow and change, too."

Joe scoffed. "Like that's so easy."

"Nobody said it was easy. But it is necessary if you want to keep the woman you love. You can start by reminding yourself that Macy is not an alcoholic bent on self-destruction. She's also not some little lost child, like that sweet, troubled girl you loved in high school. Macy's tough, with a big heart and a good head on her shoulders. She's your best friend and she's a keeper. She would never do you wrong."

"You're right," Joe heard himself whisper. He bent and

picked up Maysie, who settled on his lap and purred even louder.

His dad wasn't done. "Joe, you're not the first man to get burned by love. It's understandable that you're afraid to go there again. But son, do it anyway. Give your whole heart to Macy. I think you know deep down that she will never break your trust. You give your heart to a woman like Macy, you'll have it all.

"I'm not going to lie to you. True love is hard work. But if you do the work there's magic, too. Hard work and magic. That's what real love's about."

Chapter Fourteen

Nothing changed that day.

Joe and Macy went through the motions of living their lives same as before. They were careful with each other. They spoke quietly and they respected each other's space.

Joe wasn't sure where to go from here. He wanted his wife back. He really did. He thought constantly about the things his dad had said in the barn.

He knew his dad was right, but he was still afraid to put his heart on the line, to give up the seeming safety of not giving Macy his whole heart. He knew she was worth it. He saw now that he was cheating her *and* himself by not willingly surrendering all of himself to her.

And yet…

He just needed a little time to figure out what to say to her.

That night Joe slept on the sofa as he had the night before. The next day was Friday. Joe did morning chores and had breakfast with Macy and the kids. A while later, Macy took Ana and Cammy to the main house and went on into town while he spent a few hours repairing machinery in the tractor shed.

As he worked, he thought about how to tell Macy of his

love. *Tonight*, he thought. He would do it tonight, no more putting it off, no more making excuses for himself.

When he showed up at the store, she was already there as usual, working away on her laptop. He said hello. She said it back.

Tonight, he promised himself. No stalling, no excuses. He would make her see that he did love her in a way that was deep and true, that he was *in* love with her and that all he wanted was to spend the rest of his life with her.

Macy headed for home around three o'clock. He stayed for another hour. He had the Christmas tunes playing and the store looked seriously festive, with garlands and lights looped in the front windows and hardware-themed Christmas trees glittering with twinkle lights throughout the store.

At four o'clock, leaving Myron to close up, he headed for home.

Tonight, he vowed yet again as he spotted the Christmas tree in the front window at the house. He'd pulled into the garage and sent the door rolling down before he registered the fact that Macy's Subaru wasn't there.

Rosie greeted him in the mudroom. He bent to pet her.

"Hey, girl. Where is everybody?" By then he was starting to get a bad feeling.

Not bothering to shed his jacket or kick off his boots, he strode into the kitchen. And there it was, propped between the salt and pepper shakers on the island. An envelope with his name on it.

Dear Joe,
After all the letters we've written to each other over the years, this is the one I hardly know how to start.
   I just need a little time, Joe. A little space. Right

now, I can't be in the same house with you. The silence between us is too hard to take. I need to get away from it, from you.

I thought this would be an okay time to take a little break. Tia's moved to her new place now and she's picking Cammy up from Meggie's for the weekend.

That leaves my house empty, so Ana and Voodoo and I are heading into town. I've told Ana it's so that I can get the house back in shape now that Tia's moved out. She didn't argue. We won't stay there long—just a day or two.

I need a little time away from you, Joe. Right now, it hurts too much to be there in the same house with you. I know you don't want to hear it, but I'm in love with you. I'm in love with you and you don't feel the same for me. I need to find a way to either live with that.

Or not.

So anyway, I'll be back by Sunday and we can start deciding what our next step should be.
Macy

Joe's hands were shaking. And his knees felt like they just might give way.

He yanked out a stool and sat down before he fell down.

Then he read the letter three more times—because it took him the third time through to accept that he'd waited too long to step the hell up and now he was losing her. He dropped the letter on the countertop and put his head in his hands.

Damned if he hadn't gone and ruined everything just as he'd feared he might.

A low groan escaped him.

And then, slowly, he drew himself up straight.

What the hell was the matter with him? It wasn't too late.

He wouldn't let it be. One way or another, he would damn well make this right.

Paper. He needed paper and a pen.

With Rosie close on his heels, he ran upstairs to the spare room that he and Macy used as a home office. He grabbed several sheets from the printer's paper tray, yanked out the chair at the desk, pushed the laptop there aside, sat down and pulled out the drawer to get a pen.

*Dear Macy,
I love*

That was it. As far as he got.

Because right then, he knew the letter he needed to give to her. And the one he was trying to write wasn't it.

Macy couldn't do it. She'd driven all the way to the house in town, pulled into the driveway—and then she couldn't make herself go inside.

From the back seat, Ana complained, "Mom?" In the carrier next to Ana's car seat, Voodoo chittered to be let out. "Are we going in or not?"

Macy turned to glance back at her daughter. "I think we should just go home."

Voodoo meowed as Ana shrugged. "Okay, Mom. Let's go home."

"All right, then." Macy put the car in reverse and backed from the driveway.

Ten minutes later, they'd turned off the highway onto the narrow road that would take them to the Double-K.

And right then, a familiar crew cab came barreling

straight at them. It wasn't dark yet. Macy could see Joe's face through the windshield.

And he saw her, too.

They both hit the brakes at the same time. The Subaru skidded a bit, but then the tires grabbed and held, sending pebbles and dirt flying. When the car came to a stop, there was maybe two feet between his bumper and hers.

"Is that Dad?" Ana asked.

"Yes, it is." Macy's heart had gone into overdrive, but she tried to keep her voice even in order not to alarm Ana. "Just sit tight for a minute, sweetie. I need to...speak to your father."

"But, Mom—"

"Won't be a minute, I promise."

"Weird," Ana grumbled. Voodoo chittered in agreement as Macy shoved open her door.

She and Joe emerged from the vehicles at the same time and slammed their doors simultaneously. He headed for the gap between their bumpers and so did she.

They met in the middle.

He had two sheets of paper in his hand. They looked frayed around the edges. And so did Joe. "I love you," he said. "Macy Lynn, I'm *in* love with you."

Those words brought a tidal wave of happiness rolling through her. All that joy almost brought her to her knees. "Oh, Joe... Truly?"

"Truly. Macy Bravo, I love you."

She reached for him. "Joe..."

And then they were holding each other. His mouth came down on hers. She opened to him. Snow drifted out of the gray sky to dust their hair and shoulders. They hardly noticed.

When he lifted his head, he said, "Don't leave me."

She pressed her hand to the side of his face. "No worries. I couldn't do it. We got to the house in town—and I turned right around and came back."

"Good. That's so good." He held up the folded papers. "Remember that letter you wrote me after Becca died?"

Her breath caught. "Oh, Joe. I always wondered if you'd even read it."

"Of course I read it. And I kept it, just like all your letters." He took her hand, put the letter in it. "You remember what you wrote to me? I do. Every word. You wrote, *'You will find the woman for you, the one to spend your life with. I know you will, Joe. And I will always be there for you, I promise you, just like you've always been there for me—and for Ana, too...'*"

"Oh, Joe..."

"It's you, Macy. *You're* the one for me. I'd given up finding you, and you were right here with me all along."

Epilogue

Later, after dinner and a Christmas movie, Joe tucked Ana into bed. Downstairs in their room, Macy and Joe stayed up way too late making love and discussing their plans for the future.

On Christmas morning, Ana got her puppy, a black Labrador retriever. She named him Angus, after one of the characters in her *Dragon Slayers' Academy* stories.

By the day after Christmas, everyone was calling him Gus. Gus was lively and full of fun. He followed Ana everywhere. Yes, furniture got chewed on and house training took a while, but still. Gus was the sweetest guy ever. He and Rosie and Voodoo became lifelong best friends.

The following year, on July 31, Macy had a beautiful baby boy. They named him Justin Joseph. He had black hair and blue eyes.

Grandma Meggie took one look at him and said, "This one's a charmer, mark my words."

The days grew shorter. School started and Thanksgiving came around yet again.

In no time, it was Christmas once more. They had Camryn with them the night they decorated the tree. She was walking already and her favorite word was *no*! Camryn was a girl who liked to make her wishes known. She managed to hang an ornament or two as Justin laughed from his bouncy seat. And before bedtime, Ana insisted on reading *How the Grinch Stole Christmas!* to the whole family, including the dogs and cat.

Once the kids were tucked in, Macy and Joe sat by the fire and whispered together, making plans for the future. And agreeing that sharing forever was the best idea Joe ever had.

* * * * *

Watch for A Secret Between Friends
*coming in February 2026,
only from Harlequin Special Edition.*

Get up to 4 Free Books!

We'll send you 2 free books from each series you try PLUS a free Mystery Gift.

FREE Value Over **$25**

Both the **Harlequin® Special Edition** and **Harlequin® Heartwarming**™ series feature compelling novels filled with stories of love and strength where the bonds of friendship, family and community unite.

YES! Please send me 2 FREE novels from the Harlequin Special Edition or Harlequin Heartwarming series and my FREE Gift (gift is worth about $10 retail). After receiving them, if I don't wish to receive any more books, I can return the shipping statement marked "cancel." If I don't cancel, I will receive 6 brand-new Harlequin Special Edition books every month and be billed just $6.39 each in the U.S. or $7.19 each in Canada, or 4 brand-new Harlequin Heartwarming Larger-Print books every month and be billed just $7.19 each in the U.S. or $7.99 each in Canada, a savings of 20% off the cover price. It's quite a bargain! Shipping and handling is just 50¢ per book in the U.S. and $1.25 per book in Canada.* I understand that accepting the 2 free books and gift places me under no obligation to buy anything. I can always return a shipment and cancel at any time by calling the number below. The free books and gift are mine to keep no matter what I decide.

Choose one:
- ☐ **Harlequin Special Edition** (235/335 BPA G36Y)
- ☐ **Harlequin Heartwarming Larger-Print** (161/361 BPA G36Y)
- ☐ **Or Try Both!** (235/335 & 161/361 BPA G36Z)

Name (please print)

Address   Apt. #

City   State/Province   Zip/Postal Code

Email: Please check this box ☐ if you would like to receive newsletters and promotional emails from Harlequin Enterprises ULC and its affiliates. You can unsubscribe anytime.

Mail to the **Harlequin Reader Service:**
IN U.S.A.: P.O. Box 1341, Buffalo, NY 14240-8531
IN CANADA: P.O. Box 603, Fort Erie, Ontario L2A 5X3

Want to explore our other series or interested in ebooks? **Visit www.ReaderService.com or call 1-800-873-8635.**

---

*Terms and prices subject to change without notice. Prices do not include sales taxes, which will be charged (if applicable) based on your state or country of residence. Canadian residents will be charged applicable taxes. Offer not valid in Quebec. This offer is limited to one order per household. Books received may not be as shown. Not valid for current subscribers to the Harlequin Special Edition or Harlequin Heartwarming series. All orders subject to approval. Credit or debit balances in a customer's account(s) may be offset by any other outstanding balance owed by or to the customer. Please allow 4 to 6 weeks for delivery. Offer available while quantities last.

Your Privacy—Your information is being collected by Harlequin Enterprises ULC, operating as Harlequin Reader Service. For a complete summary of the information we collect, how we use this information and to whom it is disclosed, please visit our privacy notice located at https://corporate.harlequin.com/privacy-notice. Notice to California Residents – Under California law, you have specific rights to control and access your data. For more information on these rights and how to exercise them, visit https://corporate.harlequin.com/california-privacy. For additional information for residents of other U.S. states that provide their residents with certain rights with respect to personal data, visit https://corporate.harlequin.com/other-state-residents-privacy-rights/.

HSEHW25